RELUCTANT

ANGEL

DARCY NYBO

Darcy Nybo

For book signings and wholesale enquiries please email publisher@artisticwarrior.com.

ISBN # 978-1-987982-53-4 (paperback)
ISBN # 978-1-987982-54-1 (eBook)

First Edition

Cover by Chris Tyreman
Author Photo by Kim Elsasser, kimsphotography.com
Book Design by Artistic Warrior
Angel wing from © Can Stock Photo / benjangus

Artistic Warrior
artisticwarrior.com

Reluctant Angel

Darcy Nybo

The way people come into your life when you need them, it's wonderful and it happens in so many ways. It's like having an angel. Somebody comes along and helps you get right.

Stevie Ray Vaughan

Reluctant Angel

For my family and friends
Thank you for all your support on my journey.

Darcy Nybo

Reluctant Angel

Chapter 1: June 1976

All signs pointed to a swift and quiet death as music blared from the stereo. Ana opened one eye, unable to focus. She saw the blurry outline of Martin, her boyfriend. He was laughing and a curvy redhead was laughing along with him. Ana's jealousy barely registered and she felt at peace with the world. She sat up straight, finished off her beer, then stood up. She managed to bounce off a few walls and people on her way to the bathroom. Beer, as her boyfriend told her, can never be bought, only rented. She thought it funny at the time. Now it was annoying.

The bathroom was massive, or at least it was in her altered state. There was a huge clawfoot bathtub to the right and a toilet and sink to the left. She managed to use the toilet and then decided the bathtub would be a nice place to rest for a bit.

She made her way across the checkboard-patterned floor and grabbed a fluffy bath towel on her way there. Her feet could barely lift off the ground. The bathtub would be a safe space. After what felt like hours, Ana reached the tub, tossed in the bath towel and followed after it. The porcelain was cool and comforting. She curled into a ball, or as much of a ball as the space would allow, then pulled the towel over her head, shoulders and torso.

Much quieter, much better. She scrunched up her face and tried to remember what she took. Bobby gave them to her. He said they were leftovers from his car accident. She took one and washed it down with a beer. She remembered that. Then Martin went to talk to that damn redhead and stayed there. She asked Bobby for another pill and washed that one down with a shot of tequila. She didn't want to feel jealous, even though he gave her every reason to be. Was there a third pill? She remembered getting another beer and swallowing something with it. Bobby called them painkillers and she wanted to kill the pain of her entire life. She remembered they sounded like they were someone's name. Was it Darwin or Deon? No, not them. It was Darvon. Yes, that was it, Darvon. Peace inducers that made her no longer care where she was or what her cheating boyfriend was doing. She felt weightless and anchored at the same time.

Ana pulled back the towel and rolled onto her back. She thought about having a cigarette but couldn't remember where she'd put them. As she gazed upwards, the ceiling disappeared, and she could see clouds and stars. A faint smile crossed her face as her eyes fluttered and closed. Ana's heart rate slowed, then her breathing. She could hear the music, almost see it, as it snaked its way under the bathroom door and surrounded her in the bathtub. It was "Don't Fear the Reaper" by Blue Öyster Cult. She loved that song. She wanted to go wherever the words could take her. She wanted to leave, to be taken away by a magical creature who would make everything okay. She related to the girl in the song in that she felt sad most of the time lately and she was tired. She didn't want to go on. She opened her eyes and saw a curtain flutter and a man's hand coming towards her. She grabbed it and he lifted her out of the tub and into the night. She was not afraid. It was time to go.

Reluctant Angel

Bright lights flashed around her as the music faded into the darkness behind her. Then the lights converged into one bright beam of light heading straight towards her. She let go of the stranger's hand and floated towards it. She felt freer than she'd ever been before in her entire eighteen years of life. The light was calling, and she was content to heed its call.

There were voices behind her: a man and a woman. They were arguing. She didn't look back. She wanted the light and the peace she knew awaited. The voices grew louder. Ana turned to ask them to be quiet. She was on a mission of peace and tranquility, and they weren't helping one bit.

"I told you we should stay and watch her. But oh no, you had faith. You said she'd be fine. Peer pressure wouldn't sway her. Let's take some time off you said. Now look what's happened. She'd dead!" The voice was female, motherly, upset.

"She's not dead yet," a second voice chimed in. This one was deeper, probably male. He sounded easy-going, and gentle. "Ana, can you hear us? Can you see us, Ana? Come closer dear."

Ana ignored them. She didn't recognize them from the party. And where was Martin? He could make them go away. Then she remembered he was with the redhead with big boobs. Well, she wasn't going to pay them any attention.

"Ana, please stop!" the male voice pleaded. Ana stopped and turned around.

"Go away!" she yelled and tried to go back to the light. It was no use. Her curiosity was now piqued.

Ana walked through a thin fog towards the voices. "I'm here. Who are you? What do you want?"

"Oh, thank goodness you're still here. I've been so worried!" A woman emerged from the fog. "You really shouldn't have done that Ana dear; you scared us. I know, I know, it's our job. We should have done a better job of watching you. You were always the bold one." The woman reached out a hand and brushed a hair off Ana's forehead. Ana recoiled.

A male figure appeared through the fog and stopped beside the woman in front of Ana. "You know I've always admired that about you. The bold part, not the foolish part."

The woman tried to fix Ana's hair again. Ana pushed her hand away. "You shouldn't have taken those pills, dear. In my day you simply drank the fermented grapes and that was that. You got silly and danced and ate too much and felt horrible the next day."

The man cleared his throat.

"Yes, enough about that. We need to get you through today, so we can get you to tomorrow." The woman smiled and shook her head. "What are we going to do with you?"

"Do with me?" Ana stared at them both. "Do with me? Who the hell are you people and where the hell am I?"

The man chuckled and floated beside her. He noticed her wide-eyed stare as he settled to the foggy ground and placed his hand on her shoulder. Warmth radiated from him and into her. "Hell isn't exactly the word I would use to describe where we are; however, it can appear somewhat frightening when you first arrive." He removed his hand from her shoulder and turned to the woman. "She looks much the same out here as she does on Earth, doesn't she Dabria?" The woman nodded, stopped and

Reluctant Angel

then swatted him on the arm.

"We aren't here to chat—we have to think of something. Raphael will be very upset with us if she passes over now. So much work, so many contracts, so many lives untouched. Oh dear, what can we do, let me think."

Ana stared at the pair. "What kind of name is Dabria?" She felt the light behind her, beckoning for her to come to it. Curiosity rooted her for the moment.

"Dabria means angel, and please excuse my manners." Dabria held out her hands and took Ana's left hand between her two. "And this is Rigel, but I call him Rig, it's quicker that way." The man smiled and bowed.

"It's a pleasure to meet you person to person after all these years Ana—a pleasure indeed." He stepped forward and embraced her in a big hug. Once again the warmth spread through her. It made her aware of how cold she felt. He released her and smiled.

"Well, you seem to know me, but I don't see how that's possible." She turned and looked towards the light. "What is that?"

The pair smiled as Dabria lightly touched Ana's cheek and guided her head gently back to centre. Ana swatted her hand away.

"Don't look at that just yet Ana, we have some questions to ask and some things to do. I don't know what those things are just yet, but between Rig and I, we'll get it figured out. Then everything will make sense and we'll be right on track."

"On track for what? You still haven't told me where I am? Why is it so cold here? What on earth is that light?"

Rig chuckled again. "Wrong dear, not completely, but wrong, nonetheless. This is not Earth, nor is it Hell. Now before you say, 'What in heaven's name,' but let me stop you right there. We are at the juncture, the in-between if you will. As for the light, it's the doorway from the in-between to the otherworld. You can call it Heaven if you wish."

Ana shook her head. "Wait a minute. This is a hallucination. It's got to be the pills. I'm alive. You aren't real. I'm going to wake up in a few minutes with a bit of a headache and then Martin and I will go home. I didn't think a couple of pills would cause me to see shit like this. Wait until I tell Rose, she'll never believe me."

Ana took a step back and then lowered herself to the densest part of the fog and lay down on her back. She closed her eyes and waited. Moments passed and nothing changed. Ana opened one eye and was greeted by Rigel's smiling face.

"That won't work dear, now stand up and let's figure out what to do with you." He leaned forward and offered her his hand.

"Forget it!" Ana crab crawled backwards and stayed sitting. "I want to wake up now. Get me out of here. This is just too weird."

Dabria came forward and offered her a hand. "Ana honey, you overdosed. Those pills you took weren't just harmless Aspirin. You took too many. They slowed your heart, slowed your breathing. Your body is shutting down. We need to talk to you. We need to make a new contract."

Ana leapt to her feet. "No. No way."

She looked over her shoulder. The light was brighter,

stronger. She could see shapes inside it now.

"I am not dying or dead. I'm just freaking out in my head because of some bad drugs. I'm going to head towards that light and that light will take me home. It's like the hole in *Alice in Wonderland*, or Dorothy and her red shoes in *The Wizard of Oz*. I just head towards the light, and I'll be home in my bed before I know it."

Ana turned and ran. Figures that looked familiar materialized in the light.

The pair behind her called out her name.

"Ana please, don't go. We can work this out, I promise." Ana glanced over her shoulder—Dabria was right behind her. An arm reached out and grabbed Ana by the shoulder. Rigel took his time and caught up with them. He had a large grin on his face and his hands were in his pockets. Ana turned back towards the light and ran again as fast as her legs would take her. The hallucinations were way too real.

A figure appeared before her at the edge of the light. Ana stopped, cocked her head and straightened up.

"Grandma? Is that you?" A kindly woman with a beautiful halo of white hair stepped out of the light and took Ana by the hand. "Grandma? It can't be you, you're dead aren't you?" The woman smiled and nodded and looked towards the light.

Dabria reached for Ana again and took a hold of her other hand. "Don't go, Ana. Please, let us explain. Lives will be damaged, hopes dashed, families torn apart. Oh, this is such a mess and it's all my fault! Please, you must listen." The grandmother looked towards Dabria and let go of Ana's hand.

Rigel caught up with them. He had a perma-grin upon his face. "Ana dear, it's partially my fault this happened. I convinced Dab to come with me to see the face they found on Mars. Of course, it wasn't really a face, but you know how humans, and those who used to be human, are always trying to find themselves in everything they see. It only took a small piece of time and Dab does love to explore ..."

"Will you hush up!" Dabria wagged a finger at Rigel. "The truth is, Ana, we are your guardian angels. We should always be watching you. I thought a few minutes away would be okay, but it wasn't. We should have waited until you were asleep to go see this face thing. After all, it's been there for a few millenniums already. Can you imagine something there for two or three millennia and we didn't even know about it? It took your kind to find it and, of course, when Rig told me about it I just really couldn't say no. So, we went, and you overdosed and now you're almost dead. We need you to be alive." She paused briefly and then rushed on. "Many, many people's lives will change if you go now. We can't wait for you to come back again and grow up. Your final assignment is in ten years, which means you'll only be nine years old and nine-year-old children don't perform exorcisms on spirit doubles. It just isn't done."

"Spirit doubles? Exorcism? Coming back?" Ana shook her head and looked towards her grandmother. "Is it nice in there, Grandma? I know I'm only eighteen, but I'm so tired Grandma. Everything is just so hard. If I come with you, will it still be hard?" Tears trickled down Ana's cheek as her grandmother came forward and wrapped her arms around the girl.

Reluctant Angel

Rigel stepped forward and stroked Ana's hair. "Now, now, it won't always be this hard, I promise. You're a special one. You chose this. You signed the contract. Nothing to stop you from breaking it, but you wanted this."

Ana sniffled and poked her head out over her grandmother's arm. "What contract? Why do you keep talking about contracts? I didn't sign a damn contract."

Ana's grandmother nodded slowly and held Ana at arm's length. "We all have promises we make, Anastasia, even you. We make them before we're born and it's our right and our duty to carry them out. Dabria and Rigel are right. Your place isn't here with me. I can wait. I'll be here when it's your time."

Ana looked from Rigel to her grandmother and over to Dabria. "Let me keep her and I'll sign your contract." Rigel and Dabria exchanged glances and then looked at the soul before them. Ana stood tall and waited. "Well? Can I keep her with me? I need someone to talk to. Ever since Grandma died, no one understands me. Please, I miss her so much. Let her stay with me. If this is real, let her come back. I won't tell anyone. Not Mom or Dad or Davie or even Martin or anyone."

Dabria and Rigel shrugged. Rigel stepped forward. "It's not up to us, dear. We are, well, you see, we are part of a larger organization. A theocracy if you will. Like a council. Understand?" Rig held up his hands as if to show he had no way to comply with her demands.

"A theo what?" Ana eyed the pair warily.

"A theocracy. It's like a government run by officials who are regarded as divinely guided. The individuals would be us: Dabria and I and a few hundred million more. Our particular leader, one of our officials, if you will, is Rafael. He's like the overseer of all guardian angels everywhere. Your grandmother … she chose a different path. She's a teacher and a rescue worker. She helps others cross over. If she goes with you, we will lose one of our best workers and I'm not sure that would be acceptable. And I'm not even sure how we could send her back, after all she can't take her old body back, it's quite used up by now."

Ana rubbed her eyes until she saw spots. "Okay, you are all insane. I'm freaking out." Then Ana's body was rocked by a violent spasm, and she fell back into the fog. "What the hell was that?" Ana looked around, gazed at her hands, then up at the pair before her.

"Your heart stopped. We don't have much more time. Please, please reconsider. Don't go into the light. I wish we could make you understand." Dabria knelt and cleared some of the fog away from the floor. Ana could see a commotion below. People were moving all around, noises filtered up to her. There were sad noises, confused noises, noises of blame and shame.

"What are they doing? Wait! That's me down there. Why are they putting me on a stretcher? I'm up here? What happened to the music? Where's Martin?"

Ana stared at the chaos below and spotted Martin over in a corner. He and the redhead were crying in each other's arms. Her friend Rose was beside the gurney. She screamed for Ana to wake up, to hang on, and to come back to them.

"Rose! I'm here, Rose. I'm not dead, honest," Ana hollered into the opening. "Rose, stop Martin, he's going to sleep with that whore. Don't let him do it, Rose. I'm not dead. Martin you asshole! Get your hands off of her. I'm still alive for God's sake!" Ana looked up at Rigel and Dabria, then to her grandmother.

"Okay, I'll do whatever you ask, only one thing. Grandma gets to at least listen to me, and I get to hear her sometimes. Do we have a deal?" Ana looked from one anxious face to another.

"Deal." A booming voice shot out from deep within the light. The scene below slowed to a crawl. Ana shielded her eyes as a large figured emerged. A kindly face reflected total love and acceptance. He held out his hand and shook hers firmly. Dabria and Rigel backed away, heads lowered. Ana's grandmother gave Ana a hug and faded into the light.

"Who are you?" Ana stared into the deepest, bluest eyes she had ever seen. She habitually reached for her earlobe and stroked between her thumb and forefinger

"I believe I am what you would call, the boss." His radiant smile washed over her, warming and calming her.

"God?" Ana wavered slightly as a firm hand caught her.

"Goodness no!" The figure before her laughed until the sound of it seeped into her bones, vibrating the very core of her being. Ana giggled and then erupted into full-blown laughter. Dabria and Rigel chuckled quietly behind her. "I am Rafael. I am an Archangel and it's my duty to ensure everyone has a guardian angel or two to watch over them. Dabria and Rigel are yours. You have two because you had some big plans for yourself. Your promises were quite extensive. You were to have kept them all in the next ten years. Now, it has come to this. There is a plan, Ana. A plan larger than you can imagine right now. You are a part of that plan—you made yourself a part of the plan. Without you, the plan must be reworked, redone, renegotiated on so many levels. It would take days to explain. You can go with your grandma, but not today. In ten years, you can go. For now, we need you." Rafael smiled down upon her and cast his eyes briefly over the two guardians.

"Wait." Ana took a step back. "What's with the ten years? Are you going to give me back my life but in ten years I'm going to die anyway? I'm not sure I like that. There's got to be another way. Isn't there?"

"Yes, there is another way, but, it's only been done a few times and then only in circumstances of extreme need." Rafael shrugged and two huge wings unfolded. He ruffled them out and then let them settle down on his back. "Yes, there is another way, but you would have to become a double agent, so to speak."

"Double agent? Like a spy? You want me to spy on people? I don't get it." Ana took another step towards the light. Dabria and Rigel froze in place, each extending a hand out towards her.

"Not so much a spy. Let's call it a dual role. For the next ten years you will go about your life. You will remember none of this, except that today is the day you almost died. During those ten years your contracts will be fulfilled, promises kept. You don't need to know what they are or who they are with. You made these promises long before you came into this body. These are people whose lives you must touch, whose destiny must intertwine with yours. You needn't know you are doing it. That we know is enough. Your promise to me will be that when those ten years are up, on your twenty-eighth birthday, you can live, and you will come to work for me. I think it would be acceptable to add fifteen more years to your life. Dabria and Rigel will have their contracts with you extended. They will train you and you will be a human angel for those fifteen years." Rafael nodded once, pleased with his decision. Dabria and Rigel nodded as well. It wasn't done often, but it could work.

Ana thought about the proposal. She looked down and surveyed the chaos below. Did she really want to return to that? Then again, dead wasn't looking all that good right now. No way she was going to let Martin anywhere near that bimbo. And besides, Rose really needed her.

Ana squeezed her left earlobe between her thumb and forefinger. It hurt—she wasn't dreaming.

"Okay, let me get this straight. When I'm twenty-eight I have to go to work as an angel on Earth, but I'll still be alive, right?"

"Exactly." Rafael ruffled his wings again.

"Okay, and then when I'm forty-three I get to go back to whatever I was doing and carry on with my life, right? I'm not coming back here yet. Twenty-five years isn't a long time, especially if I'm working my ass off for fifteen years to buy back ten years I shouldn't have lost in the first place." She made a face at Rigel and Dabria, then crossed her arms in front of her and returned to hold Rafael's gaze.

"Interesting math." Rafael stretched out his wings, partially blocking the light. "How about this. I'll throw in an extra forty-three years. That takes you to eighty-six. Think of it as a bonus for a job well done."

"How do you know I'm going to do a good job?" Ana eyed his wings with suspicion and tried to look behind him.

"Because you will promise," Rafael smiled at her. "A promise is a contract with God, and I know you won't intentionally break your promise."

Ana stretched her shoulders back and looked up at Rafael. "Do I get wings?"

Rafael, Dabria, and Rigel laughed in unison. "Goodness no, dear." Rigel stepped forward and placed a hand on Ana's shoulder. "You don't get them until you've worked here for a dozen millennia or so, and maybe not even then. That's another story for another time."

Rafael nodded and produced a coral piece of paper and a quill pen. "Sign here and it will be done." Ana took the pen and signed her name at the bottom of the paper. Rafael blew on it, rolled it up and tucked it into his garment.

"It's time to go back Anastasia. Are you ready?"

Ana nodded.

Rafael gathered her up in his arms and kissed her forehead. "Did you know your name means resurrection? I believe your parents named you well."

Ana's vision clouded and her whole body hung heavy in Rafael's arms. Within moments she was back at the party, lying on a stretcher. Her first action of her renewed life was to throw up all over her best friend, Rose.

Chapter 2: December 1985

Ana inhaled deeply as she listened to the instructor's voice. "That's it, deep breaths now. In, and hold it, and out." Ana's eyes fluttered behind her closed lids. "Bring yourself back slowly. Deep breaths … in … and out."

Ana focused on the sound of the instructor's voice and brought her conscious mind back into the room. She loved her meditation classes. The energy was fantastic, and she always felt safe here. Today had been a good day. She went deep and vaguely recalled seeing her spirit guides.

"One last breath, in … and out … and open your eyes." Ana slowly opened her eyes and looked around at the group. Everyone had a goofy smile on their face. The kind you get after an extremely satisfying meal or in this case, a deep meditation.

"Would anyone like to share?" Ana's instructor, Carol, made eye contact with each of her students. Her eyes fell on Ana and Ana looked away. Today was a good day, but not to be shared yet, not yet. A petite blonde-haired woman to Ana's left spoke.

"That was the most relaxed I've even been. This time I let your voice and the music guide me. I was able to see my special house and use my key to open the door and go inside. There wasn't anyone there, just me." The woman let a small smile touch her lips and looked at her foot. "That's all."

Ana took another deep breath. Some days she wondered if

she was just plain old insane. She struggled with the concept that meditation classes were simply group hypnosis and she wasn't really getting in touch with her spiritual self. Most days she didn't care if it was real or a mass hallucination. She felt good afterwards and it was the end result that counted.

"That's it for today, then," Carol said. "Namaste. See you in a week."

One by one, the members of her group stretched and stood, then exited the room. Carol was there to send each one on their way with a blessing. Ana waited. She had questions. Ana always had questions. Carol knew Ana would be last one out. Finally, Ana stood, stretched, and walked past Carol and into her office without a word. Carol followed a few minutes later with two cups of herbal tea.

"So, Ana, how was it today. More questions? Or did you find some answers." Carol placed the cups on the desk and settled into her high-backed chair. She turned on the radio and soft Christmas music filled the room.

"Mostly questions again." Ana picked up her cup and cradled it in her hands as if she were cold. "I mean, I love what we do here, what you do here, but ..." Ana's voice trailed off as she sipped her tea.

"But you wonder if it's real." Carol finished the sentence and picked up her own cup. "Ana, we've been through this so many times before. It's as real as you want it to be. I cannot control what you see, who you see or what you do when you are meditating. You could fly to another universe and back and I would have no control over that. Is it real? If it's real to you,

Reluctant Angel

to your mind, then it's real. If you still view this as some sort of creative disillusionment, that is what it will be for you."

The two sat in silence for a moment, sipping their tea.

"I had the dream again." Ana put her cup down and stroked her left earlobe. "It was real, so freakin' real. These people said they were my guardian angels and that I was going to die if I didn't sign this contract and then this huge angel came out and filled me with hope and love and I just couldn't say no. Then, when I wake up, I'm so sad. I feel like ..." Ana's voice dropped to a whisper as the words caught in her throat. "It's like living on borrowed time. I should have died, Carol. I try to get back there. Not to the light, but to those people, and I can't." Ana gave her earlobe one last gentle squeeze as she looked to Carol for an answer.

"Ana, honey, it's been over nine years since you overdosed. You've come so far. Why not be content in knowing you're on the right path. You've had nine years of growth and discovery. You've grown into a fine woman. You do things that enhance your life instead of destroying it. You've moved thousands of miles away from your past. You have a great job and a great apartment near the ocean. Life just doesn't get much better than that hon. Trust me. It took me thirty years to get to where I am, and you're almost there."

Ana shrugged and sipped her tea. "I saw Grandma again today, in my meditation. She came to my secret house. She's always inside waiting for me at the kitchen table. A part of me so wants to believe that she's there, waiting, helping me whenever I need her. But the other part, the part that gets up for work at

7 a.m. every morning and drives to the office and does the job and pays the bills and calls home on weekends—that part of me thinks I'm nuts, and I just imagine her." She sighed and snuggled back into her chair, her mug of tea firmly held in both hands. "Am I nuts, Carol?"

Carol laughed quietly. "Hon, I am not the right person to ask that. Look at me. I'm fifty years old, twice divorced, living in a loft like some aging hippie. I teach people to meditate for a living. People like you, who aren't rich, aren't trendy, aren't into the latest fads. In other words, your basic middle-class character looking for an alternative to organized religion and/or Valium. I'll never be rich or famous. I'll tell you one very important thing Ana; I'm not crazy. A little eccentric perhaps, but I'm not crazy."

"Are you happy?" Ana leaned forward and set her cup down. She picked up a pen and started drawing on a notepad. Carol didn't answer.

"Truly Carol, are you happy? Don't you want to do something with all of this? You could move to the West End, do private sessions at fifty dollars an hour and make yourself some good cash. Why do you stay with us? Let's face it, there isn't a normal one of us in the bunch. We are the walking wounded looking for a needle and thread to put us back together."

Carol stood and walked to the front of the desk. "Well, from what I can tell we are all the walking wounded. That's why we're here—to learn. Think of me as the corner store. I can't sew you back up, but I can supply you with your own needle and thread. That makes me happy."

Carol sat on the edge of the desk and picked up the drawing

Ana had been working on. "Who is this one?"

"That one they call Rig. He's got a great smile and he's very patient. His full name is Rigel, and he has a star named for him. It's in the foot of Orion." Ana pointed to the rough drawing of the constellation behind the angel's head. "I looked it up after my dreams started." Ana shifted in her chair.

"Ana, listen carefully." Carol leaned forward. "You've been with us now for almost a year. You love to meditate, you have a natural ability to make people trust you, and you are very perceptive. Why don't you sign up for the second-year classes? They're a bit different, perhaps a little *woo-woo* as you like to call it. But I think you'll like them." Carol stood and went back to her chair. Ana chewed on the end of the pen.

"You're talking about seeing auras, talking to spirit guides, and doing psychometry and shit right?" Ana pulled the pen out of her mouth and began to doodle again. "I'm not sure that's for me. I mean, I took this class because I needed to chill out a bit. I don't want to eat pills to relax. I learned my lesson on that one. But, I don't know about the other stuff. I mean, it's just weird, ya know." Ana sketched a kindly pair of eyes looking back at her from a middle-aged face. "It's just that, I have a hard time believing any of this and yet somehow, maybe it's real. I dunno. It's all been so screwed up for as long as I can remember."

"I know, hon. I'm just asking you to think about it. You have so much potential psychically speaking and you're skeptical, so you always search for truth. It's a good combination." Carol opened her desk drawer and took out a bag of runes. She drew one stone from the bag. "Hagalaz." She sighed. "Always Hagalaz with you, isn't it." She handed Ana the rune.

Ana rubbed it between her thumb and index finger. "Yep, good ole Hagalaz. My controlled crises, coming to completion, the beginnings of inner harmony. Yeah right." Ana tossed the rune back at Carol. "If it wasn't the horrible H it would be the Tower in Tarot. I know it by heart. I know you think I'm supposed to be something magic or mystical or mythical or whatever. I don't feel it. I don't believe it and I don't want it!" Ana stood and grabbed her purse.

"I've got to go. Chris is waiting for me. Not that he'll notice if I'm late. He's probably stoned by now. I don't understand how a man can consume that many drugs and live."

Carol walked Ana to the front door. "And I don't understand what a bright, intelligent, beautiful woman like you is doing with him." She opened the door and stood aside for Ana.

"You and me both, you and me both. Must be karma or something, right?" Ana laughed, but it didn't reach her eyes. She stared out at the grey, rainy street. "Oh well, at least it's never boring. See you next week, Carol."

Carol watched as Ana made her way up the street. She had never met a walking contradiction until now.

Reluctant Angel

Chapter 3: Chris

Ana dropped her cigarette and crushed it out with her toe as she rounded the corner and headed towards Chris's house. He and his roommate rented a small two-bedroom on the edge of the downtown core. She often wondered what kind of person would rent their home to someone like Chris and his best friend, John. They always paid the rent on time, but the yard and the house were a disaster. There were holes in the walls where Chris and John got carried away and put an elbow or a knee through the drywall.

She'd met Chris at a nightclub a few months ago. He had shoulder length brown hair, a wicked smile, was funny, a great dancer, and bought her drinks all night long. Then, after last call, he escorted Ana to the back room and introduced her to the band. She was ecstatic and maybe a little drunk. The band greeted Chris like a long-lost friend and one by one they would disappear into a back corner together and come back all smiles. Ana learned later that he was their dealer. By the time she figured out he was an addict and a dealer, she believed she was in love and was determined to save him. Now, a few months into the relationship, she was wondering what the hell she was doing.

The house was dark, both inside and out. Neighbouring homes had their Christmas lights up and colour twinkled up and down the street.

Ana took a deep breath, put her key in the door and stepped inside.

"Hello, anyone home?" She turned on a light, put down her purse and walked into the kitchen. Piles of dirty dishes were in the sink. The garbage overflowed with take-out containers and empty beer cans. Ana shook her head and quickly bypassed the mess. "Hello, Chris? Are you here?" The living room was empty save for a calico cat eating the remains of the coagulated cheese and ham from last night's pizza. Ana turned and headed down the hall to Chris's bedroom. She found him sitting on the side of his bed, head resting on his chest, a candle burning on the side table.

"What are you doing in here? What's with the candle?" Ana stopped when she noticed the spoon and syringe. "What the hell are you doing? You promised me you wouldn't do this anymore! You said you'd stop. You promised, Chris!" Ana's voice was shrill, and she felt herself losing control. She walked over to the side table, swept the candle to the floor, then stepped on it.

"Jesus, Chris, you've been sort of clean for almost a month now. What are you doing? I believed you! You said you'd stop the needles, stop the junk." Ana narrowed her eyes and put her hands on her hips. "You know what you are? You are a loser, Chris. I have no idea why I'm with you. In fact, I think this is the perfect time to not be with you anymore." Ana turned and started out the door. From behind her, she heard a faint noise.

"Wait," Chris whispered. "Help me." He lifted his head slightly and then fell over on his side. His head landed on a pillow, feet still on the floor.

He brought his arms up and hugged himself tightly. "Ana, wait."

Ana turned and walked back to the bed. "Need to be tucked in Chris?" Her acidic tone was lost on the man lying on the bed. "You want help? Sure, I'll help." Ana bent over and grabbed Chris's ankles. She swung his legs up and onto the bed causing Chris to lie on his back. "Want me to fluff your pillows for you? Sure, why not!" Ana grabbed two pillows, lifted Chris's head and then let it drop. "How about a blanket? Want a blanket, Chris? Feeling a bit chilly? Sure, I'll get you a blanket." Ana went to the foot of the bed, shook out a ratty bedspread, and threw it over Chris. Only his shoulders, neck and face could be seen. His eyelids began to droop. Ana noticed a small bit of drool slip out one side of his mouth.

"Ana ..." Chris's words were barely audible "Bad shit ... too much ... very cold." Chris closed his eyes and then fought to open them again. "Get John. Help me." Chris closed his eyes and Ana watched in fascination as his breathing slowed. She timed it. One breath every twelve seconds, then one every fifteen.

Ana walked into the kitchen and found the phone underneath a pile of take-out containers. She picked it up, dialled and waited.

"Wildlife! This is where the animals party." Ana recognized John's voice. She heard the rhythmic drumming in the background and the sounds of people laughing and clapping. She never understood why someone would go to a strip club in the middle of the day.

"John, it's Ana. You have to come home. Chris is really

sick. He's asking for you. He stuck another damn needle in his arm and now he's barely breathing." Ana pulled the cord on the phone as far as it would go and peered into Chris's room. "He doesn't look good, John. He asked for you."

"Shit!" John placed his hand over the receiver and hollered for his boss. A few moments later he came back on the line. "I'll be right there, Ana. Whatever you do, don't call the cops or the ambulance. There's too much shit in the house. Got it? No cops, no ambulance. I'm on my way."

The phone went dead, and Ana placed the receiver back on the cradle. She walked into the bedroom and over to the side of the bed where she eased up one of Chris's eyelids like she'd seen on TV. The pupil was huge, unseeing. More drool had formed and was now making its way down the side of Chris's face. Ana went to the bathroom, tore off a piece of toilet paper, and came back and wiped the drool away. She left the toilet paper in the crease of his neck to catch any further drippings.

"Chris, you're such as ass. Only an ass would do something like this." Ana went back into the kitchen and grabbed a wobbly chair. She brought it into the bedroom and placed it at the foot of the bed. She rummaged through her purse, found her cigarettes and lit one, then inhaled deeply and watched the smoke rise to the ceiling as she exhaled. She grabbed an ashtray off the floor beside the bed and sat down.

"Welcome to my world. One minute I'm meditating and talking to angels and dead people and the next minute I'm watching someone die. What a weird life. No one would believe this. Do you believe it?"

Ana grabbed Chris by the foot and shook it. "Hey asshole, you gonna die? I've never seen anyone die before."

Ana watched the smoke curl up from the end of her cigarette. She continued her conversation with herself. "I think I'm nuts. Carol doesn't think I'm nuts, my boss thinks I'm great, my friends love me, but geeze, I must be nuts. Only a nut would sit here smoking a cigarette while her boyfriend ODs. Only a nut would stand by and not call 911. But, if I call, and he lives, he'll get busted and then I'll be in such deep shit I'll never get out. Oh yeah, what a good life this is. Hey Grandma, are you out there!" Ana shouted at the ceiling. "Grandma, got any advice?" Ana tugged on her left earlobe. This time it didn't make her feel any better.

Chris groaned and rolled towards the edge of the bed. "Oh shit, don't puke. No, no, no, no! I'm not cleaning up any puke." Ana put out her cigarette and got the wastebasket from the bathroom. She placed it beside the bed and then lit another cigarette.

"Well, Mr. Chris. I've learned one thing. I don't love you. In fact, I am very pissed off at you right now and it would serve you right if you died." Ana felt a tear on the crest of her cheek. "Shit," she muttered and swiped it away. "No tears for you buddy boy, nope. You don't deserve it." Ana stared at the body on the bed. Was he really dying or just really stoned? Ana couldn't tell. "You'd better really be dying because if I'm going through this and you're just having a great trip on whatever you shoved in your arm, I'm going to be so pissed at you!" Ana stood quickly and toppled the chair. She paced in the small room, then back to the kitchen, and returned to the bedroom.

"Damn it!" She sat down on the side of the bed, grabbed Chris by the shoulders, and held him in a sitting position. "Wake up damn you! Damn you to hell, wake up!" She was sobbing now.

The reality of the situation finally set in. She watched in horror as his head lolled from side to side. "No! Damn you!" Ana slapped his face. No reaction. She pushed him back onto the pillows. Where the hell was John. Maybe she should call an ambulance. This was just too real. She saw a flutter from the corner of her eye and could have sworn someone else was in the room. She turned to the doorway. No one was there.

"Shit, shit, shit!" Ana went to her purse and lit another cigarette. Then she went to the kitchen and filled a dirty mug with tap water. She came back into the bedroom and threw the water on Chris's face. He moved slightly and moaned.

"Wake up!" Ana left the room and went to look out the front window. She saw John park the car and head towards the front door.

"Hurry, hurry," she whispered to herself. "Dear God, don't let him die, please, don't let him die." She went to the door and opened it. John ran in and headed straight for the bedroom. Ana locked the door behind him and stood in the kitchen doorway, watching.

"Start the shower, Ana. Make it cold, very, very cold, no hot water. You got that?" John ripped the blanket off and began to strip Chris of his shirt and pants. "Now!" he shouted as he put Chris's arm around his shoulder and tried to help him stand.

Ana ran to the bathroom, pulled back the shower curtain and started the water. She pulled the lever and cold water sprayed everywhere. She couldn't help but notice the mould growing around the ledge of the tub and wondered if they ever cleaned this room.

John entered the bathroom with Chris. "Help me get under his other arm. Let's lift him up and get him in there." Ana did as she was told and positioned herself under Chris's arm.

"Okay. I'll lift up his left leg and get it in the tub. Once I do that you bend down and do the same with his right."

Ana watched as John maneuvered Chris's leg into the tub, then she did the same. She shivered as the cold spray drenched her top and jeans. John was standing in the shower with Chris, holding him under the water. Chris's eyes opened slightly, focused, and then closed again. He groaned as the freezing water blasted his head and then cascaded down his body.

"Go see if there's any coffee left in the pot and bring it here."

Ana found the coffeepot about half full. The coffee in it looked cold, thick, and old. She grabbed the pot and a plastic cup from the counter and brought them back to the bathroom.

"Give him some," John ordered.

Ana looked at the thick sludge in the cup.

"Gawd, how old is this coffee? It's gross!" Ana made a face, poured the brown ooze into the cup and put it to Chris's mouth.

"Drink up, Chris," Ana said as she poured the days-old coffee into Chris's mouth. Chris sputtered and then swallowed. Ana managed to get most of it in his mouth and the rest spilled down his chest, mingling with the cold water.

"Did you call 911?" John turned Chris slightly so the water now pummeled Chris's shoulders.

"No, you told me not to." Ana reached for the pot, poured another cup, and continued to feed the vile liquid to Chris. "Are you sure he's going to be okay?" Ana watched as Chris's eyes opened and closed as he tried to focus.

"I don't know but I'm not going to jail because of him." John leaned over and turned off the shower. "Go get him a T-shirt or something."

Ana took the empty pot and cup back to the kitchen and then went back to the bedroom. She stopped and looked at the candle on the carpet, crushed. What was she doing here anyway? She shook her head, went to the dresser, pulled out what she hoped was a clean T-shirt, and brought it back to the bathroom. The water was off now. John held Chris up against the wall. She helped John pull the T-shirt over Chris's head. He looked so vulnerable in his wet underwear.

"Get under his arm again. We're going to walk him." Ana complied and took her position on the opposite side of John. "We'll know in a few minutes if it's going to work. It worked last time. This guy has more lives than a cat." John and Ana took Chris into the living room where they began to walk him back and forth.

"You mean he's done this before?" Ana was shocked. "What happened that time?"

"Pretty much same as what you see here, except instead of you it was some chick named Gail. He's a lucky guy. Gets the girls and lives to talk about it." Ana stopped walking.

"So, he's almost died before, didn't learn his lesson, and now we're trying to save him. That's nuts." Ana continued pacing the floor with Chris and John.

Time passed and Chris finally held up his head on his own and shrugged his arm off Ana's shoulder. John led him to the couch, cleared a space and sat him down.

"You okay now, buddy?" John bent over in front of Chris, checked his pupils and his pulse. "Looks like you'll make it this time." John left the room. Ana stared at Chris. Moments later John reappeared, dressed in clean, dry clothes. "Well, I'm outta here. Gotta get back to work. Stay away from that shit, Chris. You're a fucking nuisance." John walked over to Chris, punched him in the arm, and left.

Ana stood there, unable to speak. Her mind was busy, too many thoughts. Chris finally looked at her. "Thanks Ana. Sorry about the scare. Man, that's good shit."

Chris stood and steadied himself by placing his hand on the wall. "I need a hot shower. I'm freezing and a little groggy. Want to have one with me?" Chris managed a lopsided wink and moved towards her. Ana stepped aside.

"You asshole!" She shoved Chris away and watched as he fell back onto the couch. "I'm soaked, cold, worried to death, and all you can think about is sex!"

Ana stomped into the bedroom and grabbed her purse. On her way back she could have sworn she saw movement in the hallway and decided it was just the cat.

"I'm leaving, Chris. And guess what. I'm not coming back.

If you want to kill yourself, do it with someone else. I'm not going to save you anymore!"

Ana rummaged in her purse and pulled out her keychain. She took off Chris's house key. "Here's your damn key. I'm outta here!" She threw the key and watched as it hit Chris in the forehead. "Merry fricking Christmas!"

Ana slammed the door as she left. Enough was enough.

Reluctant Angel

Chapter 4: A Quartet of Angels

Chris watched in a daze as Ana slammed the door. He shrugged and slouched farther down into the couch.

"Christmas?" he said to no one in particular. "I should call my sister." He grabbed a discarded shirt he found on the floor and lay it across his damp knees. He was cold, but mostly he was high and was no longer in the mood for a hot shower. It could wait.

He closed his eyes and heard an echo of voices in the room. "Huh? Who's there?" He opened one eye and thought he saw a figure standing before him, except he could see right through it. He closed one eye and then switched eyes and tried both eyes. The figure was still there. He could barely make out a second, then a third and a fourth figure, standing farther away. "Cool." was all he said as he slouched into the couch.

* * *

"There, at least she's done with that." Dabria looked down at Chris and shook her head.

"Now Dabby, no judgments here, he's not exactly had it easy you know. That was a pretty nasty contract he signed: forty-nine lessons, thirty-two karmic repayments and eighty-four connections. That's a lot to do in a short lifetime."

Rigel sat down beside Chris. He patted Chris's knee and

looked into his eyes. "Hard contract young man, but it's almost done."

Chris turned towards Rigel, smiled and then slouched back into cushions of the couch. Dabria placed herself in a chair beside the couch.

Another figure stepped forward and sat on the other side of Chris.

"Nice to see you, Donach." Rigel nodded in the angel's direction. "Tough one this."

Donach was shorter than Rigel, with close-cropped black hair and deep, dark eyes. "Toughest assignment I've had in a few centuries. Keeping this one alive has not been easy. Tough assignment for certain." He nodded towards the front door. "And with this one always hounding him it's a wonder I haven't worn myself ragged looking after the lad."

A tall figure, draped in a hooded, black cloak stood by the doorway. "Now Donach, you know you'd be bored to death if I wasn't around to make things more interesting for you."

"Oh, you'd like that wouldn't you, Nizroth?" Donach stayed seated and put a protective arm around Chris. "You and your goody basket of tasty treats and forbidden fruits. As if he could resist them after all the clauses and sub-clauses that were added to his contract. Even I would have been tempted by you if I were still human." Donach patted Chris on the hand. "You're doing a fine job lad, honest. I'll be here for you until you're done."

Chris opened one eye, then the other, and looked towards his guardian angel. "Cool," was all he said before closing his eyes again.

Rigel stood and paced the room. "I need a promise from you Niz."

The dark figure pulled the hood back from the cloak and a cascade of wavy golden hair spilled out. A bright smile appeared on his face, but never reached his eyes. "Certainly Rig, what is your wish? I have an opening in my department you know. You would have made a fine angel of temptation. We could use a hard worker like you."

Rigel shook his head. "Be that as it may, Niz, I really do need a promise, an angel promise. One angel to another. I need you to promise me you will not tempt Ana anymore. Honestly, every time that poor girl gets close to finishing her first contract you step in and give her even more to overcome."

"I'd like to comply, Rig, really I would. However, there is one teensy weensy complication in that promise."

Dabria stood and placed herself in front of Nizroth. "Oh really? A little complication? And what might that be, Mr. Nizroth?" Dabria placed her hands firmly on her hips and waited for his reply.

"Mr. Nizroth? There is no need to be insulting, Dabby. Being neither male nor female, I resent the title. Never, ever, call me a mister."

He smiled at Dabria and tried to step forward, but she refused to move. "Now that we have that straightened out, it's painfully obvious that you two have been so busy here, you haven't received the latest round of contract updates." Nizroth tossed his hair, went around Dabria, and walked towards the kitchen. "I mean really—keep abreast of things, would you." He leaned against the door jamb, arms crossed.

"What updates? What are you talking about?" Dabria unglued her hands from her hips and stared at the figure in the doorway.

"Why, it's Ana's last assignment of course. Boss says she's ready and it just so happens the only way to get them to connect properly is through me. They've added a little extra into the new contract and I get to push her in the direction she needs to go." Nizroth flashed his pearly whites and waggled his eyebrows.

"You get to be the catalyst? You? Oh, for goodness sakes. This is just too much." Dabria walked over to Rigel. "I told you we should head back and see if there were any updates, but oh no, you said you didn't want to leave her alone anymore, not now, not with him." She jerked her thumb towards Chris. "Now look what's happened. Oh dear, this is going on our record, you know."

Chris opened one eye and looked towards her. He nodded, smiled, and then mumbled, "Shush lady, I want to know about the updates. Be quiet would ya? This is the best hallucination I've ever had."

Dabria rolled her eyes and shook her head as Chris sunk back into the cushions.

Nizroth smiled and produced a rolled-up parchment from his cloak. "Read them yourselves. It's all here, plain as can be." He tossed the roll to Rigel.

Rigel opened it and studied the contents. "He's right, Dab, poor dear has to be tempted yet again. It's just got to be." He rolled up the parchment and handed it back to Nizroth.

"Keep it. I've got a copy." He patted his breast and smiled. "Well, I believe my work here is done for now. I'll see the two of you later." He turned to Donach, still seated beside Chris. "As for you and your charge, I'll be back in a few hours to see if he's learned his lesson." Nizroth strode towards the door and walked right through it.

Rigel and Dabria looked at each other, shrugged and began to fade. "Good luck, Donach. Give us a shout when he goes over, I'd like to say hello." He waved and nodded back to the pair as they faded away completely.

Donach stood, sighed, and looked down at Chris. "Well lad, only a few more months, you're almost done with it."

Chris nodded. "Damn straight man, damn straight. This is some real heavy shit." Then he closed his eyes and fell into a deep sleep.

Chapter 5: Brad Thorn

Red lights flashed on wet pavement. The west-coast drizzle created the perfect backdrop for the Channel 11 News Team. The Channel 11 van, complete with roving reporter, Brad Thorn, was filming carollers around the corner when they heard the crash. They quickly packed up and went to investigate. The crew arrived at the same time as the police, just in time to catch the whole thing.

As Brad surveyed the scene, his camera operator focused on the front door of the house with a car half in the living room. The police knocked on the door, then decided to break it down. As soon as the door opened, a small child ran out, past the police and into the street. Brad watched as the child stopped, looked around, and ran into the arms of a female paramedic. Brad ran over to talk to them. The camera operator followed.

"Hi there, Brad Thorn, Channel 11 News. Do you know this child?"

The paramedic looked up at Brad.

"Yes, I do," the woman said as she rocked the child in her arms. "This is my niece, Brittany Cranston. She was kidnapped early yesterday morning."

Brad couldn't believe his luck. A child abducted a week before Christmas, then found five blocks away eighteen hours later, and he was on the scene. He'd interviewed the parents yesterday morning when the girl had gone missing. They were wonderfully frantic and blessedly photogenic. Now, because of a drunk driver, who happened to miss the corner and slam into a house, she was free. The best part: Brad was there with his camera crew to capture it all. Brad grinned as he watched the scene unfurl. You couldn't make up stories like this. The parents would be on their way. This was top notch news.

Brad listened to the voice in his earpiece. "Five seconds to air." Brad stepped away from the ambulance and under the light of a streetlamp. He heard the Channel 11 music through his earpiece. It was show time. "Three, two, one, and we're live."

"This is Brad Thorn for Channel 11 Live at Five News. Our team has just learned that a string of chance happenings led to finding missing five-year-old Brittany Cranston." The camera panned the area. It was magnificent. The Christmas lights mixed in perfectly with the flashing lights of the four police cruisers, two ambulances, and a fire truck. Paramedics rushed about and headed into the house once the all-clear was given. The light drizzle created a surreal feeling to the west-coast scene. Brad watched on the monitor and began his narration.

"Moments ago, a driver failed to negotiate a turn and wound up smashing into this suburban home." The camera panned right, away from the lights towards the front door of the house. "When the police arrived at the scene they discovered a lot more than an MVA." The camera zoomed in as a man with a jacket over his head was escorted out of the house. His hands were handcuffed in front, his head bowed. There were armed police on either side, who guided him by his elbows. The camera pulled back, following them to the street. Brad listened intently to his earpiece to the chatter from his producer. Their inside source confirmed they even knew who the man was. Brad could barely hide his excitement. This was better than Miami Vice or Hill Street Blues. This was live TV.

Brad composed himself as the camera operator pointed to him. "We have just learned that police have identified thirty-eight-year-old Martin LaFronde as the man responsible for kidnapping Brittany Cranston from her home eighteen hours ago. LaFronde was a handyman for several families in the area. He was one of their main suspects and was out on parole for assault and unlawful detainment."

The camera pulled back and focused as LaFronde who was guided into the back seat of a police cruiser. Then the camera panned to the back end of a car sticking out of the house.

Brad looked around, somehow he'd missed the driver being taken out of the house. She was sitting on the back of the second ambulance. A paramedic shone his mini flashlight into her eyes. Brad checked his mic cord and pulled it along behind him as he headed for the second ambulance. A police officer stepped in front of him before he reached the driver of the smashed car.

"You can interview her later, after we do." Brad nodded but stayed in place, just in case. Even without an interview with the driver, it was a pretty great story. He tried not to grin. This kind of story could get him noticed on a national scale. It was perfect. The lights, the live drama unfolding, and the sound of rain falling softly. It was the perfect scene. The only thing that would make it better would be to get the parents on camera.

Brad stood a bit taller as the camera panned back to him. The camera operator pointed at him, and he began his summary.

"The most amazing part of today was, of course, finding little Brittany Cranston." The camera pulled back, Brad was now in the right-hand corner of the frame, the ambulance where Brittany was being examined, on the left. Brad provided the voiceover to the touching scene. "The woman examining little Brittany is her aunt Linda, a paramedic and the sister of the missing girl's mother."

As if on cue, a fifth cruiser pulled in and did a sideways slide-stop as the cameras rolled. Brad's excitement grew as the oh-so-photogenic, yet frantic mother and father, emerged from the police car and ran to their daughter.

"We've just learned that Brittany's parents have arrived on the scene." The camera followed the couple as they rushed through the rain towards the ambulance. As soon as Brittany heard her mother and father calling, she burst into tears. The camera panned left and caught the exact moment the little girl's parents embraced her. A cheer rose up from the now substantial crowd.

"Folks, this is a touching moment." The camera pulled back and focused on Brad as the family reunion unfolded in the background. "This poor family is now reunited after eighteen long hours of anguish." The camera pulled back farther to give the home viewers a look at the total picture: the crowds, the Christmas lights, the rain, the happy family, the flashing red and blue lights, and in the centre of it all, the brilliant smile of Brad Thorn.

Brad touched his earpiece, nodded to the camera operator and walked over to the back of the ambulance. "Mr. Cranston, how does it feel to have Brittany back?" Brad poked the microphone between the husband and wife. The camera pressed in tight for a close-up, lights shining on their faces.

David Cranston looked up and shielded his eyes. He released his daughter into his wife's arms and looked tearfully into the camera lens. "I'm just glad she's safe. We never gave up hope, we knew the police would find our little girl." He squinted into the lights once more, then turned and embraced his daughter and wife. It was the perfect soundbite, the perfect shot.

Brad turned and faced the camera. He made sure there was an appropriate amount of happiness and disbelief on his face. "Tune in to Channel 11 News at 11 for updated information on this unusual tale with a very happy ending. This has been Brad Thorn reporting."

The camera light shut off and Brad grabbed a towel from his assistant and wiped off his face. His hair was soaked, as were his shoes. He was also quite certain his tie was ruined. He didn't care. This story could give him the career break he needed. The news anchor position was posted that morning. After this great story, he couldn't see how any other reporter would get the job. He had it in the bag.

He handed his mic and the towel to an assistant and strode across the street towards the Channel 11 van. Brad waved to the crowds as he crossed. He didn't notice the woman in front of him, head down against the rain.

"Oomph." Her head came up as he crashed into him.

"Watch where you're going would you!" Ana steadied herself and glared at the reporter. She shook her head and then started to walk away.

She looked a little like a drowned rat, but she was cute. "Wait, I'm sorry. I didn't see you. Let me buy you a coffee or something." She stopped and turned to face him. He eyed her up and down, his eyes settling a little too long on her breasts.

"Buy me a coffee? Buy. Me. A. Coffee." Ana stared up at the man and his lopsided smile. "Then what? Maybe you can take me home, screw me, litter my life with your problems and then when you've decided you've had enough, just forget about me!"

Brad's grin disappeared.

"No, I don't think so. I don't care who you are, or who you think you are, I really don't need some big-toothed walking hormone deciding I'd be nice to have around right now. So, if you don't mind, I'm going home to my cat." Ana stomped her foot into a puddle and splashed even more water onto Brad's pants. "The answer is no!" Ana took two steps, then turned back to face him. "Merry frickin' Christmas, asshole!" Before he could reply, she was gone.

Chapter 6: A New Assignment

Ana stepped off the elevator and opened the glass doors to Thomas, Simpson and Parker. The advertising and marketing firm she worked for was small but growing. Ana went into her tiny office, shrugged off her raincoat, hung it up, and put her purse in her bottom desk drawer. There were three messages on her desk, all from Chris. He had phoned her repeatedly at home over the past few days. She let the answering machine get the calls. Now he was calling her at work. All she wanted was for Christmas to be over and the new year to be here. She hoped 1986 would be better than 1985.

Ana picked up the messages, grabbed the phone, then placed it slowly back into the cradle. She tugged on her earlobe as she stared at the pink slips in her hand.

"Oh Grandma, I miss you so much," she said into the empty office. "You'd know what to say, you always knew what to say."

Ana took a deep breath, then ripped the phone messages in two and tossed them in the trash. It was time to grow up and stop trying to fix people, especially him. She knew she had a bad habit of doing that—thinking she could fix men. She saw so much potential. She thought somehow she could make them better than what they truly were.

Perhaps that was why she was so good at her job. Or maybe

she was attracted to those kinds of men because of her job.

She lit a cigarette and stared out the window. She wondered if this was what she wanted out of life. They paid her to make the bland, the ordinary, the not-so-special, look fiery, extraordinary, and unique. In the relatively short time she'd know him, she'd tried to make Chris into the amazing man she knew he could be. He had such great potential. However, Ana knew in her heart that potential wasn't worth a damn if it wasn't tapped into. Moreover, Chris didn't have the faintest idea how amazing he could really be. He was a weak version of the man she hoped to marry someday. A weak, drug addicted, irresponsible version of the strong confident man who would rock her world.

She stared at the pink papers in the trash, stubbed out her cigarette, and grabbed her coffee cup off the desk. It was time for a caffeine boost. Halfway down the hallway, her boss, Mr. Gregory Parker, called to her from his office.

"Ana, I have great news!" Mr. Parker got up from his chair and walked towards the door. "But first, be a sweetheart would you and get me a coffee, too. One sugar, no cream, unless they have the real stuff, then just a splash." Ana nodded and went into the coffee room.

"Be a sweetheart would you, get me a coffee." Ana mimicked his voice. "Be a sweetheart and give me the raise you promised me, you over-bearing pompous ass." She poured her coffee first, two cream, two sugars and then grabbed a cup from the shelf. She added a sugar and then poured a splash of real milk into the cup and added a couple good shakes of powdered white stuff and stirred. She whistled and walked back towards her boss's office.

"Here's your coffee, sir, just the way you like it."

"Wonderful, thank you, Ana. Please, take a seat."

Ana took a chair opposite his desk. She crossed her legs and entwined her fingers around her coffee cup. "So, what's the good news, Mr. Parker? Did we land a big account? Are you going to send me out into the big bad world of corporate North America and let me do my thing? Or better yet, have we landed another gourmet cat food account?" She tried to keep the sarcasm out of her voice, and realized it was a hopeless cause.

Ana graduated the top in her class and was hired on four years ago at a great starting salary. The problem was that the salary hadn't changed much in four years and the only contracts the company had ever given her were pet food accounts. The kind where you make Fido's food look good enough for people to eat without really expecting them to eat it, all the while knowing that some of them do. The firm had several pet food accounts, a couple car dealerships, and some vacation destination accounts. Their biggest claim to fame was landing the celebrities who needed to be groomed a bit before taking that next step up the popularity ladder. It was more public relations than marketing, but in the end, it was all the same thing.

Greg Parker looked up at the ceiling, back to his coffee cup, and then at the young woman before him. "Now Ana, it's because you do such a good job of it that we gave those contracts to you. That's all in the past, though." He paused for effect. "We've had a call, a very important call. Channel 11 News to be exact. They need someone to help spruce up their image. Plus Expo 86 is only a few months away and they want visitors to see someone on their news team who represents our city. Someone successful, someone dynamic. Specifically, they want to improve the image of their number one roving reporter and turn him into a head anchor. It appears that 80s women find him a tad condescending and transparent.. The demographics don't lie, and Channel 11 is worried. They've dropped ten points in the market share and Channel 5 is gaining on them. They are meeting with this fellow today to offer him the position of head news anchor. He doesn't start for a month, so we have thirty days or so to turn him around."

Mr. Parker paused, took a sip of coffee and placed the mug on a coaster on his desk. "I know it's the holidays, but we can work around that. They've asked for a consultant, someone to assist them. Preferably, an independent, perceptive 80s woman to remake this reporter into someone the ladies will like. That woman is you." He picked up his coffee again and took a large gulp. "And, may I add, you do make a mighty fine cup of coffee."

Ana sat in silence. Shock and excitement flashed across her face. This could be her big break. Mr. Parker tossed a file folder across the desk. "Well Ana, aren't you excited?" Ana stared at the folder. An 8" x 10" glossy photo was paperclipped to the front. It was him, the man from the other night, the one who hit on her.

"Mr. Parker, I just don't know what to say." Ana picked up the folder and looked at the face closely. Yes, it was him. Pompous, overconfident, yes, this was definitely the man. "I mean I appreciate your confidence in me, but I don't know. This is a pretty big jump. Making processed meat by-products look good is easy, but this ..." Ana trailed off and then looked up at her boss. "I mean, have you met the man?"

He nodded and took another sip of coffee. "It's up to you. Take it or leave it."

If she left it she'd never get another opportunity like this again. If she wanted to rise up the corporate ladder, this was the next rung.

"Thank you, Mr. Parker. I appreciate your confidence in me. I'll do it and you won't be sorry you picked me. I'll make arrangements to meet with him tomorrow." Ana stood and shook her boss's hand. She picked up the folder and thought about how she would deal with this new account. She'd need to get her hair done, pick out a flattering suit that didn't show off her figure too much, and get her nails done.

"You're welcome, Ana." Mr. Parker smiled. "And you start this project today. Mr. Thorn will meet you at 12:15 for lunch at the Blue Poppy on 48th. Oh, and charge it to our account. Keep me posted. I know you can turn this one around."

Ana smiled, raised her coffee cup in a salute, and headed for her office. Her first real account and it had to be the man she brushed off the night before. This was going to be a long day.

Reluctant Angel

Chapter 7: The Voice

Brad stared into the full-length mirror in his office. The voice was back. She was his almost constant companion who whispered in his ear and told him all he needed to hear. The voice had been with him as long as he could remember or wanted to remember. It was his playmate and companion. It was there when he got brave and asked the cute girl in his class on a date. It was there when he kissed her roughly and made her cry. It was there all through high school when he tried to charm his way through the classes. Sometimes it worked, sometimes it didn't. It didn't matter, the voice was there for him. It guided him, reassured him, and told him things he shouldn't know about other people. Somehow the voice knew the secrets of others, and every now and then, when Brad needed it, the voice would tell him important information. It was just enough to give him a feeling of power over others. Just enough to get what he wanted—when he wanted it.

Sometimes the voice made him angry. It made him do things he didn't want to do. Sometimes the voice acted jealous of the women he dated. On some occasions, usually in the bedroom, the voice stopped being just a voice and took over his body. When it left and Brad awoke, more often than not, the women were angry with him. Despite all the things the voice did, and sometimes did not do, Brad knew it was a part of him. It was a part he never wanted to be without. He loved the voice. He loved what it said and how it made him feel. The voice soothed him, calmed him reassured him.

"You're a star. I always knew you were. Never forget, you're a star." The voice made love to his ego and caressed his injured soul. "You can be all you want to be. Let nothing stand in your way. I'll be here to help you. Together we will eliminate everything that stands in our way."

He nodded and made his way to his high-backed leather chair and sat down. He let his head flop back and totally relaxed. The voice made him strong. She was the perfect voice, the strongest voice in his life. Without the voice, the spirit attached to that voice, he would never have made it this far.

"Yes." The voice stroked him, pulling him deeper within himself. "Yes, that's it. Give yourself to me. We are strong together. Never leave me. Promise you'll always keep me near."

The voice was warm and sexy. Brad felt his erection straining against his pants. He and the voice both wanted the world to know the greatness of the man. He could feel his greatness, strong and pulsating. He felt it in every fibre of his being.

"I'll never leave you," he whispered softly, as if to a lover.

An intercom buzzed and a young man's voice came over the speakerphone. "Human Resources called. They want to see you now, Brad. Ask for Yvette."

Brad slowly opened his eyes and raised his head off the back of the chair. How long had he been out this time? He cleared his throat and pressed the intercom button. "Yeah, tell them I'll be up in a few minutes. I just need to get something."

"You got it boss, just don't take too long, I think this might be it." The speakerphone clicked off as Brad rose out of his chair. He walked awkwardly to the full-length mirror. It wouldn't do any good to go waving his flag up in HR.

In Brad's opinion the place was full of lesbians and frustrated wives with rich and absentee husbands. The frustrated wives he could sway to his side. However, he knew that nothing he possessed could sway the others his way. He'd tried it once. He never for a moment thought that it was his attitude or the way he looked down on them as if they were produce at a farmers' market. Brad believed that any woman who didn't fall prey to his masterful moves had to be gay. His ego, and the voice, would not allow him to believe otherwise.

Brad shrugged, stretched his neck, and closed his eyes. He willed his body to calm itself and slowly opened his eyes. He put on his 100-watt smile as he stared at himself. "Yeah," he said to his image and the voice. "I'm good."

He stepped into his private bathroom. The shelf was lined with gels and lotions, sprays and touch up. He didn't like the word makeup. Women wore makeup. Brad Thorn only needed a touch up.

He raked his fingers through his blond hair and smiled as each hair landed perfectly in place. His stylist was a genius. Then again, it paid to have talented friends that were frightened of him, of what he knew.

Brad picked up his favourite aftershave, Armani of course, and splashed a little on each cheek and behind each ear. Women loved how he smelled. He knew it. He knew it because he loved the way he smelled. The voice helped. She knew what he needed.

She knew what women wanted. She simply knew.

Brad was shocked out of his thoughts by a banging on the bathroom door. "Mr. Thorn! They called again." It was his intern.

"I'm taking a pee for gawd's sake!" To make the lie appear real, he flushed the toilet and smoothed any excess cologne off his hands and into the sides of his hair. He opened the door and stepped out.

"You look great, Mr. Thorn. Here's your jacket." The intern held up a jacket and slipped it up Brad's arms and onto his shoulders. "Good luck, Mr. Thorn."

Brad turned to the young man. "It's Danny, right?" The young man blushed.

"Actually, it's Harold sir, or Harry, but that's okay." He stood aside as Brad turned to leave the office.

"Right. Harry. Thanks for your help. I hope you enjoy working for my replacement. It's just a formality, this interview. Of that I'm sure." Brad walked out of his office, unaware that his intern was walking behind him.

"But Mr. Thorn, I thought …" Harold sped up and strode along beside Brad. "Sir, I thought if you got this promotion that you'd take me with you. After all, I know your likes and dislikes, and I've been working with you for over a year now."

Brad stopped and looked at the young man. How earnest he was. How young and naïve. How damn stupid. Brad flashed him a smile. "I'm sorry kid, but a new assistant comes with the job, I can't take you with me. Sure, I'd love to, but you know how it is in show biz." Brad awkwardly patted Harold on the back. "Cheer up, kid. Maybe the next man on the street will be a woman and you can shop for her bras." Brad grinned and winked, then turned and headed towards the elevator.

Harold watched him go and went back to his desk. Only the 8" x 10" glossy photo on his desk heard him as his muttered one word. "Prick."

Chapter 8: Operation Improvement

Brad was in a very good mood. He step was brisk as he made his way to the Blue Poppy. The day was bright—not a cloud in the sky and life was good for Mr. Brad Thorn. His appointment with HR had gone well. Yvette turned out to be one of the frustrated wives and he knew she wanted him. He had the promotion, there was just a minor thing or two he had to do. He had to meet with some image maker from some fancy uptown firm. His promotion would be made public near the end of January. Until then, he had been instructed to do whatever the image maker said. Soon he would be one of, if not the main, five o'clock news anchor. Sure, there was a catch, but it was a small catch. He could pull it off. He hoped this image person was a woman. He loved seeing himself with women, especially good-looking ones.

He paused and patted down his hair before he opened the door to the restaurant. So damn good looking. But the station wanted him to be more likeable, more approachable, more of an average Joe. He felt that average was beneath him, but that too could always be faked. He had surmised that they'd hired the marketing firm to help dull him down and make him more marketable to those less fortunate than him. Image was everything, as long as the people loved you, you were on top. He opened the door and stepped inside.

He spoke briefly to the maître d' and was shown to a table

in the back. As he approached, he saw a woman, alone. It was the perfect setting for him to take control.

She had her hair pulled back into a tight ponytail and her face had that fresh scrubbed look. There was only the slightest hint of makeup on her face. The buttons on her shirt were done to the top and the shirt was left untucked, hiding most of her curves. Everything about her screamed to be left alone, which intrigued Brad.

She stood and waved him over to their table. His approach was smooth and swift. She held out her hand.

"Mr. Thorn, I'm Ana Murphy from Thomas, Simpson and Parker. It's a pleasure to meet you." Brad took her hand and gave it an almost imperceptible squeeze.

"The pleasure is mine, Miss Murphy. It is Miss, isn't it?" He let her hand go and pulled out his chair. She did not answer. "Shall we?" They both sat. Brad pushed aside the menu, placed his elbows on the table and clasped his hands together. He leaned forward, rested his lips on his index fingers and stared at the woman across from him. She stared back. He took a deep breath, sat back in his chair, unfolded his hands and placed them on his lap.

"You look familiar Miss Murphy. Do I know you from somewhere?" Brad let a small wink escape before he could catch himself.

Ana sat back in her chair and fought the urge to tug on her earlobe.

"I don't believe so, Mr. Thorn. Since we are going to spend a great deal of time together over the next little while, may I suggest you call me Ana and I call you Brad." She shifted slightly, bent over and pulled a manila folder from her briefcase.

Brad raised an eyebrow and watched her open the folder. She placed a glossy colour photo of his smiling face on the table. Brad smiled back at his likeness. "I see you have the goods on me. How exciting. Are you sure you are up to remaking the man behind the face?" He tapped his index finger on the photograph then flashed her one of his brightest smiles. Ana did not smile back.

"Mr. Thorn, I mean Brad, you have a very photogenic face. You also have a great voice, and from what I hear you also have a great flair for reporting. The only problem is your attitude. That has to change. I propose we start with a short lesson in basic manners."

Brad sat up straight in his chair. "Manners? They're paying you to teach me manners? What about style? Grace? What about panache?" He leaned forward on his elbows again, hands together, lips pursed against his index fingers. His eyes mocked her as he waited for her reply. He would show her a thing or two.

"No one doubts you have style." He relaxed a little and sat back in his chair. "However, there is a vast ocean between style and class, and you sir, have no class."

"No class!" Brad shot up from his chair. "I don't care who you are but let me tell you one thing. Brad Thorn can outclass you any day of the week. I don't need any fresh-faced tart telling me I don't have what it takes." Brad turned as if to leave.

Ana ignored his tantrum and spoke, her voice barely above a whisper. "Sit down Brad."

Brad turned, his mouth slightly open as if to respond.

Ana pointed to his chair. "You need me. It's as simple as that. You need me to get that promotion. A classy man would not storm out on a lady. Now sit your stylish ass back in the chair and we'll discuss manners."

Brad could not believe his ears. He stared at her, smiled at a few of the patrons who had noticed his outburst, then slowly lowered himself back into his chair. He leaned across the table, his voice almost a hiss. "You are right, I do require your services, but never, ever assume that I *need* you." He pulled his napkin out of his water glass, snapped it open and placed it on his lap. "As you can see, I do know something about manners."

Brad watched her as she took a deep breath. He could tell he'd rattled her. Good. It was always good to keep them on their toes. He watched as she shook out her napkin and placed it on her lap. Each glared at the other, not willing to be the one to speak next.

* * *

Near the back of the restaurant, three angels hovered.

"Leave her alone, Nizroth," Dabria said as the trio watched the couple argue.

"Yes, this is going to be a hard enough assignment without you interfering," Rigel added.

"I don't think so." Nizroth leaned against a wall. He had changed from his previous attire and presented himself to Ana's guardian angels as a businessman. Only his long blond hair gave away the fact he was far from an 80s entrepreneur. "I rather like the way this is going. She's got spunk, or whatever they call that these days. And him, well, he's just too good to pass up. He's a twin spirit. Did you know that? Yes, this will be a delicious challenge. I have to figure out a way to tempt them both, Brad and his twin spirit, not the girl. She's going to be easy. Watch this."

Nizroth walked over to the table, unseen. He whispered into Brad's ear and then walked over to Ana. He ran his hand from the top of her spine to her buttocks. Her body involuntarily shivered, and she felt an odd sensation rush through her. Not a word was said by either of the verbal combatants. Nizroth walked back to the other angels. "There, that should plant the seed. My work here isn't done, but it has certainly started."

"You really enjoy this don't you?" Dabria asked.

"More than you will ever know," Nizroth said. He bowed to Dabria and Rigel and slowly faded away.

* * *

A waiter approached Brad and Ana's table. They still hadn't spoken a word to each other. He poured their water and placed menus in front of them. "I'll be back in a few moments to take your order. Our special today is Creole Fried Oysters. Would you care for anything to start?" Brad looked to Ana, who slowly shook her head no.

"Nothing yet, we'll decided shortly." With a wave of his hand, Brad dismissed the waiter.

Ana took a deep breath and spoke. "Mr., I mean Brad. My apologies for being so blunt. After all you are my client. What I meant to say was that a man of your distinction, with a face as well-known as yours is now, and is to become even more so." She paused and took another deep breath. "What I meant to say is, we, the TV station and I, as the one chosen for this assignment, would like to help you make that distinction one of class. In other words, Brad, we want to make you shine brighter than you ever have before. For that, we just need a few little touch ups and tweaks and you'll be good to go." She reached for her water glass and drank slowly.

Brad smiled. Yes, he was going to become even more well-known than he was now. He could put up with her for that. Once he'd mastered the anchor position at Channel 11 he'd go for the big national stations. He'd be a star all right, and it wouldn't take long. A few tweaks, as she so quaintly put it, would be acceptable.

"Well, since you put it that way." He relaxed somewhat and ran his index finger around the base of the water glass. "All right then, what little lesson did you want to start with today?"

Ana sighed with relief. Brad watched her chest rise and fall, his mind on what lay beneath.

"It really is just a little lesson. When you came in, when both of us were standing at the table, you should have pulled my chair out for me, waited for me to sit and then gently pushed it in. I know it might seem a bit old fashioned, but deep down inside, people want to see common decency and old-fashioned manners. They want to see doors opened and hats off at the dinner table."

Brad sat bolt upright. "I would never wear a hat. Unless of

course it was for a promotion, and I was getting paid to do so." As if to emphasize the point he smoothed down both sides of his hair and then repositioned himself in his chair.

The waiter approached and asked if they were ready to order.

"Yes, I believe we are." He would show her manners. He knew all about ordering for the ladies. He knew what every woman wanted was for someone, for a man, to take control.

"We'll start off with your house special salad for two, followed by your Creole Fried Oysters and a bottle of Pinot Gris." Brad dismissed the waiter with a nod of his head and turned to Ana.

"How's that for class?" He straightened his tie and sat back.

"Not bad, except you didn't ask me if I liked oysters and as it happens, I'm allergic to them. And before you start in on me, I'm not the one that chose the restaurant, my firm did. Now can we start back at the beginning? There is far too much tension at this table, and I'd like to start again." Ana stood and held out her hand. "My name is Ana, Ana Murphy. It's very nice to meet you in person, Mr. Thorn."

Brad blinked up at her and then stood. What a cheeky thing this one was. "Very well, Ana Murphy. I want you to know I think this is very foolish. My name is Brad Thorn and it's a pleasure to meet you as well." Brad took her hand, shook it lightly and let it go.

Ana stood motionless beside the table. Brad raised an eyebrow, then realized what was expected. He walked over to her chair and held it while she sat down. Just before her bottom connected with the chair, Brad pushed the chair inwards, a little too roughly. It caught Ana behind the knees and made her thump unceremoniously into her chair. Lesson one was complete.

Chapter 9: Dabria's Child

Dabria watched the scene unfold, tsking and tutting every few minutes. Rigel watched as well, chuckling more at Dabria than at the two people seated at the table.

"Dabria, you are going to wear out your tongue. Clucking away like that reminds me of the time I watched over a nice young lad just outside of Marburg, Germany. He had a fine family and a great chicken farm. People from all around would ask specifically for his chickens. You know of Marburg, don't you Dabria?" Rigel paused for a millisecond and continued. "It has that beautiful old Landgraves' Schloss overlooking the lovely medieval Old Town. Surely you remember. It's the spot where Martin Luther and Zwingli conducted their debates on the foundations of religion in 1529. He passed on just two years after that, Zwingli did. Lots of good conversation happened in that town."

Dabria looked over at Rigel and shook her head. "What are you going on about now?, Rig? Can't you see our charge is in trouble? First, she's cocky, then she's contrite, then she's cocky again. I don't know how you can just stand there and not be worried about it. And that man, what an absolute pot of fool's gold he is. This is it for goodness' sake. This is the culmination of all we've been watching over her for. This is …" Dabria tsked and tutted again as she watched Brad push Ana's chair in and Ana plop down abruptly.

"Did you see that!" Dabria fluttered around the room. "Really Rig, aren't there some days when you wish you could just materialize right in front of someone like that and give them what for? I mean, really."

Rigel took Dabria by the hand and led her out of the restaurant. They perched atop the roof, traffic flowing steadily below them. "Now Dabby, why do you say such things? Two millennia as a guardian angel and sometimes you act as if you received your appointment last week. You really must trust the plan, Dabria. What is it with this girl? I've never seen you like this before."

Dabria tried to peer through the roof to the restaurant below, but there were too many floors and too many people between her and Ana. She sighed and wandered closer to the edge of the roof. "She's just so darn fragile, that's all."

Rigel followed her and looked down. "Fragile compared to what, Dabby? Compared to us maybe, we can step off the edge and make a choice to fall or fly. For a human, she is far from fragile. She is of strong body, mind and heart. Her soul is in pretty good shape, too. I just don't see what has you so worried." Rigel put his arm around her. "What's got you so all fired up about this one, Dabby?"

Dabria paced a bit and then turned to Rigel. "Well, I suppose they'll tell you eventually, so you might as well hear it from me. She was there when I passed over for the final time. She was there, Rigel. She was present, in the same land, in the same town as I was."

Rigel removed his arm from her shoulder. "Why didn't you

tell me this before? It's not that uncommon you know." Dabria shook her head.

"You don't understand. There, in that town, when I passed over for the last time, I passed over giving birth, giving new life to a new soul. Before I left there was a brief moment when we connected. We connected and I knew her energy and she knew mine and we knew we were part of the greater whole. It was Ana, Rig. I'm sure of it. The longer we are her guardians, the stronger I feel it. Ana was my daughter." Dabria sat down on the ledge.

Rigel looked at her, somewhat confused. "So?"

"So! I tell you that our female charge is probably my daughter and all you can say is so!" Dabria walked back over the ledge and watched the traffic below. So many people, so many souls, so many life choices.

"Rig?" She walked back to where he stood. "How long before we forget what it's like to be human? How long before the longing goes away? Praise be, I am so blessed to have been given this chance to do what I do. But, sometimes, some days ..."

Rigel stared at her. "Now I see where this is going. It's not so much that the life energy that abides in Ana may be the same life energy that was in your child two-thousand years ago. You want to go back!" Rigel chuckled.

"What are you laughing at? It's not nice to laugh at another's misfortune." Dabria stood directly in front of him, willing him to stop.

"Oh my, oh dear, sweet Lord in Heaven, Dabria. Being an angel is a misfortune? Don't let Gabriel hear you say that, or he'll put you on border patrol before you can wish for wings. Can you imagine it? You, as a human, after two-thousand years as an angel? With the stresses of the twentieth century you'd worry yourself to an early grave before you knew it had even happened."

Dabria straightened up and jutted out her chin. "It just so happens that I have a great deal of caring in me. It's just my way of thinking things through. And speaking of my caring, what about Ana? We really should get back to her."

Dabria willed herself into the restaurant and Rigel followed behind her. They deposited themselves at a table beside Ana and Brad's table.

"See Dabria, everything is just fine. They are talking like civilized individuals, and all is well. It will be a few more months before we are really needed. Until then, just enjoy the moment."

Dabria reached over and ruffled the hair on Brad's perfectly shaped head. The hair stuck up at the back like Dennis the Menace. Dabria laughed, then smoothed them back down again. She had to trust the process.

Chapter 10: Meditation Time

The sound of flute mixed with sitar filled the room. Candlelight flicked across the faces of the women who breathed in and out in almost perfect unison.

"I want you to take three deep breaths and on your third breath I want you to bring your conscious selves back into the room. One. Deep breath in and slowly exhale."

Ana inhaled deeply as she felt herself becoming more aware of her surroundings and her body.

"Two. Breath in through the nose, out through the mouth. Almost back now."

Ana inhaled deeply, filling her lungs, expanding her chest, holding it ever so slightly, and then exhaled through barely parted lips.

"Three. Big, deep breath." Carol watched as eyelids started to flutter. "Hold it. Now exhale slowly. Welcome back ladies." Carol grinned as she watched the faces around her slowly become more animated. Their eyes opened, glazed and then focused. Smiles formed on some faces, others looked puzzled, and others, like Ana, looked sad.

"Excellent session everyone, now let's all stand up and shake out those arms and legs. Arms first. Wiggle your fingers, feel that energy move all the way up to your shoulders. Let the energy flow. Now lift up your left foot and wiggle your toes.

Reluctant Angel

Give your leg a shake. That's it, now the other foot. Wiggle those piggies ladies! Shake those bones. Now you've got it. Drop your head to your chest and slowly rotate left. That's it, hold it. Now rotate to centre and slowly rotate right. Perfect. Drop to centre and heads up." Carol led the group through their steps and then sat down at the edge of the group.

"Okay class, who here would like to share their meditation with the group? Sheila?" A mousy looking woman with thick glasses smiled sheepishly.

"Sure, um, okay. Well it was just so peaceful, just like the other ones. Only this time I found myself by a lake instead of a pond. It was so pretty and relaxing, and there were ducks on the lake. That's pretty much it. I just sat there, listened to the music and watched the ducks." Sheila lowered her eyes to her hands on her lap. "It was nice."

Carol smiled at the woman. "Excellent Sheila. It's wonderful that your visuals are becoming so clear. Thank you for sharing. It sounded lovely. Anyone else like to share?"

Carol scanned the room. Some eyes met hers, others looked away and others became very busy with straightening their clothing and picking imaginary pieces of lint off their laps.

"I'll share if you like, only because I'd like some interpretation of it all." Ana looked around the group and then cleared her throat. "It was the same as the other ones, lots of hallways and brightly coloured doors and I went in one and found some paints and I just painted the walls all these great colours. Then I went out and down another hallway, only this time things weren't so bright or so warm. I had to go deeper and deeper into this maze of hallways. The hallways slanted downwards, and every turn brought me beneath the layer of hallways before. Only now there were no colours, just greys and darkness. I was afraid to open the doors. So I just stood in the hallway looking at them. Then I came back when you started counting. It just felt so, I dunno, odd."

Ana searched the room for a glint of understanding in someone's eyes. Most of the women met her gaze, but none offered any suggestions. Finally, a black-haired woman spoke.

"Maybe you're finally uncovering a part of yourself you've never admitted to having before, or maybe you didn't even know it was there? That's all I can think of. I love the bright colourful hallways but the darkness and cold of the other hallways is a little scary. If I were you I'd take some imaginary breadcrumbs in there with me to make sure I could find my way back!"

The group broke into soft laughter at the idea.

"I think Shanda may be right." Carol stood up and walked towards the front of the room. Sometimes things we don't understand show up in black and white or shades of grey, in our dreams and our meditations. Or maybe the black and white is a symbolism of how you see yourself when faced with decisions, or," Carol paused for effect, "maybe you ran out of paint from painting the last room you were in." The group twittered and then fell silent.

"All right class, that's it for this year. See you all in two Saturdays after Christmas, same place, same time. We'll be doing a guided meditation. I'd like to get us all to the same place Sheila was at. That lake sounds very relaxing. Sheila, would you mind putting yourself into a meditative state and bringing us along with you?" Sheila blushed and nodded.

"Great, it's a plan then. Next session, we are going to the lake. See you then ladies." Carol turned and walked into the outer room. She greeted all the women by name as they left, hugged them and wished them a Merry Christmas and Happy New Year. As usual, Ana was the last to leave.

"Hey kiddo, how're you feeling now? A bit better, I hope. Come into the office and we'll have a nice cup of tea."

Ana nodded and followed. Lately her meditations had been giving her more questions than answers. Carol poured water from the water cooler in the hallway into a large carafe. She came into the office and filled the kettle and plugged it in.

"Carol, I just don't get it. Everyone else has ducks and fluffy clouds and nice cottages and streams in their free flow meditations." Ana gave her earlobe a gentle tug. "I get dark, spooky hallways. Just doesn't seem right. Is there something wrong with me?" Ana sighed and crossed her legs beneath her. She touched her thumb to her baby finger and frowned.

"Oh Ana, stop your worrying. There's nothing wrong with you, in fact there's probably more right with you. Those other women are just touching the surface, not going beneath, no one sees under the lake or looks into the basement of the cottage. They will get there soon, but you just dive right in and get into the muck and start looking and searching. That takes a lot of courage."

The kettle whistled. Carol stood and made a fresh pot of chamomile tea.

"Remember Lucy, the college professor with the shark meditations? Talk about having your fears stalk you. She beat it in the end, though. She transformed that shark into a beautiful dolphin and rode it up to the surface. She never had that meditation again. Most importantly she got rid of her fears of confrontation." Carol poured two cups of tea and placed one in front of Ana.

"You must understand Ana that meditation is a lot like dreaming except you are totally in the here and now. You are exploring your sub-conscious, your super-conscious and the great unknown all at the same time. It's a free-for-all of information and you get what you need." Carol took a sip of her tea and sat back in her chair.

Ana reached for her cup and held it in her hands. "I guess so. I just have this sinking feeling that I'm going to have to open those doors sooner than I want to and it's not going to be pleasant."

Carol laughed. "You are such a pessimist! Lighten up, girl. Behind that door is simply the unknown and it can't hurt you because you are in control of the journey."

"If you say so." Ana smiled at her mentor. "Doing anything special for the holidays?"

"Nope, just me and some friends and a large turkey and several bottles of wine. You?"

"Oh, my parents want me to come home, but to be honest, I'm just not up for it. I'm looking forward to time off work and sleeping in and cuddling my cat. It just doesn't seem like Christmas without small children around and there aren't any left in my family. My folks are upset but I told them I was spending part of it working and Christmas day with you."

Carol laughed. "Well, you are more than welcome to join us."

Ana smiled and took another sip from her cup. "To be honest, I'm really looking forward to some alone time, but thanks."

"Your call, let me know if you change your mind. So, what else is new with you? You seem a little off today."

Ana shrugged. "I dumped Chris last Saturday night and I got a new assignment Monday morning."

Carol whooped with excitement. "That's great! I'm so proud of you on both counts. Excellent news. Tell me about the new assignment."

"Well, it's human, or so it appears to be on camera. Our first meeting was a total disaster, but I've met with him a couple times since and things seem to be going better. It's my job to smooth out the diamond in the rough and boy, is this one rough." Ana took a sip of her tea. "Aren't you going to ask who it is?" Ana put down her cup and stared at Carol.

"Okay, I'll bite. Who is it?"

"It's Brad Thorn, the Channel 11 roving reporter." Ana grinned from ear to ear. "I've graduated from dog food." Ana picked up her cup again and took a sip.

"That is brilliant news. He's gorgeous if you go for that sort of thing. Any sparks between the two of you?"

Ana almost spit out her tea. "Sparks? Between Mr. Perfect and me? I hardly think so. He's not exactly my type but I think I am his type." Ana paused and waited for Carol to speak.

"Okay, I'll bite again, why are you his type?" Carol waited for the punchline.

"Because I'm breathing and have nice boobs." Ana laughed and put her cup down. "Honestly, he put the hound in hound dog. The weird thing is, I think it's all a show. Somehow, somewhere, underneath that macho pig is a really nice guy. He's got potential." Ana stood and stretched. "I really gotta get going. Mudo will be waiting to be fed." She grabbed her purse and headed for the door.

"You don't want to keep Mudo waiting. Why did you name your cat Mudo anyway?"

"It means dumb in Spanish and he is the dumbest cat I've ever known. Could be from all those dog food samples I fed him, you never know. Thanks for the tea." Ana waved as she walked the door.

Carol shook her head. Ana had found yet another man with potential. At least this time she was getting paid to see if it was really there.

Chapter 11: Realizations

Ana headed towards the seawall walkway that skirted the downtown area and bordered the ocean. Christmas and New Year's had come and gone. She'd quit smoking for the eighth time in her life, but this time she felt it would stick. So far she had no cravings at all. She felt happy about the promises and potential 1986 held for her. She'd managed to avoid all invitations and had spent a quiet week with just her, the cat, and her walks by the ocean.

She quickened her pace and headed downtown when she remembered Mudo needed some cat food. She'd been feeding him all her dog food samples, and she decided perhaps Mr. Kitty needed some real cat food.

She reflected back on the past month as she gently tugged twice on her earlobe. It hadn't been as bad as she'd thought. The first meeting was almost a total disaster, but somehow they had made it through lunch and four other meetings the first week. The weeks flew by, and she could hardly believe that he was growing on her. Every now and then she'd catch a glimpse of someone real, someone who wasn't all cocksure of themselves. Ana liked what she saw during those glimpses.

Even her meditations had improved. She'd been brave enough to open one of the darker doors and there wasn't even anything inside, just some dust bunnies in a corner. Meditation classes had resumed and the group meditation where Carol guided them to the lake with the ducks, had been quite pleasant. Ana was surprised to realize that everyone in the room had made it to that same place, seen the exact same things, and experienced the same sounds and feelings. It was the first time she'd gone into someone else's personal meditation space, and she found it quite refreshing. The meditation may not have been as deep as the ones she normally experienced, but it certainly was refreshing.

She'd spoken to Carol about Brad and how they were getting along. Carol was her usual self and simply pointed out the obvious, that Brad was a client and having potential to be a great person, didn't mean you were one. She could always count on Carol to give her a reality check.

Then, last night Ana and Brad had gone out for a post-Christmas and New Year's, working dinner. Sandy Shores was one of those trendy, on the waterfront, high-priced, small-portioned restaurants that everyone wanted to be seen at. Being with a celebrity did have its benefits. They simply walked past the line to the maître d'. Brad smiled at him, whispered a few choice words in his ear, shook his hand, and they were immediately escorted to a window table overlooking the harbour.

Ana smiled. He'd progressed rather nicely. He held her chair for her, deferred to her on the wine list and let her order her own meal. He'd even made enquiries about her family and her work. She knew it was all about the lesson, not about her, but it was still nice to be sitting with someone who wasn't stoned out of his mind.

Ana rounded the corner and stepped into the pet food

store. She had no idea what kind of cat food Mudo would like. She'd rescued him from the SPCA a few months ago. He was about six months old then, long and skinny with the most pitiful meow. She'd landed the dog food contract just the week before and had samples at home. Mudo was so hungry he ate it all. Ana continued to bring home samples and Mudo continued to eat it. He'd filled out a bit but was still terribly stupid. He was the only cat she'd known that could fall off the couch when he was laying in the middle of it.

Ana picked up a can with an orange tabby on it. It looked just like Mudo, so she bought it. She found a similar cat on a bag of dry food and purchased that as well. Cat food in hand, she headed back to her apartment.

Ana looked out over the ocean as she walked. It was such a beautiful city and an even more beautiful day. Life was getting better. No more layabout stoners for boyfriends, no more dog food makeovers. Her people makeover had been a success.

She smiled to herself, turned her back on the ocean, and headed for home.

Chapter 12: Celebration Time

"And we're clear!" Lights were turned off in a cascade until only two dim lights remained on the set. The red lights on the cameras blinked and then disappeared.

"Nice job, Brad," a voice called from the dimness in front of the anchor desk.

"Yeah, good job, Brad. Not bad for a first day," another voice said, farther off, walking away.

Brad sat at the anchor desk, hands stroking the edges. He'd done it. Another voice approached him from his right.

"Damn fine piece of reporting, Brad." Brad turned to see Executive Producer, John Scanlon. He stood and shook the man's outstretched hand. "If we get another good disaster to report on in the next year or two I can see you being nominated for an Emmy. I don't see that in many people, Thorn, but I see it in you."

"Thanks John, I appreciate the vote of confidence. You won't be sorry you put me in this chair." Brad beamed. He'd made it to the top. Nothing could stop him now. Today Channel 11, tomorrow the National News. Scanlon's voice nailed him back to the ground.

"Don't make me sorry, Brad. I don't handle disappointment well." Scanlon smiled, patted Brad on the back, and left the studio.

Brad's smile slowly faded as he sat back down into his chair. Scanlon was a hard ass, and everyone knew it. He'd also made Channel 11 one of the best, if not the best, news hour programs in the country. Now Brad was part of that. More than part of it, he was the figure head of Channel 11 News. He rubbed his hands across the desk again. The wood was still warm from the lights.

He straightened out his papers, stood and stared into the bank of darkness in front of him. He should celebrate. After all, tonight was his big night. He'd made it. Thanks to his dazzling smile, charm and wit, along with some damn fine reporting skills, he'd made it. Sure maybe that Ana woman had helped him a bit, but he knew it was all his doing, him and his companion. He listened to see if she was awake. Nothing. No sound, no stirring deep within. She'd been quiet lately, his internal companion, his teammate. That was okay. He needed to be all man right now, needed to make it on his own. She would help him when he needed it.

Brad walked into his dressing room and peeled off his jacket. A quick clean up and he'd be ready to celebrate. But where? And with who? Brad sat down at the table and stared into the mirror.

"Damn," he said to the empty room. "I am so good looking. What say you and I head out on the town for a night cap." Brad winked at himself, then grabbed a tissue and began wiping the makeup off his face. They used far too much of this stuff on him. All he wanted was to avoid the glare. His skin did not require painting. Brad sighed and threw the tissue into the trash. Who was he kidding? He didn't want to go out alone and he had no friends. Sure there were the latest news groupies, but lately he wanted something more. He wanted someone more like Ana. Ana had substance and some great assets.

He looked at himself again in the mirror and then checked his watch. "Call her," he said to his reflection. "Ask her out. Tell her you want her to share in the success of your first night as head anchor."

It was a little late notice. He anticipated she'd decline. His voice took on a higher pitch as he spoke to himself.

"Brad, you can't just call someone at a moment's notice and expect them to drop everything for you. Plan ahead. People need to feel special." Yep, that was what she'd say.

Brad shook his head. Screw special, he wanted to go out and he didn't want to go alone. Sure he should have thought of it earlier, but he was very busy prepping for the big night.

Brad grabbed his jacket and reached for his cell phone. The last month with her had been highly entertaining. She had a certain vulnerability about her that he liked. She was also one of the most stubborn, opinionated, direct women he had ever met. Even the way she tugged on her earlobe was charming. Most importantly, he'd known her for almost five weeks now and had never slept with her. That was probably due to the fact that she was always telling him what to do, how to sit, how to act, how to talk. It was enough to drive a man insane.

All their hard work had paid off. Brad was as polished as marble, and he knew it. Wouldn't it be ironic if all her work made him more attractive to her? It was the ultimate power trip. She found a man and changed him, made him into what she wanted.

Now, tonight, it was time to get a little of what he wanted. He wanted some of Ana's assets.

Brad punched her number into his cell phone. He'd been very proud when he bought the phone. One of the first at Channel 11. It was a bit heavy, but the convenience was worth it. Ana picked up on the third ring.

"Hello." Brad closed his eyes and imagined that she'd just stepped out of the shower, water dripping down her skin, a towel loosely wrapped around her waist, her breasts perched atop her perfect waist, waiting for him.

"Hello, is anyone there?"

Brad opened his eyes. "Hey Ana, it's Brad. Did I catch you in the shower?" He closed his eyes again, recapturing his vision.

"No, I just came in from a walk and I'm in desperate need of a shower. How did it go tonight?"

"Great, really great." He paused for effect. "Listen Ana, I know you aren't officially working for me anymore, and I know it's late notice and all, but I was wondering if you would like to go out to a late dinner with me. You know, to celebrate the occasion."

There was a pause at the other end of the line. He waited for her to scold him. He wasn't disappointed.

"Brad Thorn, did you not learn anything from me? First of all I never did work for you, I worked with you. Secondly you can't just call someone up at a moment's notice and expect them to drop everything for you. Plan ahead. People need to feel special." He pictured her pacing at the other end of the phone. He waited, his answer already planned out.

"You are special, Ana, and now that we don't have a working relationship, I'd like to show you how special." Silence. Had he come on too strong? Would she fall for it? Damn, he should have tried the lonely soul tactic. There was no way she was going to fall for the special line.

"Brad Thorn, you are a complete and total jerk. I think you need a quick refresher course." He could hear her moving around on the other end of the line.

"So what time should I pick you up." Brad grinned from ear to ear. Not quite the response he'd hoped for, but it was a start.

"Give me twenty minutes. Pick someplace semi casual, not too stuffy. You're going to want someplace where your demographic hangs out. They'll have watched you tonight, might as well keep the PR machine going. I'll see you then." Ana hung up the phone before Brad could say another word.

He didn't want to go somewhere to face his fans. He wanted her, and the more he thought about it the more he wanted her naked in his bed. He wondered if *she* would be there to help him with the seduction. His companion always knew what to say and the right time to say it. Why had she been so quiet lately. He turned back to the mirror and heard her whisper. "I'm here. I'll never leave you."

"Will you help me tonight? Will you help me with her?" Brad stared into the reflection in the mirror and then closed his eyes.

"You don't need her, you have me." Brad felt the stirring within him. The voice purred in his ear. "Yes, that's it. Give yourself to me. Promise you will never leave me." The voice was warm and sexy. He could feel himself getting harder, pulsing, pushing against his trousers. "Touch it. Be my hands, be my mouth, touch it with me."

Brad pulled down his zipper and moaned. "No. Not now, please. I promise I will never leave you. We're a team you and me. Please, not now."

Brad opened his eyes. She was gone. It was time to go pick up Ana.

Chapter 13: One Drink

Ana stared out the window as the car lazily made its way up the street. She glanced over at Brad and smiled. Dinner had been wonderful. He'd picked the perfect spot. It was just casual enough for the yuppies to be there and just busy enough for their fellow diners to recognize him. To top it off they served just the right amount of food and the service was outstanding.

Brad handled the attention well. He paid very close attention to Ana, not acting at all like the pompous ass she'd begun to work with five short weeks ago. He was really very charming, even though Ana suspected some of it was being put on for her sake.

Brad took his eyes off the road and turned to her. "Night cap at my place? I make a mean martini. I'll even spring for a cab to take you home after."

Ana hesitated. So far this had been a perfect date. She didn't want to ruin it by getting drunk and maybe losing her sense of sanity and ending up in bed with the guy.

"No, I don't think so, but thank you, it's been a great evening. I'd say you passed with flying colours." Ana patted him on the knee and looked back out at the street.

"You think I'm going to try and seduce you, don't you?" Brad laughed and shook his head. "Don't you think that maybe, just maybe the guy you first met was the one with all the defenses, the one who was trying to hide. Do you think you made me? You didn't make me. This is who I really am. Do you think I would try to seduce you after all we've been through together? I am hurt." Brad slowed for the corner and then turned right.

"Oh, don't be silly." Ana turned and watched his profile. Was he really upset or was this just another Brad Thorn pick-up line?

"I'm not silly, and I want an apology," Brad continued to stare straight ahead.

"An apology?" Ana thought about it for a moment. She didn't want to ruin a perfectly good evening. He did offer to send her home in a cab. She'd never been to his place and was a little curious. "All right then, I'm sorry and I will accept your offer of a drink and a cab home."

Brad grinned from ear to ear. "Right then, martinis it is, and you get to pick the music." Ana tugged on her earlobe as Brad turned into his underground parking and pulled into his stall.

"How did? I mean …" Ana looked at him. "You brat, you were headed here all along." Ana playfully punched him in the shoulder. "No hanky panky, you understand? Just one drink and I'm going home."

Brad stepped out of the car and went over to open her door. "I can't believe I've invited a woman to my apartment who uses words like hanky panky. But since you put it so quaintly, no hanky panky."

They rode the elevator in comfortable silence.

Ana was pleasantly surprised when the doors opened onto

the penthouse suite.

"Nice digs," she said as she entered the living room. "Very nice indeed."

"Make yourself comfortable," Brad hollered from the kitchen. "I'll make us that martini. Stereo is over by the balcony. Pick out something you like."

Ana looked through the albums, picked out *Voyeur*, and put it on the turntable. She walked over to the full-length sliding glass doors and stared out at the city below. "You have a great view from here. How long have you lived here?" She turned and was startled to find Brad at her elbow, a large martini glass in each hand.

He offered one of the glasses. "About a year now. I'm glad you like it." He put his free hand on her elbow and steered her towards the oversized leather couch. "Have a seat, I'll put on the music."

Ana sat, being careful to balance the overfull glass in her hand. "These, ummm, glasses, well, they're a little large don't you think?" Ana stared at the amount of liquor in the glass in her hand.

"Not really, it saves me from having to get up and mix more, besides, you said only one drink. That's your one drink." Soft music surrounded them, and Brad joined her on the couch.

"You have good taste in music too. I just love David Sanborn." He leaned over and clinked his glass to hers. "Cheers and thank you. I've never thanked you before for all you've done for me."

The sounds of a soulful saxophone wafted over Ana. "You're

welcome, Brad. Thank you for being such a fast learner. You've come a long way." Ana took a sip of her drink. It was delicious. "Shaken not stirred, right?" She reached in, took out an olive and popped it in her mouth. She was running out of things to say.

"A martini connoisseur, I see. Very good. What else don't I know about you? What other secrets have you been keeping while we've been having our business relationship." Brad shifted slightly and Ana felt his thigh press against hers. It was warm, comfortable. Ana decided not to move. She took another sip of her drink.

"Well, let's see. I have a cat, I believe in reincarnation, and my favourite colour is the rainbow. I won't eat lamb or veal, but I have been known to rip the ear off a pig on a spit and chew it with great relish. I go to meditation classes, sometimes twice a week, and I don't jog or drink decaf." Ana sipped her drink and stared at Brad. "Your turn."

"My turn? I thought you knew everything about me. What more is there to learn?" He placed his drink on the table and turned so he was facing her. "All right then, you asked for it. My favourite colour is green, I'll eat anything if it's prepared properly, and I've never ripped the ear off anything except my teddy bear when I was four. I prefer whiskey to beer and red wine to white and I drink all things caffeinated. I don't have any pets, but I do have a companion that no one else can see."

Ana spit out some of her drink. Brad pulled a napkin off the coffee table and handed it to her.

"Did you choke on an olive?" Brad grinned devilishly at her, picked up his drink and raised it slowly to his lips.

"You have a what?" Ana took another drink and waited. This was starting to get weird.

Brad winked. "I have a companion, a friend, that no one else can see. She speaks to me when I need her." Brad rolled the rim of the martini glass from side to side on his bottom lip.

"Like a guardian angel or something?" Ana's curiosity was piqued.

"Oh, she's no angel, quite the contrary. She advises me on matters and helps me through my days, but it's hardly an angelic voice or angelic thoughts that come to me from her." Brad grinned.

Ana squirmed slightly. Was this guy for real? But then again, she spent two days a week trying to contact the unseen, the unknown, to venture into the other spaces of the world.

"Are you frightened of me now?" Brad sipped his drink and placed it on the table. Ana watched as he stood and went over to change the music.

Ana hesitated. "Well, honestly no, I'm not. It's just that it's not every day someone you think you know fairly well comes out and tells you they have a demon advisor, and a female one at that." Ana's lips felt dry, and she took another sip of her drink. She realized it was going down a little too quickly.

"She's not a demon, more like a spirit without morals."

Brad positioned himself on the edge of the couch directly in front of Ana. She realized she was getting drunk and tried to place her glass on the table.

Brad stopped her and guided it back to her lips. "You promised me one drink." The glass rested against her lips, and she opened her mouth. Her tongue darted into the glass and lapped at the liquor like a cat.

Ana finished it in one gulp and placed the glass on the table. "Brad Thorn you are filling my head with weird stories and getting me drunk. What will your fans think?" Ana laughed at the thought of Brad doing the newscast with his amoral spirit running the teleprompter. "I think it's time you called that cab for me."

Brad leaned forward and cupped her chin in his hand. "I'm going to kiss you."

And he did.

Chapter 14: Malfunction Junction

"There she is." Dabria's voice filtered across the dark room. "She looks upset."

Rig nodded in agreement. "She'll get over it." He crossed the living room and approached the figure standing motionless in front of the large sliding glass balcony doors. He reached out and placed his hand on her shoulder. Ana shivered involuntarily and shrugged. Rig removed his hand and gazed out at the city below. "You know, it had to be this way. This is always so rough on them. It's always hard just before the final contract is completed."

Dabria came over and stood on the other side of Ana. She attempted to smooth a stray hair out of her eye. It didn't move. Dabria sighed. "Now we have to wait. How much longer do you think?" She lifted her hand as if to try moving the hair again, then stopped and dropped her hand to her side.

Rig looked over at Ana, then to Dabria and back to the city lights before him. "A few days, maybe a couple weeks. Maybe she'll wait until her birthday. Either way, it won't be long now."

There was slight whooshing sound as Nizroth appeared. "Good evening fellow angels. How are we tonight?" Nizroth let the hood of his cloak fall back, the flowing golden hair surrounding his face. "I've been rather busy tonight, but everything appears to have worked out rather well, don't you think?"

Nizroth waved his hand in front of Ana's face and laughed.

"Poor dear is stunned by the whole thing, isn't she?" He walked through Ana and positioned himself in a semi-reclined position on the leather couch. He looked over at the trio. "I must say it was a bit nasty for poor old Bradford as well. Can you imagine having Mr. Happy take a holiday right before entering vacation land?"

Dabria shook her head and stomped over to the couch. "How can you be so crass? You never cease to amaze me. How on earth did you get that to happen? I thought angels of temptation let their victims receive the fruits of their labour."

Nizroth sat upright. "They do my dear. This was not of my doing. It was the other in him that caused the little malfunction at the junction."

Dabria rolled her eyes and walked back over to Ana. "Poor dear. Bad enough to let yourself be seduced only to have things fizzle. She must feel terrible."

"EXACTLY!" Nizroth stood and paced around the room. "You really must pay attention, Dabria. This is exactly how it's supposed to be. Now she feels terrible. She has so many reasons to feel terribly guilty that it will motivate her to complete her contract."

Nizroth continued to pace the room, stopping to emphasize each sentence.

"Understand, that part of her feels guilty because she knows she should have sympathy for the man. She knows how fragile this male's ego is. She feels guilty because she really, really wanted the big O and never got it. She's ticked that she didn't get it and feels guilty because she put her needs ahead of another's feelings. Then vanity is added for a more potent guilt. She feels that maybe, just maybe, he couldn't complete the job because of her. What has she done wrong? And yet, he seduced her and should have completed the job. Not to mention the weird conversation he had with his internal companion just before everything went kaput."

Nizroth rubbed his hands together and smiled up at Dabria. "So you see my dear, everything is going wonderfully. It couldn't be better!" Nizroth threw his head back and laughed. "I just love it when a plan comes together." He headed towards Ana, walked through her again and turned around. "Better luck next time dear." With another faint whooshing sound he was gone.

Dabria tsked after him. "Can you believe that one. No sense of decency at all."

Rig chuckled. "Well now, he is the angel of temptation. I assume it would be very hard to tempt people if you had to abide by the same set of rules we do. You keep forgetting that we all have jobs to do. His is just a little more distasteful than others, but you've got to admit, without him, contracts would be harder to fulfill."

Ana stepped away from the window and walked into the bedroom. She looked at the sleeping figure on the bed, picked up her clothes and made her way to the bathroom. Dabria and Rig waited patiently by the window.

Moments later she emerged, picked up the phone, called a cab, and looked out at the city below her.

She dug through her purse and pulled out a business card. She found a pen and scribbled something on the back and placed it on the coffee table.

Ana jumped as the buzzer to the apartment rang. She took one last look around and headed out to the waiting cab.

Rig and Dabria watched as she left.

"Shall we head out this way?" Rig tilted his head towards the balcony doors.

Dabria shook her head. "In a moment. I want to make sure he sees this." She went to the card and propped it up against a large, empty martini glass. Two words were scribbled on it. "Call me."

Chapter 15: Ana, the Morning After

After a sleepless night, Ana got up and gathered her things for her meditation class. Perhaps a little deep breathing would help her sort out her confusion. She pulled on her loose pants, pulled a clean T-shirt over her head, and padded barefoot into the kitchen. Mudo rubbed up against her, meowing.

"I'll feed you little fellow. Just hang on." Ana grabbed the cat's dish and poured out a small amount of kitty kibble. Then she opened the fridge, took out an opened tin can and mixed in a tablespoon of a smelly salmon concoction. "I'm glad you like this Mudo, but it sure smells awful." Ana put the dish down and watched as the cat ran to it and chowed down.

"Mudo, I envy you." Ana opened the fridge and gazed inside. She didn't really want to eat but knew she should. A slightly wrinkled grapefruit lay at the bottom of the fruit crisper. She picked it up, looked at it and put it back. Maybe tomorrow it would look better. She closed the fridge and poured water into the coffee maker. She added enough grounds to make a good strong pot and flicked the switch. The sound of gurgling and hissing water competed with the sound of the cat crunching on his breakfast. Ana stared out the window and sighed.

"Mudo, you've got it made. You got neutered, no worries for you. No wonder they call it being fixed. I need to be fixed." Ana went to the kitchen table and sat down. Mudo finished his

Reluctant Angel

breakfast and jumped onto her lap. She absently scratched the cat behind his ears as she thought of the night before. She had been so stupid to go to his apartment. Even more stupid to drink that rather large martini, and then, to let him kiss her. That was the stupidest thing of all. No. There was the other thing that took the stupid prize. She looked down at Mudo.

"At least you don't want to get it up. Brad couldn't get it up, well he could, but it certainly wasn't staying up. I can't believe it got that far and then: poof! A failed fornication fiasco. What the heck did I do wrong? Or was it him? And was he talking near the end? Mudo, you just wouldn't believe it." She scratched the cat under the chin, and he obliged by closing his eyes and positioning his chin perfectly under her fingers.

"It was like he was talking to me, but he wasn't. He said, 'go away' and then he said 'no, not you' and he grabbed my wrist and pulled me close and kissed me. Then he let me go and moaned and up it would go and then he'd open his eyes and whisper 'go away' again. He pulled me close again and down it would go. He let me go and up it came. It was rather fascinating. It was like watching someone blowing up one of those long clown balloons and forgetting to tie the knot at the end and then blowing it up again. It was very weird, Mudo, very weird indeed. Then he fell asleep. Did I mention it was weird?" The cat nodded and moved his head so that Ana was scratching behind his ears again.

The coffeemaker gave one final hiss to announce the arrival of a mighty fine cup of coffee.

Ana picked up Mudo and placed him on the floor. He lay down where she placed him and stretched out on a sunbeam. His eyes slowly closed, his face a picture of kitty content.

Ana grabbed a large mug from the cupboard and poured her coffee. There was no use thinking about it anymore. She'd thought about it all last night. She wasn't sure she wanted to see him again, but what if, just what if, it was her, and not him that was the cause of it all. Today, she was more certain it had nothing to do with her, and she was a bit annoyed that she had left the card asking him to call her. After all, a gentleman shouldn't have to be prompted to call the morning after the night before. Ana brought her coffee back into the bedroom and placed it on her bedside table. She rummaged around for a warm pair of socks, found some and pulled them on. She sat on the edge of the bed and stared at her feet.

There was nothing more to be done about it now anyway. He'd call or he wouldn't. Either way, she'd deal with it when it happened. She stood and faced herself in the full-length mirror, then scowled and wagged her finger at her reflection.

"Just what did you think you were doing last night young lady? You know you shouldn't have gone there. You never, ever sleep with a client. You never slept with the dog food manufacturer, why sleep with the gorgeous hunk of a TV star?" Ana took a sip of her coffee and continued to lecture herself.

"Granted, the dog food fellow was a little paunchy, and a little bald, and his teeth were a little yellow, but that's not to say he wasn't a nice man. Now, I'm not saying you should go try and sleep with him since you tried to sleep with Mr. Handsome, I'm just saying that you shouldn't have been so done in by a pretty smile and a little bit of charm."

She gave her head one quick nod as if to announce to her mirror image that she was finished with the lecture. A small smile tugged at the corners of her mouth as she left the bedroom. Mudo met her in the hallway and followed her back to the kitchen. She finished her coffee and put the cup in the sink. The clock on the stove read seven a.m. on a Saturday morning. Maybe she should go for a walk on the seawall. That might clear her head. Meditation class didn't start for two and a half hours. She had to find something to do.

Mudo looked up at her and meowed. "No, no more food for now. You can have some later. Why don't you go stalk a fake mouse or something? Ana reached down and grabbed a pink toy mouse from the floor. She noticed the tail was missing.

"Go get it boy, go get the mouse." Ana flung the tailless plaything across the kitchen and into her living room. The cat looked up at her, stretched and yawned and sauntered after it.

"Lazy cat." Ana muttered as she reached for her sneakers. A walk might do her good. She grabbed a light sweater and her keys and headed for the seawall.

Chapter 16: Inside Another's Mind

Even with the leisurely two-hour stroll, Ana arrived a full half-hour ahead of schedule. She rapped on the door. A few moments later Carol appeared, a carafe of water in her hand. She opened the door and let Ana in.

"Ana, what a pleasant surprise. You're early, come on in." Carol locked the door behind her and followed Ana into the office. "I was just about to make a pot of tea. What's up, why are you so early?"

"Couldn't sleep so I went for a walk and came here." Ana sat herself in her favourite chair.

"Are you saying you need my classes to put you to sleep? And here I thought I was helping you on your path to enlightenment." Carol laughed and poured the water into the teakettle and plugged it in. "Seriously, you look like hell. What's up?"

Ana shrugged and tugged on her earlobe. "Not much really. I almost got laid last night but it fizzled out in the end, and he fell asleep. So, last night, nothing was up." She managed a small smile.

Carol rummaged through her drawer, found the tea she was looking for and put it in the teapot. "Well that doesn't sound like much fun."

"Believe me it wasn't!" Ana folded her legs underneath her.

"I've never had a guy weird out on me like that. One second he was acting like he was really enjoying what we were doing and the next he was pissed off and I think he was telling me to go away. Really weird, really, really weird."

The teakettle whistled and Carol silenced it with a quick tug on the cord.

"Well, sometimes people don't know what they want. Maybe he was confused about his feelings for you. Maybe he had too much to drink."

"Maybe he's a nutcase," Ana added. "Whatever it is, I feel like I need to be with him again, like there is something unfinished between us, and I don't mean sex.

Carol put an old brown teapot on the desk, tossed in two teabags and poured in the hot water. She opened her bottom drawer and took out two china cups. "Can't have my morning tea in a coffee mug." She placed a cup in front of Ana. "Maybe you two have some past life difficulties to work out."

"Or maybe I'm not used to having someone fall asleep on me mid-coitus." Ana laughed and shook her head. "Carol, have you ever had a man fall asleep during foreplay?"

Carol lifted the lid off the teapot and gave it one quick stir. "I can't say as I have, but I have had them fall asleep just before foreplay and of course immediately after, whether I was through or not." She poured tea into both china cups. "Don't let it get to you. If you really like this guy, see him again and if it happens again, reconsider the relationship. Who is the sleeping beauty anyway?"

Ana picked up her teacup and mumbled into the amber

liquid "Brdthrn" She kept her eyes down, hoping that Carol wouldn't ask again.

"Who? Did I hear you say Brad Thorn? *The* Brad Thorn. He who was assigned to you and brought you out of dog food hell? That Brad Thorn?"

Ana looked up. "Yes, that Brad Thorn. And I wasn't assigned to him anymore. We finished our working relationship a couple days ago. He called me up and asked me out to dinner to celebrate his first night as anchor for the News at Six and things just went from there. It wasn't like I planned it or anything. Let's just drop it. It really wasn't that big a deal anyway."

Carol let the silence fill the spaces between them while she sipped her tea. "Want to help me set up the mats?" She set her cup down and stood. "Today I'm going to teach you all how to bring someone into your meditation space, your headspace. It should be interesting to see how each of us perceive Sharon's peaceful place. I hope she's feeling brave enough to take us there."

Ana put down her cup and followed Carol to the meditation room. They set up the mats without saying another word. Carol left briefly, brought back a cassette player and plugged it into an outlet. "Sage or Sandalwood?" She held up two sticks of incense.

"Sage," Ana replied.

"Sage it is then." Carol pulled a pack of matches from her pants pocket, lit the incense and placed it carefully in the burner. "Time to open the doors and let the party begin."

Ana stayed in the room, got herself comfortable on her mat and waited. She was probably making too big a deal out of the whole thing anyway. In a few days she was turning twenty-eight, which meant only two more years to the big three-oh and still no stellar career, no husband on the horizon, and definitely no buns in the oven. Her mother would be calling asking about prospects on the career and the husband front. She hated to disappoint her, but at least her career was looking up.

Two more ladies came into the room looking freshly showered and scrubbed clean, ready to face the weekend. Before long the room was full, and everyone had settled in and was ready to chill out and meditate like nobody's business. Carol locked the front door and came into the meditation room.

"Good morning, ladies. Today we are going to go one step farther than our regular self-guided meditation or the standard guided meditation. Today we are going to experience what it's like to be in someone else's meditation, someone else's head. I'll start you off and then I'm going to ask Sharon to open herself to us and let us in. It might get a bit crowded and perhaps a little uncomfortable, but we must always remember this is Sharon's meditation and she is in control."

Carol paused to let the last sentence sink in. "If at any time she asks us to leave, we must do so immediately. One of the things you must understand about this type of meditation is that we must all be connected here and now, before we can go any deeper into anyone's mind. I want you all to get comfortable and reach out and hold the hand of the person beside you. As you relax, keep your eyes closed and feel the energy flow as you all connect as one."

Carol sat between Ana and Sharon and turned on the cassette player. She reached out and held each of their hands.

"Are you ready to do this Sharon?" Sharon nodded. "Very well then ladies, let us begin. Bring yourselves down and then we'll go for a little joy ride." Soft flute and harp music filled the room. Breathing became deeper, eyes closed, muscles relaxed. When Carol felt everyone had reached the proper state of relaxation, she began.

"I want you to picture a beautiful rolling meadow. You can hear a stream in the distance and see a small arched stone bridge over what you assume to be the stream. As you come closer you realize that you are not alone. In this beautiful meadow you sense all the ladies in this room are with you. You can feel them beside you as you approach the gently sloped bank of the stream. Now you can see the stream. Now you can see Sharon walking ahead and away from you. Can you all see Sharon now?" Fourteen heads nodded in unison. "Good. Now Sharon, do you sense the other ladies in your meditation with you?"

Sharon cleared her throat. "Yes, I do. It's very weird because I can't really see them in here, but I know they are there. They're behind me, but I don't feel the need to turn around."

Carol smiled. "Very good, very good indeed. Now Sharon, would you be so kind as to lead our merry troupe through this beautiful valley of yours?" Sharon cleared her throat again.

"Okay, ummm yeah. I've never actually crossed over the bridge before, but Carol said for today I should try. I've seen very lovely flowers over there. I'd like to take you there."

Sharon verbalized her journey, walking up the bank and over the bridge.

"How are you feeling, Sharon?" Carol asked.

"Good, really good. It's like I'm here and there too and it's like I'm watching myself and everyone else walk towards the bridge. But I can't see them, yet I sense them. I can't tell what is real, what is imagined, and what is really in this shared meditation."

"Good, this is good Sharon. Keep going, guide us with your voice." Carol's words were barely a whisper.

"If I cross that bridge now, you will all be in my head won't you?" Sharon took a deep breath and slowly exhaled.

"Yes, we will. If you don't want us to follow, tell us now." Carol waited.

"Okay, let's do this." Sharon, eyes still closed, took another deep breath. "We are going to cross the bridge now. The stones feel cool under your feet. We can hear the water gurgling under the bridge." Sharon stopped speaking and Carol's voice penetrated the silence.

"Once you get to the middle of the bridge I want you all to look into the water. Don't tell us what you see, just remember, we'll compare notes later. Whenever you're ready, Sharon, take us further."

Sharon smiled and when she spoke her voice was stronger, more confident. "Okay, now we are walking down the other side of the bridge and into the field. There are hundreds of flowers here. It's so pretty! There's just so much to take in. Let's sit and relax for a bit."

The music played on in the background. Harp mixed with flute, rose to a gentle peak and fell back down again.

Fifteen women breathed in unison as they sat and enjoyed

the tranquility of Sharon's special meditation place.

The final song on the tape began to play and Carol opened her eyes. She spoke softly so as not to startle the women. "Now I want you to find Sharon in your meditation. Bow to her and make your way back across the bridge. Sharon, you need to wait until all the ladies have crossed the bridge before you come back." Carol paused and waited a moment. "Are you all back across the bridge and at the spot where you first arrived?" Fourteen heads nodded. "Good. Breathe in deeply through your nose and exhale slowly through your mouth. Inhale and exhale. Sharon, you can come out of the meditation now. Two more deep breaths and come into this space, stretch and relax."

One by one eyes opened, glassy, disoriented, smiling. Carol passed around pencils and preprinted sheets of paper.

"Sharon and I spoke at the end of class last week. She gave me a general idea of what she sees in her meditation and that she wanted to take you all across the bridge to the other side and see what kind of flowers were there. Now, on each sheet you will find three questions. Answer them as best you can and put your name on the upper righthand corner. When you are done, pass the sheet to the person on your left."

The women did as they were asked and began filling out the questionnaires. The questions were easy enough to answer. Did you cross the stream? What was in the stream? What was in the field on the other side of the bridge?

A few minutes later everyone had filled out their forms and passed them to the left.

Carol looked to the woman directly across from her. "What

Reluctant Angel

answer is on the sheet for question number one?"

The woman looked down at the sheet. "The answer was yes. The stream was crossed."

Carol smiled. "Good, does anyone here have a sheet that says, no?" Fourteen heads wagged from side to side. It was unanimous; everyone had crossed the bridge. Carol looked over to Ana. "And what does your sheet say for the second question."

Ana looked down at her sheet. "Salmon, pink and red salmon spawning in the stream."

"Excellent!" Carol looked around the room. "Does anyone have a different answer than salmon?" Again, fourteen heads moved from side to side, this time a little more surprised than the last.

"And Sharon, as it was your meditation, would you kindly tell us what you saw on the other side of the bridge."

Sharon cleared her throat. "Hundreds and hundreds of pink and white daisies."

Carol watched the expressions of the women as they heard this simple statement. "Did anyone have something other than a very large amount of pink and white daisies?" The heads shook no for the final time, and everyone was silent.

"So now you know how easy and wonderful it is to join into another's meditation space. Remember ladies, this must be done with love, trust, and respect. It isn't something to be taken lightly. Being invited in should be considered sacred." Carol stood and brushed imaginary lint from her pants. "Any questions?"

The women looked from one to the other, down at the answer sheets and then at each other again. They all shook their heads, there were no questions. Each of them stood and said a quiet "thank you" to Sharon and Carol as they left the room.

Ana went into Carol's office to wait. Her tea was cold, but she drank it anyway.

A few minutes later Carol appeared.

"So, how was it Ana? I always enjoy going into someone's special place." Carol flicked a switch on the coffee pot and sat down. "I pre-fill these things in the morning, makes the coffee much quicker that way." Carol picked up the teacups and placed them on a shelf. She took two coffee mugs from the bottom drawer and sat as she waited for Ana to speak.

"Carol? When we were with Sharon, in her meditation, we weren't really deep in her mind were we? I mean, it was pretty much like a fairy tale meadow, is that what she's really like inside? I mean, well, do you know what I mean?"

Carol laughed. "No, and I don't know, and yes I know. I would never have let any of you ladies go to or take anyone into the deeper parts of yourselves. That could be dangerous. As for Sharon really being like that, well on the level we were at with her, yes she is really like that and yes I do know what you mean." Carol glanced at the coffeemaker and strummed her fingers on the desk. "Darn thing. You'd think someone who taught people how to relax wouldn't need coffee, but I do."

Ana leaned forward. "What do you mean by being dangerous when you go deeper? I mean it's not like we can die or anything. It's all pretty much us using the creative part of our brains, our imagination, and running with your pre-planted ideas and suggestions isn't it?"

Carol shook her head. "You never cease to amaze me. How can anyone have such deep, introspective and life-changing experiences and mediations, and yet still be so damn skeptical? Yes it's real. Most people try to separate the human brain from the metaphysical. I believe they are joined. I believe the brain is a direct path to the mind and the mind is the gateway to the soul and the universe. I believe in a fifth dimension and possibly more. I believe there is so much more to life than what we as humans can see, or experience. I believe in angels and alternative realities and time warps. I believe in all of it because if I don't, I'd go crazy thinking this was it. Because if this is it, I don't want to play anymore. Gawd, I need that coffee!" Carol grabbed the dirty teacups and left the room. A few moments later she returned with a small tray with cream, sugar, and spoons.

"Sorry about that. I really do need my coffee." Carol chuckled and prepared her cup and passed the tray to Ana. She slowly poured the coffee in over the cream and sugar and stirred it slowly. "Did I mention I love my coffee?"

Ana followed her lead and held out her cup for the brew. The two sipped in silence. Ana put down her cup and cleared her throat.

"You are the most un-zenlike spirituality/meditation instructor I have ever met. Of course, you are also the only one I know, but that's another story. Seriously, how could bringing someone into your head space be dangerous?"

Carol sighed and relaxed a bit. "Yeah, I'm great at being calm and cool when I'm not passionate about something. This is one thing I am passionate about. Here's your serious answer.

When you go deep into your mind, you are in effect exploring your subconscious. It's a wonderful, exciting place because it's normally hidden from us."

"I believe we'd go mad if we lived totally from our subconscious. It doesn't respond to logic, it responds literally to almost everything it's given. If you tell your subconscious mind that you are hot, you can make yourself believe you are hot. Yogis all over the world have proven this when they manipulate their body temperature, their blood pressure, and their heart rates. So imagine if you let a stranger in a deep meditation. That stranger would be entering your subconscious mind with their subconscious mind. Two entities that take things literally."

Carol paused and took a long, slow drink of coffee. "What would happen if you died in your mind? There is a very good chance that some major physiological changes would occur in your body at that time and depending on the strength of perceived reality of the moment of death, it's possible that someone could die. So to answer your questions, although highly unlikely, yes, it could kill you."

Ana pondered Carol's answer for a moment. "But what if it wasn't a stranger? What if it was someone you knew pretty well?"

Carol finished off her coffee and reached for the pot. "Ana, just what are you planning on doing?"

"Nothing. Why do I have to be planning something? I'm curious is all." Ana held out her cup for a refill. "You know, I like you better on chamomile tea, but you're far more interesting on coffee."

Carol smiled and shook her head. "Only the heavens know

why I put up with you. Look, whatever your reasons, whatever your ideas, just don't. If you really want to explore deeper with someone, let me know. I've got a friend coming with me to a big conference next week in San Francisco. I'll ask him about it and maybe he'll agree to come exploring with you. Until then, just let it alone, okay?"

"Okay, I will. Is there going to be a whole bunch of woo voodoo folks there speaking in tongues and channeling Elvis?" Ana laughed and gulped the coffee down. "Don't answer that. I have to go." She gathered up her things and headed for the door.

Carol followed. "Just be careful okay, promise you won't do anything stupid. I'll be back in a week. See you next Saturday, okay?" Carol gave her a hug and held the door open.

"You bet, boss. No stupid things to be done, not a one. I'll see you when you get back." Ana returned her hug and walked out the door.

Chapter 17: Brad, the Morning After

Brad rolled over and opened one eye. There was no one in the bed beside him. He sat up on his elbows and looked around the room. His head hurt. He looked at the bedside clock. It was 9 a.m. Slowly he remembered what happened the night before. He moaned and fell back onto the pillow.

"Oh gawd. Tell me last night didn't happen." He pulled a pillow over his face and screamed into it. Then he tossed it across the room and watched it sail out the door and land in the hallway. "What were you doing?" There was no answer.

He groaned again and then threw back the covers. He grabbed his robe off the back of the door and made his way down the hallway and into the kitchen. He opened a cupboard and swore.

"Damn, no coffee. How can there be no coffee?" He slammed the cupboard and headed for the living room. He flopped down on the couch, his arm draped across his eyes to stop the dagger-like pain of the morning sun.

"Where are you?" He lay there for a moment, still, waiting. There was no answer. "Damn you! I really liked this one. Why do you have to interfere? I wish you would just leave!" Brad sat up and rubbed his face with his hands.

She wasn't going to answer him. She only came out when she wanted to. No matter how desperately he needed her, no

Reluctant Angel

matter how much he cajoled, sat quietly or raged inside. She came on her own time, on her own terms. Sometimes she came when he called, but it only lent itself to the illusion that he had some control.

"I hate you," he whispered as he took his hands from his face and lay them helplessly on his lap. He noticed the card propped up on the table, next to the empty martini glass.

He picked up the card and saw her quick scrawl, *Call Me.* Maybe she wasn't pissed off after all. He certainly would have been if he'd been her. Could be she just wanted to scream at him and tell him to his conscious face that she never wanted to see him again. If he were her, he'd do that.

His mouth was dry, and his eyes burned. He ran his tongue across his lips and grimaced. He needed a shower, a shave, and a huge cup of coffee. Maybe she'd come to him then. Maybe she'd explain. Maybe he didn't want her to explain. Maybe it was time to have just one woman in his life. Maybe, just maybe, it was time to rid himself of the companion. She'd been inside him since he could remember. He would miss her, but then again, he couldn't have her controlling his physical self when another woman was present. She would have to go.

Brad reached for the phone and punched in a number. Ana's answering machine picked up on the third ring. Brad hung up. No use leaving a message.

He pushed himself off the couch and made his way towards the bathroom. On his way he hit the buzzer to the intercom. The doorman answered.

"Send up a maid would you, but before you do, send her

out for some coffee. Large, latté, easy froth, lots of cinnamon, oh and Ben, have her grab you one, too. I'll pay her when she gets up here." He released the button on the intercom and reached into his robe pocket. He always put extra cash in his robe, as it was easier to have cash at the ready at any given moment. He pulled out a fifty, walked back the living room, and placed it beside a martini glass. He picked up Ana's card and put it in his robe pocket. She still might be interested. Who was he to say what she thought? Most women usually gave men a second chance. He didn't find that a very appealing trait, however it served him well.

Brad whistled as he headed for the shower. She'd forgive him, he'd drive by and take her out for brunch, and all would be right again. He vowed that before the weekend was over, he would bed Miss Ana Murphy.

Reluctant Angel

Chapter 18: Birthday Surprise

Ana looked at the file folder in her hand. Brad Thorn. Assignment completed, lousy lay. She sighed and opened the filing cabinet, filed him under "T" for thoroughly through with, and closed the door.

She had seen his car in front of her apartment building on Saturday after class. She had called out, but he didn't hear her and had driven away by the time she'd ran up the street.

She spent the rest of Saturday and the entire day Sunday sitting by the phone. She was too stubborn to phone him and too hopeful that he would call her.

Carol called to invite her out for an early birthday dinner, but Ana declined, putting Carol off until Monday for the birthday celebration.

Now it was Monday. Ana looked out her window. Here she was twenty-eight-years old today. She had wanted so badly to grow up and with each passing year she realized that growing up took forever and growing older had a much faster pace to it. Twenty-eight. Almost three decades of living.

At ten she was a precocious child with the world in the palm of her hand. By twenty she had awakened to the stupidity of her teens and scared herself into making something out of her life. Now, at twenty-eight, she found herself in a job that bordered on a career. Her marriage prospects were slim to nonexistent, and her mother was still making noises about settling down and making her a grandmother.

Ana was glad for work today. Work always had a sobering effect on her and helped her place the past into the past and get on with the future. Working with dog food accounts and dating dogs of the humankind had her longing for a better future.

It was almost lunchtime. Definitely time for one more cup of coffee before she met with Mr. Parker and discussed her next assignment. The door to the coffee room was closed and Ana almost walked into it. She turned the handle and before she was completely in the room, she was met with a chorus of "Surprise!"

Ana jumped and dropped her coffee cup. The entire room was filled with her coworkers. Someone blew up balloons, and perhaps that same someone had strung a huge birthday banner across the wall near the ceiling. Ana stood there with her mouth open as she was regaled with a rousing chorus of "Happy Birthday."

She bent over to pick up her cup and heard someone whisper in her ear. "Happy Birthday beautiful lady."

She turned abruptly and came face to face with Brad Thorn. "What are you doing here?" She knew it sounded rude, but he was the last person she expected to see in her coffee room at work.

"It's your birthday and I came to give you your present." He gently turned Ana around so her back was to him. She felt something slip around her neck and she gasped as she realized he was placing a tear drop shaped turquoise pendant with a gold chain, around her neck.

"What? I mean, how did you know turquoise was my favourite stone?" Ana fingered the pendant and looked around the room. Happy faces beamed at her from every corner.

"I have my sources," Brad said into her ear, and then without warning, gave her a peck on the cheek.

As she turned to chastise him she found herself face to face with her boss, Gregory Parker.

"I don't know what to say. This was really a surprise everyone. You are just too wonderful." Ana reached out to shake Mr. Parker's hand. "Thank you, sir."

"We'll have none of that sir stuff here young lady." He draped his arm over her shoulder and coughed loudly. "Everyone listen up. I have an announcement to make." The room was dotted with whispers. Parker stayed silent until the last word faded away.

"Here at Thomas, Simpson and Parker we've always believed in promoting from within. It was our dream that someday, someone would come along that would be worthy of becoming a junior partner. Ladies and gentlemen, that day is today. I am pleased to announce that Ms. Murphy here has single-handedly increased business revenues by over 23% in the past year and as her reward, she is becoming what I hope to be the first in a long line of junior partners."

The room erupted with clapping and cheering. For the second time in just a few minutes, Ana was speechless. It was a bit too much.

She turned and shrugged Parker's arm off her shoulder and extended her hand. He turned and shook it. "Thank you so much Mr. Parker, you don't know how much this means to me."

"Nonsense," Parker grumbled. "And call me Gregory from now on, better yet call me Greg." He shook Ana's hand enthusiastically and cleared his throat for another announcement.

"In honour of Ana's promotion and her birthday, I'm giving her the rest of the day off. The rest of you, get back to work within the hour!" Parker turned, saluted to Ana and left the room.

Before Ana could say anything, a Styrofoam cup was thrust into her hand. She took a sip. "Champagne!" She took another sip, smiling, letting the surprise celebration and the promotion sink in. People came up to her, congratulated her, then moved back into their cliques. Ana scanned the room for Brad.

"Looking for me?" She felt his breath on her shoulder.

"As a matter of fact, yes, I was." Ana turned and smiled. "Thank you for my gift, it's beautiful. I don't know how to thank you."

"No thanks necessary. Besides, there's more to come. Let's get out of here."

Brad took the cup from Ana's hand and placed it on an empty spot on the counter. He extended his arm to her. "Shall we?"

Ana nodded, took his arm, and the two headed towards the elevator.

Reluctant Angel

Chapter 19: Birthday Treat

Brad opened the door to his car and waited as Ana got settled. He was frustrated when he didn't find Ana at her apartment on Saturday. He'd called twice but didn't leave a message on her machine. On Sunday he was sulking at his foiled plans. By Monday morning he was refreshed and ready once again to conquer the elusive woman. A quick phone call to the personnel office had given him the birthday information. More calls followed to a few influential people, and a final call made to Mr. Gregory Parker. Before 10 a.m., Thomas, Simpson and Parker had obtained three new high-profile clients and Ana's promotion was in the works.

"Are you going to get in?"

He shook his head slightly as he gazed down at Ana, his eyes going from her face to her long, shapely legs.

"Of course, I'm coming. We are going to celebrate!" Brad closed her door and got in on the driver's side. Within moments they were headed out on the freeway, whizzing past the city and into the country.

"Where are you taking me?" Ana asked. "How did you know it was my birthday?"

"I'm taking you out and I knew it because I asked. I'm not totally without my faculties, you know." He turned the car onto a side road and drove it up a winding gravel driveway.

"Where are we? What is this place?" Ana looked out her

window as a Tudor home came into view. To the left of the house was a swimming pool and hot tub. To the right a beautiful flower garden complete with a gazebo. "This is beautiful, but why are we here?"

"It's your birthday present and you will find out soon enough." Brad pulled the car into a parking spot under the trees. "It was a little hard to arrange on such short notice, but I believe you are worth it. Besides," Brad let his voice drop to almost a whisper. "I think I owe you this after what happened."

He got out and opened Ana's door. A plump, rosy-cheeked woman came down to greet them.

"Chou must be Hana." The woman took Ana by the hand and led her up to the house. "We will take good care of you, don't chou worry one l'il bit."

Brad watched as Ana was taken away. He waved as she disappeared into the house. This plan could not fail. After a two-hour massage, a pedicure, a manicure, and a facial, he felt Ana would be putty in his hands. She'd better be, this was costing him a lot of money.

Reluctant Angel

Chapter 20: Meet the Companion

Ana was very relaxed. Three hours of pampering could make a person feel that way. Brad picked her up and drove her back to the city with few words exchanged other than "thank you" and "you're welcome." Not a word was spoken as his car pulled into the underground parking at his apartment. She nodded and smiled playfully as he took her arm and led her upstairs.

Today was a lucky birthday. She had a party, a promotion, and now she just might get lucky again.

"Can I get you a drink?" Brad smiled down at her as she curled up on his leather couch.

"Yes, please. Water is fine. It's been a great birthday. Thank you so much for everything. I haven't been this relaxed in a long time." Ana let out a contented sigh and let her mind wander. She began to think about the group meditation and how she was able to see what Sharon had seen.

She called to Brad in the kitchen. "Do you believe we can travel from this dimension to another dimension?" She didn't expect an answer straight away and waited while he fetched her water and returned to the living room.

"What do you mean by another dimension?" He set a crystal goblet down in front of her and put his beside it. "Do you mean like time being the fourth dimension. You know, depth, width, height, and time?"

Ana picked up her glass of water and ran her fingers over the crystal pattern. "No, not like that. More like past, present, future, and other places. More like there are things around us that we can't see with the naked eye but if we looked in a different way, we could see them, really see them."

Brad turned sideways on the couch and tucked his legs underneath him. "I'm not sure what you mean. Do you mean the world of spirits and things that go bump in the night?"

Ana sat up more, faced him and crossed her legs underneath herself. Their knees almost touched. She reached forward and gave him a playful tap on his knee. "Well, not really, but kind of. So do you?"

Brad took a sip of his water and placed his glass carefully on the coffee table. "What would you say if I told you I had warlock-like powers and I was in league with the dark side." He smiled at her, winked and returned her playful tap with one of his own.

"Ohhh, the dark side. Are we talking Dracula dark side, or the devil himself dark side, or Stephen King dark side?" Ana leaned forward, elbows on her knees, chin nestled in her hands.

"I'm talking about the power my companion gives me. The power to travel into other realms. You do remember me telling you about my companion don't you?"

Ana wrinkled her nose. She vaguely recalled a warped conversation laced with plenty of vodka.

"So you weren't kidding when you told me that? I thought you were yanking my chain. You really believe you have some sort of connection between here and another world through this companion of yours?" Ana sat up straight and reached for her drink. She missed her mouth and spilled a little down her top. When Brad reached over to wipe a drop off her lip she pulled away. He smiled and let his hand fall to his lap.

"Yes, I seriously believe I have that ability through my companion. It's how I've gone this far in life and it's how I plan to continue on in life."

Ana stared at him for a moment. "Prove it." Her eyes never strayed from his. "Prove to me you can do this."

Brad stared right back at her. "And how do you propose I do this? Do you have some magic ability that will enable you to see what I see, feel what I feel, go where I go?"

Ana nodded. "Magical, no. But I think we can do this. I'm going to take you on a guided meditation through my mediation. I think I can bring you inside what I see. If it works, you can come in and let me see what you see. Or I think that's how it works."

Brad raised his eyebrows. This was intriguing. However, it was not what he had in mind when he planned the day. He wanted to get into her pants, not into her psyche. Then again, it just might be a completely new form of foreplay he'd never even thought of.

"Sure, why not. How do we do this." He shook out his shoulders, placed his hands palm up on his knees, and began to hum.

"Well that's close but not quite. Here, move a little closer so our knees are touching. Now get comfy and hold my hands. That's it, now close your eyes and let's see where we can go. Let me know if you can see what I'm seeing, and we'll take it from there."

Ana guided him through deep relaxation exercises. Within moments their breathing was synchronized. "Imagine a field with a stone bridge going across a little stream. Can you see it in your mind?"

"Yes, I see it." Brad smiled and wondered if what he was seeing was his imagination or hers.

"Excellent." Ana sat up even straighter. "Now imagine yourself walking across the bridge and once you get to the other side you can see me standing there. Can you see me?"

Brad nodded and then realized she probably had her eyes closed, too. "Yes, I can see you. There are tall purple flowers over to your left."

Ana giggled. "That's right! Oh this is so cool that you can see this. Maybe you are connected. Okay, now look over to my right. There is a small cottage. We are going in there and once inside we are going into the basement. Follow me."

In Ana's mind she saw the perfect summer cottage nestled in among the trees. She could still hear the stream gurgle and birds in the forest beyond the cottage. She felt Brad behind her, following her into the cottage. Once inside, she closed the door and headed towards the back of the small house.

"Okay, do you see a kind of white door in front of us?" Ana waited for confirmation. A few moments later Brad spoke.

"Weird as this sounds, I do not see a white door. I believe the door is closer to a sunshine yellow." Brad smiled, eyes still closed, somewhat amazed, and totally amused by this new journey she was taking him on.

"Oh my God! You are with me. It's a yellow door. Okay, take my hand." In Ana's mind's eye she saw Brad reach out and take her hand. She felt his hand tighten in hers as they sat together on the couch. "Here we go. Welcome to my world."

In Ana's mind she saw the door opening and the stairs descending down into the basement. She stopped briefly, remembering her promise to Carol. But she was so close she didn't want to stop.

They made their way down without a sound and stopped at the bottom. A long, well-lit hallway stretched out before them. Every three or four feet there was a closed door on either side of the hallway.

"Whoa. This is some weird psyche you have young lady. Do you always keep everything shut up inside? There must be a million doors in this place." Brad's eyes moved rapidly as if in a dream state. He scanned up and down the hallway and saw nothing but brightly coloured doors.

"It's not all locked up. All the doors are open, you just have to choose which one you want. I come here often to remember. Some doors have childhood memories, some have hopes and dreams and others are just day to day stuff I file away. Care to look in one?"

Brad chuckled. "Sure, why not. I've never seen such a neat brain before, might as well explore it."

Ana squeezed his hand even tighter. "Good, let's try the third door over on the left." She saw herself and Brad walk over to the door, open it and step inside. In the next instant she was inside the room, marveling at all the books and stuffed animals. "This is my collection of best loved things from grades one through four."

Brad looked around, careful not to touch anything. He recognized a few of the books from authors he loved as a child. There were a few well-worn teddy bears and dolls with dainty dresses and over in the corner, a shiny pink bike.

"Are you ever a girl." He teased as he look around the room. "Let me try this. Can I drive?"

Ana hesitated for a moment. "Sure, why not. It's not like there's anything here that can hurt us. Beam me up, Scotty." Ana giggled and waited for Brad to lead the way.

They exited the room and stood in the hallway. "I want to go to the deepest, furthest part of this hallway. I want to find a door you've never been in."

Ana jerked as she felt herself being pulled rapidly down the hallway. It felt so real yet at the same time she could hear Brad's even breathing in front of her. She gave his hand another squeeze to make sure she was still where she should be. When she looked around again she was in a dimly lit alcove off the main hallway. The floor was a grey and white checkerboard, and the doors were all black. She broke the silence.

"Wow, this is depressing. What the heck have you found." Ana squinted to see in the dim light.

Brad nudged her knee with his and let out a small laugh. "You mean to say you've never been to your dark side. It's where I am most comfortable some days. I believe it's time for you meet my companion. Ana, this is my companion, Fauvé. Fauvé, meet

Reluctant Angel

Ana."

A dark presence formed in a puddle at Brad's feet. It oozed over to Ana and then began to envelope her. She found it hard to breathe. Her body shivered and then it was gone.

"What the hell was that!" Ana opened her eyes. Brad sat motionless in front of her, his eyes closed. She could see him clearly. As clearly as she had on any other day, and yet there was this haze, this gauzy thickness that pulled her back to the dark alcove. She struggled briefly and then closed her eyes. She hoped today was still her lucky day.

Chapter 21: Darkness and Light

When Ana looked around she could only see grey. No real light penetrated the place where she stood. She could still feel Brad's hand in hers, yet here, in her mind, she could not see him.

"Brad?" Ana looked left and then right, wondering how to get out. "Brad, are you still in here?" She tried to speak aloud and felt her throat tighten. She squeezed Brad's hand and then felt it slowly slip through her grasp.

"Oh my God. Brad!" Ana's breathing became more laboured as she struggled to maintain calm. "Brad, this isn't funny anymore. I can't feel you or see you, where are you?" The silence was all enveloping. Ana heard a pounding noise and realized it was her heartbeat. "Brad, this is really going to waste all that relaxation I had today. Come out, please. I don't feel very well."

Ana turned to her right, then hesitated. Maybe they had come through on the left. She wasn't sure. She took a deep breath, turned right, and started down the hallway.

"You won't find him here." A woman's voice, silky, menacing, close.

"Who are you? Where is Brad? Why can't I open my eyes?" Ana glanced around nervously. This was getting out of hand. "Fauvé? Is that you?"

A shadow appeared before her, a woman's shadow, yet no woman was there. "Yes, it is I. Brad is gone. I've put him to sleep. He's out there on the couch, with you, but he's not in here anymore."

"What do you want with me? Why are you here? Who are you?" Ana stared at the shadow and lifted her hand to touch it. The instant she connected the shadow enveloped her, sucking the air out of her lungs, taking the light out of her life.

"No!" she screamed and tore at the filmy darkness. "I want the light!" Ana struggled and fought until she found a small opening. "Help me!" she called out, but no one answered. "Dear God, somebody help me!" The tear opened further as Ana clawed at it in her mind. Finally there was an opening big enough to crawl through. Bits of ashen mist clung to her as she stood and ran down the hallway. She saw a light up ahead and ran with all her might. She heard a voice.

"How long has she been like this?" It was male, businesslike, yet urgent. Then she heard Brad's voice.

"I don't know. I must have fallen asleep. She was at the spa. We came back here, sat to talk, I must have dozed off. It's her birthday for God's sake. Do something!"

Then another voice—a woman. "Calm down, sir, we're doing all we can. Is she allergic to anything, on any medication? Is her purse here?"

Ana listened for a moment more, then stopped when she realized she was back in her familiar hallway. She opened a door and found her bike and dolls and stuffed animals. She walked over to the corner, picked up a chocolate-coloured teddy bear, and hugged it to her chest. She sighed and slid down the wall until she was sitting amongst her toys. Safe, safe for now.

Darcy Nybo   123

"Yes it's there, beside the couch. That's her purse." She heard Brad from a distance. He sounded concerned, confused. Where was she? Why couldn't she wake up.

A knock on the door startled her. "Who is it?" No answer was given. "Who's there?" Ana stayed curled in the corner. "Go away!" she sobbed and buried her face in the teddy's chest. "Just leave me alone!" The door opened slightly, and a man entered the room.

"Hello Ana." He closed the door behind him, then opened it again. "Almost forgot, I'm expecting someone else. She'll only be a moment. She had to deal with some unpleasantness down the way there."

"Who are you?" Ana quivered and tried to make herself even smaller.

"I'm Rigel. Don't you remember me?" He stood in front of her and then sat in a squat position. "No, I suppose not. It will take some time for you to remember." He picked up a doll with blond curls and a little teddy of its own. "Remember when you lost her? You were so upset, I thought we'd never get you calmed down. You were more worried about the tiny teddy than the doll. You left her at the park, you know." Rigel lowered himself completely to the ground. "Another little girl found her. She knew it was yours and didn't tell anyone. She watched you run to your parents when they called. She waited for you to come back for the doll, but it started to rain. Do you remember that day?"

Ana shook her head. "No, well kind of, not really." She stroked her bear's head and relaxed a little. "How do you know these things? Why can't I open my eyes?"

Just then a petite blonde bustled through the door. "Goodness gracious that was messy!" She shut the door behind her and then floated over to Ana. "Hello dear, so nice to see you again. Are you all right? How's the head? Does it hurt? Oh look, Rig found Missy and Mister." She pointed to the doll and the mini teddy.

"That's right!" Ana smiled. "I called them Missy and Mister and I forgot them at the park. I never knew what happened to them. We looked for days and even put up a poster, but they never came back to me." Ana looked at the two strangers and furrowed her brow.

"Who are you and what is going on? Why can't I open my eyes and why does my head hurt?" She tried to stand and steadied herself with one hand on the wall. "Actually, I'm a little dizzy but, wait a minute. We're in my head so you can't be real unless you're a memory that somehow got lost. Do I know you? I mean, did you come from another one of the rooms?" Ana straightened the bear's bow tie and put him back on the floor. "This is so weird. One minute I was having fun with Brad and taking him through my meditation, and the next he's gone, and that thing is here and then it's gone, and you are here. I feel like I'm in that *Twilight Zone* show."

Dabria took Ana by the hand and led her out the door. "There's another room that's safe, just down the hallway. Let's go down there and sit and chat a bit dear." Ana nodded and let Dabria lead her to a smaller room, this one with a white table and chairs. She sat at one of the chairs and looked around the room. Everything was white; floors, walls, ceiling, chairs, table, doors, absolutely everything, stark white.

Ana watched without feeling as Rigel and Dabria sat with her at the table. Dabria patted her hand and spoke. "Now dear, it's time to explain what has happened. Are you up to it?"

Ana nodded.

"Well, I guess it's best to start at the beginning. First of all, you aren't dead, although you would have been if you hadn't almost died once already and then made the deal to come back and do what would have killed you anyway, but this time didn't kill you. Are you following dear?"

Ana shook her head and looked back and forth between the two. "Who are you?" she muttered.

The man smiled. "You'll have to forgive ole Dab there Ana, she keeps forgetting that you haven't been able to see us for some time now. I am Rigel, and this is Dabria. We are your guardian angels." Rigel paused to let his words sink in. "Now, about ten years ago you accidentally almost died. Dab and I were off on a little exploration of our own and we weren't there to guide you and well, you came very close to leaving before your time was up."

"I remember that." Ana studied their faces. "And I remember thinking how lucky I was, but I don't remember you two."

"That's okay, we remember you." Rigel patted her hand and continued. "Everyone signs an agreement before they are born as to what lessons they will learn, what their life path shall be and what, if any, is their task. Your task was to be here and rid Brad of his companion. Once that was completed your reward was to take your place amongst us and continue on as a newly incarnated angel."

Ana scowled, trying to understand what he said. "You mean I'm supposed to be dead for real, but I get to be like an angel or something?"

Rigel laughed. "Yes, or something like that. But it didn't happen that way. You rewrote your contract and now you aren't going to live on the other side. However, the world does need another angel and your services are required. That's why Rafael made sure you signed on as an Earth angel for the next fifteen years."

"Fifteen years! You're telling me I'm going to be some sort of angelic emissary for the next fifteen years!" Ana stood and paced the room.

Dabria watched her and smiled. "Yes dear, that's pretty much it. Today is your twenty-eighth birthday, the day Rigel and I begin your training as a human angel. You made a fine bargain with Rafael. You came back, fulfilled your original contract and for doing so he gave you fifteen more years to live as an angel on earth. In that time you will do some marvelous things. Then when that time is over, you'll go about your life without direction from us or …" Dabria looked upwards and smiled.

"And then what!" Ana stopped and stared at the duo. "Then I die again. This is just way too much. Way too much." She stopped pacing and strode from corner to corner to corner of the room.

Rigel stood and smiled. "My turn." He walked beside Ana, matching her step for step. "No you don't die again. It's in the contract. I can get a copy if you like. On your forty-third birthday you get your own life back. You can do what you like, when you like, with who you like. I believe Rafael threw in another forty-three years or so. So, actually you aren't leaving here until you're eighty-six or something. Unless you want to leave of course. The last forty-three years are up to you." He stopped pacing and watched Ana as she slowed, turned and faced the two angels.

"Okay, so if this is all true, where the hell am I now! Answer me that, Mister Angel man." Ana glared at the two of them. How could this be happening? Where was Brad? Why was she hearing voices? Why did her head hurt?

Then the room faded away. She heard urgent voices, a pin prick in her arm, noise, like a drill, an odd sensation in her head, lights flashing, the smell of something burning. She heard and felt all of this and yet was unaffected by it. The most pressing matter in her mind was to find out where the hell she left her purse.

Reluctant Angel

Chapter 22: Meet the Guardians

"Oh, I hope she's going to be all right!" Dabria fussed with the bedcovers and fluttered about the room.

"Relax. After two-thousand years you think you would have learned how to relax by now. Go check on the patient in room 321, I think Henry may need a little help in convincing him to stay here. He's not at all pleased about only having one foot now." Rigel gazed out the window.

A nurse came in and checked the bandages around Ana's head. She looked small. Her eyes were closed, there were tubes in her nose, and an IV in her arm. She'd regain consciousness soon. All that was left to do was wait.

A doctor entered next and checked her chart, then scribbled something on the bottom. The room was silent, save for the steady hiss of oxygen. The doctor, head bent to the nurse, whispered something. She smiled, nodded, and the two of them left the room together.

Ana's parents and brother were somewhere high above in an airplane, winging their way to the hospital. For now Ana was alone. Rigel hoped she would awaken before the family came. It would make it easier.

He walked over to the side of her bed and stroked her hand. "Time to wake up, Ana," he whispered. "Your new life is about to start and there isn't a moment to waste." Ana's eyes fluttered slightly. "Come on now, sweetheart, come out and meet us. We've waited so very long for you to see us on this side of the veil."

Dabria re-entered the room. "Henry is doing just fine without me, and it was a thumb not a foot you fool. Sometimes I wonder how you ever get anything straight." Dabria looked down at Ana. "Any change?"

"She'll be here in a moment. Have a little faith, would you." Rigel ran the back of his hand slowly across Ana's forehead. Her eyes fluttered again, and this time opened.

"Where am I?" She looked at Dabria and Rigel. "I remember you, from a dream I think, or at least it felt like a dream. Where is Brad? Was there an accident? Is he okay?" Ana tried to sit up and moaned. "Ow, my head, geeze that hurt." She eased her way back onto the pillows.

Dabria moved closer to the bed and patted Ana's hand. "Ana, it wasn't a dream, We were there, in your room with you and now we are out here in your room with you again, only it's a different room of course. Do you remember what we talked about dear?"

Ana looked from one face to the other. "A little I think. I remember my stuffed animals, Missy and Mister, and something about a contract. Oh, and I was supposed to be dead but I'm not. Wait, you said something about being my guardian angels. If that's true, why did I get hurt, why am I in the hospital? Where's Brad?"

Rigel chuckled. "Heaven's Ana, guardian angels don't stop you from being hurt, or even dying. They are there to help keep you on your path. They aren't bodyguards. What would life be without the odd bump and scrape here and there?"

Ana gingerly touched her head. "This is not a bump or a scrape. What happened?"

Dabria jumped in with an explanation. "Well, you see dear, there was this entity that should not have been inhabiting a certain body of a certain person and since you prearranged to help this person out it was your duty to go in and help remove that entity, or at least occupy it long enough to have it expend most of its protective energy so that I could go in a do a little clean up. And if you hadn't done that foolish thing with the drugs ten years ago you'd have succumbed to a brain aneurysm and today would have been your last day on Earth for this lifetime." Dabria paused for a millisecond. "But that's all water under the bridge now because you did succeed, the entity has gone back to the light to remember who it was and you made an excellent deal with Rafael and now we get to show you the ropes and teach you how to be an Earth angel and how to see things as we see them and help people out, by keeping them on their path because when we come down into the Earthly lifetime we tend to forget how to use our other senses because these human ones are so overwhelming and then there's the whole brain chemical addiction that happens sometimes which gets complicated indeed." Dabria smiled at Ana, expecting her to understand everything she'd said.

"How can you talk so much without taking a breath?" Ana asked. Then most of what Dabria said, sunk in. "Wait, am I supposed to be dead?"

Rigel gently moved Dabria aside. "Our Dabria is a bit

excited that you can see her. Suffice it to say that you should have died today, we actually prefer the term graduated. We are your guardian angels and as of today, we also get to be your guides and teachers. Over the next few days you will make a miraculous recovery and we'll be on our way." Rigel moved in closer and looked Ana in the eyes. "One other thing. No one else can see us. Well, some can but they are hush hush about it. I highly recommend you don't mention this to your family or the doctors. It will be difficult to convince the doctors and your family of your recovery if you tell them you are seeing and hearing people they can't see or hear. Understand?"

Ana nodded. "I think so." Just then her nurse entered the room.

"Good to see you awake, Ana. How's the pain?"

Ana grimaced slightly and looked back and forth between the nurse and her guardian angels.

"Do you have a sore neck?" The nurse moved in closer and began to palpate Ana's neck.

"No, no, I'm okay, but my head really, really hurts. What happened? One minute I was at Brad's, and then I remember voices and darkness and light and then I was here." Ana looked at Dabria out of the corner of her eye. She looked real enough to her, but she still couldn't be sure.

"I'll page the doctor for you. He'll explain everything." The nurse did a quick check of the readouts from Ana's monitors and quickly left the room.

Dabria swooped in to occupy the space the nurse had vacated. "See, that wasn't that hard was it? A little uncomfortable but you'll get used to it." Rigel stood off to the side, arms crossed in front of him.

A moment later, Ana's doctor entered the room.

"Ana, it's good to see you awake." He shone a small flashlight in her eyes. "Excellent, very excellent. I'm Dr. Naton. My team and I operated on you earlier today. You had a brain aneurysm. Now you may find it hard to do basic things for some time, like talk and walk, but I assure you we have an excellent physiotherapy department here and we'll have you up and around in no time."

Ana watched him as he wrote in her chart, glancing up now and then to look at her. "I think I can talk okay, Dr. Naton, and except for the odd visual oddity, everything appears to be okay, except for this massive headache." Ana glanced over at her guardians, then back at the doctor.

"Well then, it appears you are a very lucky lady. There was a lot of internal bleeding in your brain. We thought we'd lost you at one point. Can you sit up? I'd like to do a quick neural exam on you."

Ana gingerly lifted herself up onto her elbows, then sat upright as she moved her legs over the side of the bed. "How's this?"

Dr. Naton smiled and ran his finger down the sole of her foot. "That tickles." Ana giggled as he did the same to the other foot. Next, he tested her knees and elbows. He shone a light in each eye and made mmm hmm noises the whole time.

"Looks amazingly well, Ana. I'll have physio come up and evaluate you later this afternoon. Your family should be here shortly. Get some rest before they arrive. How's the pain? Do you need something stronger, or can you live with the level it's at right now?"

Before Ana could answer, Rigel stepped in front of her and placed his hand on her crown. Ana closed her eyes and let out a little yelp. When she opened her eyes, the pain was gone.

"Ana, what happened just now? Do you feel dizzy, nauseated?" Rigel stepped aside as the doctor reached for her wrist and took her pulse. It was fast but strong.

"Ummm, actually no." Ana blinked and looked in his eyes. "The pain seems to have gone since I've sat up. I'm okay now." She looked over to Rigel and Dabria. Rigel winked and Dabria gave her a thumbs-up sign.

"All the same, I'm going to schedule another MRI before physio today to make sure everything is okay. Now lie down, get some rest and I'll be back to see you this afternoon."

Ana lowered herself into the hospital bed and snuggled into the pillow. "Wow, that was really weird." Rigel stood beside her bed and brushed a stray hair off her forehead. "Sleep now Ana, sleep the sleep of angels and when you awake, your new journey will begin."

Reluctant Angel

Chapter 23: And So it Begins

Ana's recovery was nothing short of amazing. She spent the next few days surrounded by her family. She told the nurses not to give Brad any information or to let him see her. What happened between them was just too weird and she wasn't up to seeing him. She just wanted to be left alone and tried to ignore the angels only she could see. They fussed over her when no one was in the room, touching her head, smoothing her hair, smiling and nodding to one another.

She asked for a TV and a small portable was brought into her room, mounted on a moveable arm. Right after her bland breakfast of what appeared to be scrambled eggs and dry toast she turned on the TV to watch Challenger take off. It was an exciting time as there were two women, an African-American and an Asian-American on board. She thought it was a little cold to be launching a spacecraft, but what did she know. Until recently she promoted dog food for a living. Ana put on the headphones, plugged them in and settled in for the launch.

Dabria and Rigel appeared just as the countdown started. Ana tried to ignore them and listen to the announcer. "T minus thirty-one seconds. Ground launch sequencer is a go for auto sequence start."

Dabria removed the headset from Ana's left ear. "Let's go for a walk, get you moving around."

"No!" Ana pulled the headset back on. "I want to watch this."

The announcer's voice could barely hide his excitement. "T minus sixteen seconds. Launch pad sound suppression system is activated." He took a deep breath. "T minus ten seconds, nine, eight, seven, six, five, four, three, two, one. We have ignition and lift-off!"

Dabria moved between Ana and the TV. "Okay, you saw it, let's get you moving now."

Ana tried to see around Dabria. "What the hell? How come you are invisible, but I can't see through you. Please move, I really want to watch this."

Rigel came to stand beside Dabria. "We think you've had enough excitement for now, and we simply want you to get some exercise. You can watch the rest of it on the news later."

Ana still had her headphones in and could hear the chatter from NASA as well as the odd comment from the announcer.

"Move!" Ana demanded, which caused a nurse walking by to poke her head in the door.

"You okay?" she asked.

"Yah, just excited about the launch." Ana pointed to the TV.

The nurse nodded and continued down the corridor. Ana glared at her so-called guardians. "Please, move."

Dabria and Rigel both shrugged and moved aside. Ana watched as she continued to listen to the chatter from NASA and the announcer.

"Altitude is four point three nautical miles. The twenty-fifth space shuttle is now on the way after more delays than NASA cares to count. This morning it looked as though they were not going to be able to get off . . ."

The announcer quit speaking as the screen filled with a huge cloud of smoke. Rigel and Dabria looked away. Ana gasped and leaned closer to the TV.

"What the heck?" She watched as one part of the shuttle went left and the other went right. It looked to her like horns on a devil. "Did it explode?" She looked toward Dabria and Rigel. "Did it? Did you know about this!" The smoke horns kept growing, only now the smoke was falling downwards, back to Earth. She listened intently to the announcer.

"It looks like a couple of the solid rocket boosters blew away from the side of the shuttle in an explosion." Ana blanked out for a moment and then heard the muffled voice of someone from NASA, ". . . obviously a major malfunction."

She watched as the camera followed several tendrils of smoke downwards. Now the horned devil looked like a massive jelly fish with dozens of arms.

"That's enough," Rigel said as the TV shut off.

"But . . ." Ana had no words. She knew a little about the crew from news reports. Some had black belts, some liked to paint, one was a teacher. How could their lives be gone, just like that, and on live TV?

Ana laid back on the bed, rolled over and sobbed into her pillow. The hospital ward was eerily quiet. Then the noise level picked up with sounds of disbelief and shock. Bad news travelled fast.

Dabria tried to comfort her. "Let's go for a walk dear, you'll feel better if you move around."

"Move around? You think me getting up and walking around will make me feel better. What the hell! I almost died, twice. Now for some reason I can see invisible ghosts or angels or whatever and I just watched seven people blow up. They are dead and I cheated death twice! What kind of a messed-up world is this? You think a walk will make me feel better? Go away!"

Rigel motioned for Dabria to move away from Ana. They stood at the foot of the bed as she pulled the covers over her head and tried to make some sense of it all.

* * *

By the end of the week the doctor proclaimed Ana ready to go home. She could return to work in a week if she felt up to it.

Ana's mother breathed a sigh of relief, her father looked at his watch and her brother gave her a grin.

"So, everything is okay then, Dr. Naton? I can really go home and get back to my life?" Ana glanced at Dabria and Rigel out of the corner of her eye.

Dr. Naton looked over her chart one last time, signed the bottom and placed it on her tray. "Young lady, you've had an amazing recovery. I'm not suggesting you start running marathons or working fifty hours a week. Pace yourself. I'll see you at my office in a week and we'll see how you are doing then."

Ana's mother thanked the doctor profusely, her father nodded and muttered something about catching the 4:30 p.m. flight and her brother picked a stray cat hair off his shirt.

Ana swung her legs over the edge of the bed and grabbed the small bag her mother had brought her.

"That does it then, I am out of here."

Ana heard Dr. Naton speak to her family and heard words like, amazing, miracle and astounding. She heard her father thank the doctor again, and as before he mentioned if they hurried they could catch their flight home. Ana's mother fussed a little then agreed perhaps it would be best to let Ana get on with her life. Only her brother offered to stay over, despite his dislike of her mangy cat and her small west end apartment.

Ana emerged from the bathroom, fresh faced and grinning from ear to ear. "What are you waiting for? Let's get out of here." She grabbed her get-well cards and a small stuffed animal and tucked them into her overnight bag. The flowers were almost dead, so she left them in the room.

When they reached the front door of the hospital, Ana and her family stood for a moment, not knowing what to do next.

Ana broke the awkward silence. "Look guys, I really appreciate you coming out and all the worry I've put your through, but honest, I'm fine now, even the doctor said so." Her parents looked at each other and then at Ana. "Go on. I know you've got meetings to attend and places to be. I'll be fine. Mudo and I will keep each other company and I promise I won't go back to work right away. I've got more sick days coming. I'll just hang out at the beach or something."

Ana's mother hugged her and kissed her forehead. Her father gave her a quick hug and pressed a fifty-dollar bill into her hand. Her brother embraced her in a full bear hug and then held her at arm's length.

"You take care of yourself now sis. Don't go blowing up

any other parts of your brain, you hear."

Ana smiled and watched as they all got into a taxi and headed off to the hotel to get their luggage and then fly home. She waved at the next taxi as it pulled alongside her. "Corner of Beach and First Ave. please." She settled into the back seat, happy to be alone and away from the hospital.

"We aren't going home, Ana." Rigel appeared on her left. Dabria appeared on her right. "We're going to Paris!"

"No, we're going home." Ana crossed her arms.

"Actually we're going to Paris. Dab was right. It won't take long. You've already got a bag packed and Mudo was given an extra helping of food this morning. His litter box is clean, and the toilet seat is up. One more day won't hurt him."

"But," Ana protested, "I just got out of the hospital. I'm supposed to be recuperating, not going to the airport!" She looked from one to the other, then at the cab driver through the rear-view mirror.

"Excuse me miss, did you say you wanted to go to the airport?" The cabby waited for her answer. Ana opened her mouth to say no, but the word yes came out instead.

"Which airline, miss?" The cabby kept his eyes on the road.

"I'm not sure really." She looked from Dabria to Rigel and to the cabby. "Whichever one is going to Paris, I guess."

"International flight then." He glanced in the mirror and caught the nod of her head.

Ana dropped her voice to a whisper. "Are you two crazy? I can't go to Paris, I don't have a passport with me, I don't have a plane ticket and I don't have any reason to go there."

"Actually, you do dear." Dabria reached into Ana's purse and pulled out her passport and a plane ticket. "And you have a very good reason to go there. He would have been your first assignment if you'd come over instead of rewriting your contract. Now, we'll just have to get there in a four-dimensional way. Takes a bit longer but the scenery is breathtaking."

Rigel nodded. "Don't forget to tell them your reason for travel is for a quick business trip. For now just mention your current employer if they ask. Consider this your first research assignment."

Ana sighed and looked out the window. The airport grew larger as the cab approached the international departure level.

"Here we are miss, that will be $18.50."

Ana reached into her purse and pulled out a twenty-dollar bill. "Thank you and keep the change." She grabbed her overnight bag and her purse and looked around for the airline listed on her ticket. Within a matter of moments she had cleared customs and was seated on the airplane.

Twenty minutes later, as her plane cleared the runway, Ana's family boarded their plane for home.

Chapter 24: The First Assignment

Ana dozed through most of her flight, awakening only to eat the bland meals served on the flight. Nine and a half hours later she found herself standing amidst a crowd of people, all of whom were waiting for tiny little Parisian taxis to take them to their destinations. Rigel was by her side. Dabria was nowhere to be found.

"Where is she?" Ana looked around the busy terminal. "Does she do this often? Will she be able to find us?" Ana searched the crowd for a moment.

Rigel guided her out the door and towards a waiting taxi. "Don't worry yourself about Dab, she'll be along any moment now. She tends to wander off now and then."

Ana clutched her bag close. "Where are we going? Who am I supposed to meet?"

Rigel said nothing as she opened the door to the taxi and got in. The taxi driver said something rapidly to Ana in French.

"Tell him the Louvre Museum." Rigel settled in beside Ana just as Dabria appeared on her other side.

"What? Where have you been? Don't leave me like that!" Ana's voice grew louder, and the cabby repeated his request again in French.

"The Louvre dear, tell the nice man, the Louvre." Dabria patted her hand and smiled.

"The Louvre," Ana muttered. The cabby sped away from the curb and barreled into the traffic. Ana held on to the inside door handle as the cabby whipped in and out of lanes, careened around traffic circles, and sped through yellow lights.

"Woah!" Ana's body was flung to the right as the cabby narrowly missed another car. She steadied herself on the seat with a hand on either side. Once she got into the rhythm of it, staying upright was easier. "Do they always drive like this or am I getting special treatment?" Ana held on as the cabby took a right turn, barely slowing for the corner. She held her breath and closed her eyes as cars whizzed all around her, horns honked, voices shouted.

"Isn't this exciting?" Dabria had her head out the window, her eyes squinted against the wind.

"Fun?" Ana felt she had to shout to be heard above the traffic, the horns and the excited voices all around her. "This is nuts!"

She turned to see Rigel sitting serenely, arms crossed over his chest, eyes closed, breathing calmly.

Suddenly the car screeched to a halt and the driver turned to her, grinning. "Voila, Dix-sept Franc s'il vous plait."

"Pardon?" Ana looked at the driver as she opened her purse. Inside she found some bills and started to hand them to the driver.

"That's a little too much dear, one bill will do, the top one will be fine." Dabria had pulled her head in and was now outside the door to the taxi, ready to explore.

Ana peeled the top bill off and handed it to the driver.

"Ummm, mercy misyer."

She had barely exited the cab when the driver sped away.

"Now what?" She looked around at the milling crowds coming and going into a massive building.

"What's this? Is this the Louvre? I've read about it but never thought I'd actually be here, not now, not this soon, I was thinking maybe for my thirtieth birthday, but this is good. So, now what am I supposed to do?" Ana found herself walking with a tour group.

"Just stay with the group, you'll do just fine. Rig and I will be nearby if you need us." Dabria gave Ana a quick hug and then disappeared into the crowd. Rigel was nowhere to be seen.

Ana knew she should be tired, what with the transatlantic flight, the time changes and the fact that it was already tomorrow even though she knew it was the middle of the night, last night, back home. She found herself enjoying the tour and following along with the English-speaking guide. No one asked her why she was with them, or if she was lost. She simply blended in with the crowd and enjoyed the tour.

"Over here we have *The Persistence of Memory* by Salvador Dalí." Ana listened to the tour guide intently. The painting fascinated her. "It's one of his most famous works and is sometimes called *Soft Watches* or *Melting Clocks*. This particular work was the first of his surrealistic images of the soft, melting pocket watch. The general interpretation is that the soft watches represent the falsehood that time is rigid, solid, and unchangeable."

Ana became absorbed in the history and the beauty around her and almost forgot why she was there and what strange circumstances had brought her to this point. They came to Da Vinci's *Mona Lisa* and Ana listened intently to her history.

"Over here we have one of the most famous paintings of all time. It's the *Mona Lisa*, painted by Leonardo da Vinci sometime between 1503 and 1506."

Ana looked at the smile, the face without eyebrows, and understood why people were so fascinated with this painting.

The guide continued. "She continues to motivate, arouse, and of course, confound, most who try to unravel her mystery. As art critic, Alessandro Vezzosi once said, 'Her legendary indirect gaze provokes a reaction known as the Mona Lisa Syndrome: the viewer is enchanted by her smile, which becomes increasingly enigmatic and indefinable, transforming the painting as a whole into a mysterious mirror.' This painting is, of course, the most reproduced painting of all time."

Ana stood in front of the painting. She found herself smiling back at a woman, who if real, was long gone from this world.

The guide continued with his informative spiel. "On August 21, 1911, *Mona Lisa* was stolen right off the wall of the Louvre. It was such an inconceivable crime, that the *Mona Lisa* wasn't even noticed missing until the following day. Two years went by with no word about the real *Mona Lisa*. And then the thief made contact."

The guide paused for effect.

"Then in December of 1913, through a series of incidents, Vincenzo Peruggia, a former employee at Le Louvre, was arrested. His motive was to return the painting back to Italy where he felt it rightfully belonged. He was thrown in jail, the *Mona Lisa* took a tour of Italy, and she was returned to France on December 30, 1913."

The tour guide moved on and the group followed closely behind. Ana found herself standing transfixed, staring into the face that had produced a thousand questions, most left unanswered by the death of the man who created her. She cocked her head to the left and closed one eye, seeing if a different perspective would give her a deeper understanding of the enigma before her.

"She won't give me any answers either."

Ana jumped, startled out of her own private world. She turned towards the voice and saw and young man standing there. His hair was disheveled, a good week's growth on his face, his eyes red around the rim. Despite his unkempt appearance, he was still rather handsome.

"Pardon me?" Ana looked around and realized they were the only two people there. Everyone else had moved on and she could hear another tour approaching.

"Mona." The man motioned with his head towards the painting and spoke in unaccented English. "She won't give me any answers either. I've come here every day for a week now and each day I stand here and watch her and each day I leave without an answer."

"Maybe she's not supposed to give you any answers." Ana looked from the painting to the man. "Maybe she was painted to create questions, like a riddle without an answer. Maybe her sole purpose was to get people to think, to question, to talk to each other, to wonder aloud, alone and in groups, as to why she was made with all these seemingly odd bits and pieces. Maybe Da Vinci just had a warped sense of humour."

"Hmmm." The young man pondered this for a moment. "You really think so?"

Before Ana could answer, Dabria and Rigel were at her side.

"Hello dear." Dabria linked her arm into Ana's. "Time to go or we'll miss our flight."

"But," Ana looked at the two of them and smiled weakly at the young man, "but I thought I had some research to do here, someone I had to meet, something I had to do." Ana's voiced trailed off to a whisper. "What are you doing? He's really cute."

Rigel linked his arm into Ana's free arm. "Yes, time to go Ana, you don't want to keep Mudo waiting." The two angels turned Ana around and marched her out the doors of the Louvre and into the street.

"What?" Ana dug in her heels, but the two angels simply lifted her up enough to carry her along without it appearing they were doing so. "Hey! Wait just a minute here!" The two ignored her as they guided her into a waiting cab.

"L'airport s'il vous plait," Rigel instructed the driver.

"Hey? What? Okay, how come you can talk to him, and he can hear you? I thought I was the only one who could see you and hear you." Ana crossed her arms and sat back in the cab. "Would somebody please tell me what is going on here!" The cabby glanced at her and barely missed a car that turned left in front of him. Some expletives filtered back to Ana, but she didn't understand them.

Dabria leaned into Ana and tried to explain. "First of all, you did what you came here to do, and if I must say so you did a very fine job of it, no prodding or coaxing needed. We are very proud of you dear. Your first assignment and you carried it off like a pro. We need to get back because it's already becoming tonight here, and you need to get back to this time tonight later today at home and get some rest. As for Rigel, pay him no never mind. Every now and then he likes to flex his angel muscles and let himself be heard. We'll be at the airport in no time and before you know it you'll be in your own bed, and we'll debrief you on your first mission."

Ana closed her eyes and slowly opened them. Her jaw clenched. "I don't want to go home yet. I'm not some secret agent who needs to be debriefed. I want to know what the hell just happened and how my being here made any bit of difference to anyone, anywhere!" Ana did her best pout. "Besides, just in case you didn't notice, he was cute! And for your information I am not dead, I am very much alive, and I've had a rough few weeks, and in case I forgot to mention this—he was really cute!"

The cabby turned to look at Ana just as he was taking a corner and barely missed a large tour bus. More expletives rang out from the front seat and were accompanied by some horn honking and fist shaking.

No one said another word, not at the airport, not during the flight, and not even on the cab ride home.

Reluctant Angel

Chapter 25: The Debrief

By the time Ana opened the door to her apartment it was dinner time the day after she'd left. She ignored the messages on the answering machine, ignored the flowers and plants that lay about her apartment, and ignored her very lonely and hungry cat. She walked past it all, tossed her overnight case onto her bed and locked herself in the bathroom.

"Ana dear, may I come in?" Dabria had been fussing over her ever since she stopped talking to them in Paris.

"No!" Ana turned on the shower and peeled off her clothing, wrinkling her nose as each piece fell to her feet. "I'm tired, I stink, and I have no idea what just happened. Just leave me alone!" She stepped into the shower and let the water soothe her shattered nerves and aching body. Flying across the Atlantic and back and catching cat naps while sitting upright in an airplane was not something she suspected Dr. Naton would call taking it easy.

"We'll talk when you get out, dear. I know you must be tired." Dabria fussed around the apartment trying to arrange the flowers. At times she succeeded, and at others she watched in frustration as her hands failed to grasp the stems and instead, slipped right through them. Rigel found some cat food, fed Mudo, and then settled into an easy chair for what appeared to be a nap.

Ana emerged from the shower, her hair wrapped in a towel. She glanced into the living room and quickly went into her bedroom. She returned, dressed in an oversize T-shirt and panties. She sat down opposite Rigel and began to brush her hair.

"So, is that it? You just make money and airplane tickets appear out of nowhere, fly me all over the world to meet people I can never have relationships with, and I end up at home smelling like day-old socks and feeling like I have feathers on my tongue. What a life this is."

Rigel opened his eyes and began to speak. Before he was able to get one word out Dabria appeared beside him. "On no Ana dear, it's not like that, not like that at all, I promise. First of all, we can't just make money and airplane tickets appear, that just wouldn't be right. We exchanged those airplane tickets and the foreign currency with your money and some days you won't have to go anywhere at all, and you'll be able to meet people and have relationships. It's just that you might have to leave them at a moment's notice, for you see from here on in it's a blank slate and we aren't quite sure what your human life holds for you. It's like an unwritten symphony waiting to be heard."

Ana blinked twice and then got to her feet. "What?" She began to pace. "What!" She stopped and faced Dabria. "You took *my* money to buy those tickets and get me French money?"

Dabria and Rigel nodded. "You took my savings, my nest egg, to have me fly halfway across the world and back in one day, just to have me traipse through the Louvre and come home again without even so much as a T-shirt!"

Dabria and Rigel nodded again.

Ana stormed into the kitchen and opened the fridge. "I supposed all the food here came out of my pocket as well."

"Yes, dear," was the soft reply from the living room. "But your brother bought the beer and some cat food, and your friends and co-worker and family gave you the plants and flowers."

Ana plunked herself down again, beer in hand. "Might as well have something I'm not paying for." She downed half the beer in a few swallows, gave a small burp and stared at the two of them. "So, debrief me then, spy angels. Tell me what wonders I've achieved by spending money I was saving to buy a house, for a two-day adventure where the only thing I did was briefly look at some great art and almost meet a cute guy."

"Well, technically the flight there and the flight back cancel each other out, almost," Dabria explained. "We left here at noon, flew for fourteen hours and we were only there for three hours so it was really only seventeen hours. Then the fourteen hours back and the one hour from the airport, we were really only gone for one and a third days." Dabria caught a sideways glance from Rigel and stopped talking.

Rigel leaned forward in his chair, elbows on his knees, and addressed Ana directly. "Ana, think of money like you do wind or water. It's continually moving, flowing from one place to another. When you get too much water or too much wind in one place it can get destructive. Same with money, if you trust that money is part of the universal flow, it makes it much easier to let it flow instead of trying to hang on to it. You will attract that which you need the most in life, whether it's a lesson, money, friends, or even angels."

Ana looked doubtful. "So, if what you say is true then when I need the money to buy my dream home, it will somehow magically be there."

Rigel chuckled. "Well, it's not magic, it's a law, the law of attraction. If you need it and it serves your higher good, it will come to you."

The phone rang, catching Ana by surprise. "Who would be calling me now?" She picked up the phone on the second ring. "Hello." The voice on the other end sounded relieved.

"Oh thank goodness you answered. I was worried about you. We called as soon as we got home but you didn't answer. Your father headed straight for the office, your brother's out on a date somewhere—a nice girl, you'd like her. You know this aneurysm really has me worried. I hope it isn't hereditary, honey."

"I'm fine mom. I was sleeping, that's all. I feel great and I'm sure it's not hereditary." Ana sighed. She loved her mother and her family, but they could be trying at times.

"I didn't want to ask you in front of your father, but who is that Brad fellow. He sent some lovely flowers and a plant, but he never came up to the hospital. Your brother told me about the flowers. I hope you don't mind that he stayed in your apartment. That poor cat of yours was lost without you."

Ana reached down and absently stroked Mudo's chin. Bits of dry food clung to some of his fur.

"Mudo is fine, Mom. He's purring at my feet." Ana hoped she could avoid the Brad conversation but knew it would be futile. "Brad is a client I was working with when I got sick. I'm sure the flowers are simply a business gesture."

"I've never known a client to sign a card with 'I hope that wasn't our last night together. Love, Brad.'" Ana's mother waited for the answer.

"Oh Mom, just stop it please. He's interested in me and I'm not so sure I'm interested in him. Let's just leave it at that."

"All right dear, call me if you need anything, anything at all. We're here for you, sweetie."

"Thanks Mom." Ana hung up and looked at the answering machine. There were twenty-three messages. "Oh geeze, who the heck left all these?"

Rigel popped his head into the kitchen. "Brad called three times. He's very concerned, said something about how he'd never had a woman react that way with him before. Your boss called twice, told you to take the rest of this week off and call him next week. You had fourteen calls from co-workers and friends, all wishing you well. Oh and four people called to see if you wanted to—now let me get this right—get a lower rate credit card, donate to a kids' camp, join an organic co-op, and the last one was just some marketing firm wondering if you would call them. They have some new position open and want to talk to you."

"You listened to my messages? Is nothing sacred anymore?" She moved back into the living room and sat down. "Someone wants to hire me at a different firm?" Ana looked from one angel to the other. "Oh, never mind, I'll listen later. Let's just get on with this shall we?"

Rigel re-seated himself and spoke slowly. "Ana, what you did today wasn't just some random trip to see if you'd listen to us. You saved two lives today. Remember the young man at the Louvre?"

"Remember? Of course, I remember him. I wanted to know more of him. How did I save his life? It wasn't like I stepped in front of a speeding car for him or anything."

"No, the speeding car was the other woman dear." Dabria smiled from her chair. Rigel gave her a look that told her to let him speak.

"The young man is a struggling writer and student, trying to find his place in the world. The questions posed by the *Mona Lisa* have tormented him for years. He's always felt he should be able to answer the questions, solve the riddle. He couldn't. Today was his self-imposed deadline, unravel the mystery of the *Mona Lisa* or leave this world. He was fixated on her, her creator, and the questions surrounding her. He felt he was the one to answer some of those questions. Your little chat with him about how perhaps Da Vinci made her that way simply to make people think, gave him a whole new perspective with which to view his life. He'll go on to be a great scholar, a well-known writer and eventually marry, have children and grow old. With time, he will answer each one of those questions well enough to satisfy himself."

Ana was silent for a moment. Finally, she spoke. "Wow, that's pretty cool."

"It's very cool." Dabria couldn't contain herself. "Rig isn't telling you the whole story. You see, as a teacher he will spark the imagination of some of the great minds of the next decade, on top of that his books will bring pleasure and spark controversial discussions for all who read them. He will do with his books, exactly what you suggested Da Vinci did with his painting. They make people think, ask questions, and talk to each other."

"Wow." Ana finished off her beer and relaxed a little. "What about the second one, how did I save her?"

"That one was a bonus." Rigel sat back again. "We just happened to be there at the right time. You distracted your cab driver. The other car that he barely missed, gave the driver, a young lady, a bit of a start and she slowed down and pulled into a café to compose herself. Had she kept going, she would have been hit by a tour bus. It wasn't so much that you saved her life, more like you ensured her quality of life. It wasn't her time, and she has a pretty solid contract, so she'd have to stay here. The accident would have been very messy with a long recuperation time, however, she would have survived. Fortunately, she didn't need those lessons in this lifetime, she'll be fine without them."

"Wow," was all Ana could say. She took her empty into the kitchen, picked up Mudo and headed for her bedroom.

"I need to sleep in a horizontal position on something that isn't traveling at 570 mph at 36,000 feet."

Ana closed the door to her bedroom, climbed into bed and pulled Mudo beside her. Within moments Mudo was purring and Ana was softly snoring.

Chapter 26: Goodbye Brad

The next few days were about as uneventful as they could be considering the circumstances. Friends came by to visit and wish her well. She answered her phone messages and assured everyone that a brain aneurysm wasn't much to be concerned about, at least in her case. She did all this under the watchful eyes of Dabria and Rigel who would pop in and out at a moment's notice and sometimes stay for hours, only to disappear again. When she'd asked them where they went, they just smiled and said, "In good time dear, all in good time."

She was now accustomed to being called dear, and their comings and goings were startling her less and less. Even Mudo was comfortable with them around. Brad had called her every day for four days and she feigned exhaustion every time. She wouldn't be able to put him off much longer.

Ana sat down with a cup of tea and went over her finances. All in all, considering the spur of the moment plane ticket purchase and spending money, her accounts didn't look as bad as she'd feared. Some of her investments had doubled in value while she was in the hospital, and although the amounts weren't great, it was enough for her to let go of the anger she felt at first after having her money spent without her permission.

The phone rang and startled Ana. She rose, grabbed her teacup from the table and went to the wall phone in the kitchen.

"Hello, this is Ana." She leaned against the door jamb and looked out her kitchen window onto the city below.

"Ana, it's Brad. I hope you're feeling better today. I really do want to see you." Ana heard the sincerity in his voice and realized she couldn't put him off forever. She would have to tell him the truth.

"Hi Brad. Thanks for calling, but I really am okay. I'm not up for company is all." She inhaled slowly hoping he would take the hint. Ever since her last night at his apartment she had felt no attraction for the man. She chalked it up to the blood vessel that exploded in her brain, figuring it must have knocked out the neural net that made him attractive to her in the first place.

"But Ana, I really need to see you. I want to make sure you're okay, especially after our last night together." Ana paused a moment and gathered up the courage to tell the truth.

"Brad, I appreciate your concern, and the fact that you want to see me again. The truth is, I'm just not interested in you in that way. I have no explanation for it, it just is and I'm sorry if I've hurt you." She took a few sips of her tea and waited. The silence was almost palpable.

"Is it because I'm lousy in bed?"

Ana choked and a spray of tea splattered against the mouthpiece of the phone. She coughed, put her tea down and wiped off the receiver with a tea towel.

"Ummm, geeze Brad, I wasn't expecting that. Truth is we never really had sex, I mean that first time, you didn't actually, well you know, it wasn't like you, ummm, you know, got it up enough."

Ana felt her face flush. She was glad that Dabria and Rigel weren't around.

"I'm not talking about the first time. That was different, there were, well there were circumstances then that I'll explain some day. I'm talking about the night you were rushed to the hospital. We were joined in that weird meditation thing you were doing and then you took my hand and kissed me. Things just went from there and you sure did act like you were enjoying it. Truth is, I've never felt like that before, with anyone. I was so there, so with you, it was amazing. Are you telling me you don't remember that?"

Ana held her breath. She didn't remember that at all. She remembered meeting Dabria and Rigel in the white room. She remembered Dabria leaving, then returning, and then things became a bit blurry until she awoke in the hospital.

"Brad, I am so sorry, I really don't remember. I have a vague memory of wondering where my purse was and that's it." She waited for his response. There was none. "Brad, I don't know if this really happened or not, but even if it did, it doesn't matter, I really don't have any feelings for you. I'm sorry." She waited to hear the cockiness return in his voice, the easy way he used to brush people off as if he didn't care. It never came.

"Ana, I know you may find this hard to believe, considering what a self-centred jerk I've been in the past, but something changed that night, something good. Whatever you did to me that night, it worked. I need you. Please let me come and see you." Ana heard his voice catch and then there was silence.

"I'm sorry, Brad, really I am, but you don't need me

anymore. I have to go now. Goodbye." Ana placed the received back on the cradle and walked into her living room. She sat looking at nothing, shocked yet relieved at the same time.

"Ana, grab your purse and come with us!" Dabria and Rigel were standing directly in front of her.

"What? Where are we going?" Ana jumped up and ran her fingers through her hair. "I'm not dressed for going out. Where are we going?"

"Never you mind the details dear." Dabria grabbed her hand and ushered her towards the door. Rigel picked up her purse and followed behind.

"But, where are we going?" Ana turned as Rigel handed her purse. Rigel just smiled.

"It's so exciting, dear, you've been given your third assignment, it's all so exciting isn't it?"

"My third what? Who? Is it in town? Do we have to go far?" Ana locked the door behind her and hurried down the hall to the elevator.

"Just a ways from here dear. It's so exciting, her guides did something to have her listen and she's here, right now! We thought this one would take forever to get to you, what with the distance and all the other differences. This is so exciting!"

Dabria walked right through the elevator door before it opened. Rigel waited for the doors to open and stepped in with Ana.

"But who is she, what do I have to do? Give me a hint for gawd sakes!" Ana adjusted her purse strap and hiked up her jeans.

"Just a few seconds more, oh this is so much fun!" Dabria

waited this time for the doors to open and rushed out of the lobby and into the street.

Ana could do nothing but follow.

Chapter 27: Change for Change

What followed wasn't exactly the stuff that movies were made of. Dabria and Rigel were giddy as they exited the building and rounded the corner. They rushed ahead of Ana, then ran back to her side, all the while chattering and saying how excited they were. Three blocks up the street was Ana's corner store, a quaint little grocery store with fresh fruits and vegetables and lots of ethnic foods to choose from. Dabria stopped short and had she not been in a state of flux, Ana would have bumped directly into her. Instead, Ana had the slightly unpleasant feeling of walking right through her.

"I'm never going to get used to that," Ana muttered and then looked around to see what she was supposed to see. "So, now what?"

She shifted from her left foot to her right foot and glanced up and down the street.

"Any second now," Dabria almost gushed. "Oh, I can't believe she's really going to be here! This is so exciting!"

Ana shrugged and opened her purse to look for a stick of gum. When she glanced back up, a young woman was standing in front of her. She looked lost, disheveled and fairly upset. "Look, I hate to bum money from a stranger, but if I don't call my agent, I'm in deep shit. Could I borrow some change?"

"Ummm, yeah, sure." Ana dug around the bottom of her

purse and scooped out a couple of quarters, dimes, and nickels. "Will this do?"

The young woman smiled and took the change. "Yeah, this is perfect. Thanks. I'm so excited, I may have a part in a movie my brother is in! If things work out, I'll find a way to pay you back some day." With that, the woman dashed back down the street the way they had just come and plunked the coins into a payphone.

Dabria was grinning from ear to ear. Rigel stood with his arms crossed, his head bobbing slightly, a small smile on his face.

"Well, where's my assignment?" Ana looked at them and waited.

"Let's go dear, you've done well." Dabria started walking back towards the apartment, giving the young woman an appraising glance as she passed by the payphone. The woman looked up, smiled and gave a thumbs-up to Ana as she walked by.

"What is going on here?" Ana looked back at the young woman who let out a whoop of joy. "Who was that?"

"That," Dabria stated emphatically, "was assignment number three."

"That was it? I had to be on a corner to give some woman a buck's worth of change for a phone call. That was my big assignment? Gawd this just gets weirder and weirder as the days go by." Ana sighed and rounded the corner to her street. Without looking back she entered the building, got into the elevator, and headed for her apartment.

Dabria and Rigel were right behind her, Dabria chattering away and making less sense than usual. Ana tried to block her out, but it was no use. Dabria's voice carried its way across the room and into her head.

"Wasn't that exciting, to be there, at the very beginning? How absolutely wonderful." Dabria clapped her hands together. "Oh what a glorious day! It's just so exciting, don't you think? To be here, right at the start, to be part of the day—the day that made her who she is about to be. Oh, I can hardly believe that we got this to work, well not that we did it, after all it was her guides that got her to come up here, which is very good because I was trying to figure out how to get you, Ana dear, down there to her but you see we didn't have to do that after all because she was able to come here and by coming here she got the good news at exactly the right time on the right day, because you know dear, if she had called any earlier, and she would have if she hadn't lost her purse on the bus. My that was a fantastic manoeuvre on Gustav's part, don't you think so Rigel?" Dabria paused looked at Rigel and waited for his answer.

"Yes, quite. Very much so. He's getting the maneuvers down pat now. I wouldn't have believed he'd learn so quickly, he's becoming quite a strong guardian angel. Yes, very proud indeed."

Ana sat down on the couch and let out an audible moan. "For the sake of my sanity, will someone please tell me what just happened?" Mudo jumped up on her lap and began to purr.

"Why Ana dear, I just told you." Dabria looked hurt. "Weren't you listening?"

Ana stood, let out a sound of pure exasperation, and stomped into her bedroom.

"Oh my, I think she's upset." Dabria sat down on the

couch. "Did I not make myself perfectly clear? I thought I did. I was just thinking I was getting so much better at this."

Rigel sat down beside her. "Well Dab, you did leave out the part that she is destined to play one of the greatest roles ever created for an actress. You left out the fact that without Ana there, she would have been a few minutes too late for the call, and her agent would have called someone else. But, other than that, you did a fine job, Dab." Rigel patted her on her knee, got up and went to the bedroom door.

"Ana, would you like to come out and join us for some ice cream?"

"No!" was the terse reply. "You make my head hurt!"

"All right then, we'll be out in the kitchen if you need us." Rigel headed for the kitchen and took three bowls from the cupboard. He proceeded to the freezer and took out a pint of Rocky Road ice cream. He scooped exactly the same amount into each bowl and then put the ice cream away.

He carried the bowls past her doorway into the living room. "I've made a bowl for you. Rocky Road, your favourite."

An audible groan was heard from behind the closed door. A few seconds later the door opened, and Ana stomped out, her eyes narrowed. Her lips pursed in a reasonable facsimile of anger. "You just had to have Rocky Road didn't you? No other kind but my favourite. I can't win! I've got two invisible freak friends who've known me since birth, how can I win?" Ana sat down on the couch and unceremoniously folded her legs beneath her. She held out her hand and took the proffered bowl, complete with the right sized spoon and the right amount of ice cream.

Rigel said nothing and began to savour the chilly treat. Dabria smiled and reached for her bowl. Her smile widened when she realized she was able to hold onto it and scoop some ice cream onto the spoon. Her smile faded when she realized her grip was slipping and the spoon tumbled back into the bowl.

"Oh, some days I wish I could just get the hang of this!" She looked at Rigel with a mild expression of exasperation.

Rigel looked over at her and put down his bowl. "Dabria, you keep forgetting to stop trying so hard. You are so worried that it won't happen, that it doesn't."

Dabria looked over at Ana and then back to Rigel and said in a whisper. "I know that Rigel, I just don't … I just can't …" Ana looked over at the pair and froze, her spoon inches away from her mouth.

"You mean to tell me that after two thousand years you still haven't got the hang of things? Gawd help me. Here I am beating myself up because after two weeks I don't seem to understand what the hell is going on and you can't get your shit together after two thousand years. Unbelievable." She shook her head and went back to her ice cream.

"Ana, do you think that being harsh like that will somehow make your frustration less?" Rigel drew her attention back up to his eyes. "Dabria does her best with what she came here with. Like you, she is an evolving being, like all of us. Sometimes it's best to give ourselves patience in order that we may share it with others."

Ana dropped her eyes back to the ice cream in front of her. "I guess, maybe you're right, I don't know."

"This isn't just about you, Ana," he said, his voice somehow commanding her to look at him again. "It's about all of us, every single one of us. Not just you, not just Dab, not just me, not just anyone we meet. It's about every single one of us on this planet and beyond. It's about all of us that have been, all that are now, and all that are to come. You can't separate yourself from any of it, no matter how hard you try. Remember that when you get frustrated with yourself, we all feel it to some degree. What you give out, what you allow, will manifest and we all feel it."

Rigel turned away and gave his full attention to Dabria. "Dab, remember Henry?" Dabria looked puzzled for a moment and then her face lit up.

"Oh yes, he was just as much a teacher as we were, he was marvellous to work with." Her smile was back.

"Do you remember what he said?" Rigel picked up his ice cream and began eating again.

"Well, he said a lot. I mean, he was a man with a lot of words to say and lots of great ways to say them, and—"

Rigel cut her off. "Whether you believe you can or believe you can't—"

Dabria finished the sentence. "Either way, you are right." They both nodded in unison.

Dabria reached down for her ice cream. "I believe I can." She grasped the bowl, picked up the spoon and quickly sunk a mouthful of cold, gooey ice cream into her mouth. "Oh, that is so good."

"Henry who?" Ana finished her ice cream and placed the bowl on the coffee table in front of her. She unfolded her legs and stretched them out. "Who is Henry? Was he another angel?"

"Well, he wasn't then," Dabria began. "And I can't really say for sure if he is now or not, but I know that he sure could be, but not maybe a full-fledged angel, perhaps more of a helper or guide or perhaps even a rescue worker, actually, I'm not sure which way he went after he left, I know he said he was excited when he did go because there was so much for him to do."

"But, who was he."

"He," Rigel said. "Was Henry Ford."

Chapter 28: Ana the Hero

Work was actually easier now that she was a junior partner. Her days consisted mostly of going through research that had already been done for her clients and suggesting changes to them. She had a few people to deal with, but none of them were like Brad. Mr. Parker was pleased with her work, and he even hinted at a full partnership in a few years.

The weeks went by fairly quickly and Ana became accustomed to a routine of dropping everything and following the instructions of her guardian angels. Fortunately, most of it happened on weekends and didn't interfere with her work. There was the odd assignment where she had to deal with it during working hours. These were the simple assignments that only took a few moments, and all of them were within an hour of the office. She simply told the receptionist she had to go out for a bit. No one questioned her. More often than not her tasks consisted of speaking a kind word to a stranger, lending money for the bus or helping someone find their car in a parking lot. By far the most exciting assignment of them (aside from flying to Paris) was reuniting a cat that had followed her home with its elderly owner. It was pure luck that Ana spotted the poster. Her guardian angels begged to differ.

Rocky Road ice cream became a staple in her small apartment, and Mudo became a little fluffier around the waist as he always got to lick the creamy leftovers in the bowl.

"Does this ever get exciting?" Ana asked one day. "At first I was all concerned that I was losing my mind and this whole angel helper thing was going to be too much, but so far I've barely done more than walk to the store and back and stuff myself with ice cream.

Ana got up and went to the fridge for her second helping of the day. She was craving dairy and chocolate lately and couldn't quite figure out why.

"It's the little things in life that count," Rigel reminded her. "One kind word, one well-timed action can make all the difference in the world to someone's entire life."

Ana hollered from the kitchen. "I know that, you've drilled it into me. I get it okay. It's just that, well the company wants me back, and I'm ready to go back. Plus a head-hunter has been calling and asking me to come in for an interview. I know that by my next check-up the doctor will pronounce me fit for work and my insurance claim will run out and it's back to work for me. Quite frankly, I'm looking forward to it. Promoting pet food never looked so good!"

Ana returned to the living room with her second bowl of ice cream. "Besides, if I keep eating like this, I'm going to look like a beached whale. Heck I won't even be able to go to the beach. Look I'm already getting a little belly!" Ana lifted her T-shirt and showed Rigel a slight roundness in her mid-section.

"Don't worry about that dear," Dabria said. "It's a sign of being a true woman. Back in my day women prided themselves on the slimness of waist and the slight roundness of their belly. It was quite pleasing to the eye then, just as it's now. That Twiggy really messed things up for the curvy ones." Dabria stopped and looked shocked. "Oh my, did you hear that, I actually didn't run off at the mouth and go on about everything."

Rigel stood up. "And before you do, I believe it's time to go. Come now, Ana, put on your swimsuit, put on a nice summer dress, and let's head out and enjoy the sunshine."

Ana shrugged but complied. Ten minutes later they were in her car and on the way to the beach.

"Turn left," Rigel directed. "We aren't going to the beach by the ocean. We are heading inland to a park with a picnic area and a nice stream running through it."

Ana shrugged and did as she was told. Her constant questioning had never gotten her anywhere before, and she knew it wouldn't get her any closer to an answer now. If anything, she was learning to be a bit more patient.

"I think there's going to be a party there today!" Dabria clapped her hands together like a schoolgirl, her face beaming as she anticipated the festivities. "Yes indeed, cake and balloons, a birthday I believe. This is so much fun, I do love a good birthday party. Why, the last time I was at a good party, back when I had a body, was over two-thousand years ago and what a party that was. There was much celebration, in a quiet way anyway, even if what happened afterwards wasn't very pleasant, I mean with the killing of the babies and all the confusion over what did or did not happen and of course the magi came and went so quickly no one could really confirm or deny if they had really been there."

"Turn here." Rigel pointed to a parking lot that bordered a

regional park. "This looks like the spot."

Ana found a parking stall closest to the trail, got out and locked the car. Dabria and Rigel started ahead. Rigel stayed on the path. Dabria wandered along in a zig zag pattern, sometimes keeping to the path, and at other times walking right through small shrubs and trees.

"Oh look, this one has fresh buds on it." Dabria became as solid as she could, reached up and pulled the branch down for Ana to see. Ana looked over at the buds, nodded and continued walking. Dabria let go of the branch, turned to catch up with the pair, and walked firmly into the trunk of a huge maple, which was also rather solid.

"Ow!" Rigel chuckled but didn't look back. Ana looked back just in time to see Dabria give the tree a dirty look.

A few moments later they emerged into a clearing complete with fire pits, picnic tables, and off to one side, outhouses. A small but swiftly moving stream flowed to the left of the picnic area. A family had gathered and set up for what indeed was a birthday party. There was cake on the centre of the picnic table. Balloons floated on the breeze, attached to various trees and a few streamers hung from branches. Parents chatted while children ran to and fro in a wild game that looked to be a cross between tag and hide-and-go-seek.

Ana found a shady spot and sat under a tree a few yards away. "Oh, not there dear. No, no. That will never do. I think you should be over here." She walked Ana a short distance past the partiers, down a small path and near a bench by the creek. The water looked cool and inviting, but Ana could tell it was moving fairly fast and was in no way tempted to go for a swim. "This will do nicely." Dabria put her hands on her hips and surveyed the area. "Very nice indeed. Now we wait."

Ana pulled out a book, set it on the table and settled in for a read. She could hear the children laughing and screaming behind her, and the steady murmur of adult voices, mingled with laughter and squeals as if someone had told a risqué joke. She barely heard the little girl go by, and had it not been for her soft giggle, she would have missed her completely. Off behind her she could hear a little boy counting. "Twenty-one, twenty-two, twenty-three."

She looked to see where the little girl had gone and heard a rustling in the bushes next to the bank of the creek. The boy continued to count. "Twenty-four, twenty-five! Ready or not, here I come!"

The little girl let out a stifled squeal. The bushes moved ever so slightly and then Ana heard a scream and a splash. She looked towards the partygoers and then back to the creek. She saw the little girl's arms flailing as the current carried her past her vantage point. Ana jumped up and ran to the water's edge.

"Help! Help me! A little girl has fallen into the creek!" Ana looked over to Dabria and Rigel, but they had disappeared. "Great, never an angel around when you need them." Ana remembered someone had told her once that in order to get someone's attention in an emergency you had to yell fire. Help wasn't working so she bellowed at the top of her lungs.

"FIRE! Somebody help me! Damn it! Fire!" Ana looked back to the little girl. She was even farther downstream, her frightened eyes barely visible above the surface, her arms thrashing wildly.

Ana looked around. Not a single person in sight. "Oh, for God's sake!" she muttered. She didn't bother to take off her dress, instead she kicked off her shoes and jumped into the chilly waters.

Ana gasped when the full brunt of the cold hit her. Then she swam as best she could in the three feet of water. She winced as she caught her toes every few feet on outcroppings of rocks. She could feel the skin was pulled away on a few of her toes as the cold water rushed around her. The child was just up ahead. Ana watched in horror as the little girl sunk beneath the swift flowing water and didn't emerge. Frantic, Ana began to half run and half swim towards the spot where she last saw the little hands go under. She reached down and found nothing but more rocks. She plunged her hands back in, scraping the tender skin away from her knuckles, backs of her hands and wrists.

"Help!" she screamed again, her arms churning up the water, searching, grabbing for anything that might be the little girl. "Will someone please help me," she screamed and plunged her head under the water. The murkiness made it impossible to see. She gasped for air as she resurfaced and noticed a small hand floating palm up a few feet ahead of her.

"Gotcha," she said to herself and rushed to where the girl was. She grabbed her by the waist and tossed her over her shoulder in an effort to expel water from the little girl's lungs. The current was strong and buffeted her legs as she made her way to shore. She grabbed on to some reeds to help pull herself out of the water. The bank was slippery, and Ana tumbled back into the water. She held the little girl above the water as Ana felt herself sink lower. She tried to move but her foot was lodged under one of the larger rocks.

She struggled to hold up the child and free her foot at the same time. The current was stronger here and it tugged mercilessly at her. The captured foot held her fast, causing her to sink farther beneath the surface. She stretched as far as she could and was able to take one short breath above the water before being pulled under again.

"We've got her, hand her to us!" Ana heard a man's voice and let go of the child's waist when she felt a strong tug upwards.

"We're coming to get you. Hold on!" The voice was farther away now, somehow floating off. Ana realized her foot had come loose and she was bobbing, face up, down the stream. She saw a face in the clouds and smiled.

Reluctant Angel

Chapter 29: A New Life

Ana opened her eyes and tried to rub a stray hair away from her forehead. A soft, mummified hand touched her temple. She looked at it in disbelief. She raised her other hand and was met with another bandaged appendage. She raised herself up on her elbows and winced. Her head hurt, her back hurt, everything hurt. She wiggled her toes and knew that when she looked, she would find gauzy white lumps on both her feet.

She lay gingerly back on the pillow and tried to remember what happened. Her memories were scattered and out of order. There were paramedics and she couldn't find her purse, and then there was a little girl and angels, yes the angels were there.

"Hello Ana, nice to see you again." A pretty nurse came in to check Ana's pulse. "We were wondering if it was you when they brought you in. It looks like you will make another miraculous recovery, with only minor scarring." The nurse patted her shoulder and went to find the doctor.

A few moments later another nurse popped her head in the door. "Ana! So nice to see you again. Well not under these circumstances, but don't you worry, we'll have you out of here in no time."

Just then a doctor came into the room, grinning from ear to ear. "You certainly are keeping us busy young lady. You sure know how to bang that ole noggin' of yours around."

Ana looked up at him, recognized his face, but could not remember his name. She felt like Norm in *Cheers*, her favourite sitcom, where everybody knew her name.

"Excuse me, Doctor, I don't remember your name." Ana gave what she hoped to be a beseeching smile.

"It's Naton, Dr. Naton. I worked on you when you had your aneurysm last month. You do remember that don't you?" The doctor shone a light into Ana's eyes, then asked her to follow his finger.

"Looks good to me. I wouldn't normally be your doctor; however, you did have a slight concussion and it gave me an excuse to come in and check on my fastest recovering patient. You're quite the hero you know. There are some people waiting to see you. I've told them to come back tomorrow and let you rest today."

"Oh gawd, not my parents, please tell me my parents aren't here again," Ana groaned and tried to pull the covers over her head.

"Actually, we haven't been able to reach them yet, but we are trying."

"No! Please, don't get them, it's just a few cuts and scrapes. I'm sure I'll be all right in a few days. No use them coming all the way out here for a few scraped up knuckles and toes."

Ana tried to waggle her finger to show the doctor she was healing very nicely. She winced in pain as she tried to move them.

"Oh, it's a bit more than a few scrapes I'm afraid." He looked at her chart and flipped over a page. "Multiple contusions to all phalanges on both hands and feet, a sprained ankle, mild concussion, haematomas on the spine between C5 and T4 and of course the mild pneumonia you've developed as a result of bravely, yet foolishly plunging yourself in the water to save that child. You should be out of here in a week or so. We have to watch your hands and feet for signs of infection and to see if any skin grafts are needed."

"Skin grafts?" Ana groaned and this time succeeded in pulling the covers over her head. "Stupid angels and their stupid assignments."

"Pardon me? What angels? Are you having hallucinations?" The doctor gently pulled down the covers.

"No, I didn't say angels. I said, stupid fa-angeles—isn't that what my toes and fingers are called?" Ana plastered on a cheerful grin and stared directly at the doctor.

"Phalanges, yes." The doctor looked at her chart once again and placed it back at the foot of her bed. "You'll have another doctor in shortly; my colleague, Dr. Charles. He'll fill you in on the rest."

"The rest? What rest? I'm a banged-up mess, what else is there to say?" Ana quizzed the doctor to no avail.

"He'll be along shortly. Just remember if you have any prolonged headaches, double visions etc., ask them to call me." With that, he turned and left the room.

Dabria and Rigel appeared the moment he left. "Wasn't it nice to see all your old hospital friends again? And wait until you meet Dr. Charles. He's quite handsome if I may say so myself. Rugged in a doctorly way."

"Oh stop that, Dabria," Rigel chided. "Dr. Charles is not

here for Ana's visual pleasures. We have some very serious things to discuss."

"What serious things? What are you two talking about?" Ana turned to see a couple standing in her doorway.

"May we come in?" They looked vaguely familiar, yet Ana had no idea who they were.

Ana nodded and said, "Sure, who are you?"

The couple rushed to her bedside and immediately began speaking. "I'm Dane McCurdy and this is my wife, Dana. You saved our daughter Dalene today, at the party, by the creek. Do you remember?"

Ana nodded as the woman spoke. "We just don't know how to thank you for all you've done. We should have been watching her more closely, but you know how kids are. She was just out of our sight for a moment."

Ana looked from one face to the other. "It was nothing," she said. "You would have done the same thing."

"We want to thank you somehow," the woman gushed. "I mean just look at you. Your poor hands and feet. Dalene is a bit groggy and has a few scrapes on her feet, but nothing like you, I just feel so terrible. There must be something we can do."

Dabria and Rigel stood over in the corner grinning from ear to ear. Ana looked towards them but got nothing in the way of a hint as to what to do.

"Honestly, I don't want anything. It was a reflex. Anyone would have done it. I'm just glad the little girl, Dane, er Dana, ummm Dalene, is alive." Ana struggled to sit up more and grimaced as she used her palms to push herself up. "Just go be with your daughter."

The McCurdy's thanked her profusely and quickly left the room. Dabria and Rigel took their places at her bedside.

"Children are such precious gifts. You did a wonderful thing today, Ana." Dabria brushed a stray hair out of Ana's eyes.

"Precious gifts that should stop running around like wild animals and mind their parents." Ana sighed and let herself sink back into the pillows. "I'm glad I don't have one, the way things are going I'm having a hard enough time looking after myself."

She closed her eyes and began to drift off just as Dr. Charles entered the room. She opened her eyes again and gazed into the deepest, greenest eyes she had ever seen. He had tussled blond hair, a rumpled white coat, and reminded her slightly of Don Johnson from *Miami Vice*.

"Ana, so good to see you're up and chatting. I just passed the McCurdys in the hall. You're quite the hero. The press wants to come in, but I told them to wait until tomorrow. Let you freshen you up a bit." The doctor grabbed her chart and began looking over the notes. "I'm Dr. Charles. I'll be looking after you while you enjoy your stay here."

"Um, hi." Ana wasn't sure what else to say. He was handsome. She could think of nothing more enjoyable in her condition than to have this delicious doctor tend to her needs.

"When we brought you in we ran some blood tests, standard procedure, typing, white count etc. We also did a pregnancy test."

Ana's eyes opened wide. She stopped concentrating on his eyes and focused on his words.

"A pregnancy test?" She waited for more information.

"Yes, a pregnancy test. It appears you are about six weeks along. Now, fortunately the baby wasn't harmed during your ordeal, but we did want to keep you here a few extra days to monitor you. Sometimes there can be a delayed reaction to trauma."

"Pregnant," was all she could mutter. "I'm pregnant." She thought back to her conversation with Brad and how he had told her they'd made love the night she had the aneurysm, which was about four weeks ago.

"I can't be six weeks pregnant, I had my period six weeks ago."

"Well, that would make sense then. We calculate pregnancy from the first day of the last menstrual period. I trust this is good news?"

Ana's eyes welled up with tears. The strain of the last six weeks weighed heavily on her shoulders. "No, it's not good news, as a matter of fact it's horrible news. I can't look after a baby! I can't be a mother. I don't ever want to see the father again. My parents won't be of any help, and I certainly can't advance my career with a kid latched onto my boob, now can I!" Tears rolled down Ana's cheek and she swiped them away with her mitten hands.

"Look at me." She held up her hands for effect. "I'm a mess. I can't even keep my own life together without messing up. How the hell can I look after a baby!"

"Judging from today, you already have great instincts. Ana, it's not that bad, you'll get through this, and whatever you

Reluctant Angel

decide, just make sure it's right for you." Dr. Charles eased her back under the covers and tucked her in like a child.

"Sleep now, and I promise that in the morning things will be a little better and you'll be able to think clearer. Just give it time to sink in."

Ana groaned and rolled onto her side. "I should have stayed dead," she muttered as the doctor left the room.

Chapter 30: Changes and Choices

The next few days were uneventful. Ana healed quickly and was up walking around within four days. The press came on the second day, took pictures, touted her as a hero and by the next day she was almost forgotten. The McCurdys sent her flowers and when she arrived home there were gift baskets filled with fresh fruits, jams, and exotic pastries. She hadn't told anyone about the pregnancy. The doctors assured her that everything was proceeding normally and that she should find an OBGYN as soon as possible. She had a list of doctors taking new patients but hadn't called anyone for an appointment yet.

The truth was that Ana didn't know what to do. She was just barely twenty-eight, had cheated death twice in the past ten years, and talked to angels that guided her daily life. On top of that she had to prove herself as a junior partner at her firm. It was stressful knowing she was apt to be told to fly to London or Rome with a moment's notice. The entire situation had her rather confused and a little rattled. The news of a baby on the way was added to the already confusing array of life-changing moments thrust upon her. Even her beloved cat, Mudo, didn't seem to think all these changes were something to fret about. He went about his daily business as if everything were exactly the same.

Ana lay in her bed, flipping pages of a magazine, not even

looking at the pictures. Any decision she made would have to be made soon or it would be taken out of her hands.

"Ana, make sure you wear rubber gloves when you change the kitty litter." Dabria literally popped her head through the door. "I heard somewhere that litter germs were bad for developing babies."

Ana made a sound to acknowledge that she had heard but did not look up or engage Dabria in conversation. Dabria gave a weak smile and went back into the living room.

"I'm worried about her, Rig. She's just not snapping out of it. She's barely spoken a word since she found out. I thought she'd be overjoyed with a new baby on the way. She's bringing a brand-new life into the world, protecting it with her own life force. It's just so exciting!"

Rigel crossed the room and took Dabria by the elbow. "Let's go outside and talk and give Ana some space and some time to rest."

The two appeared to float and propelled themselves out the window and up onto the roof of the apartment building. They sat on the ledge and looked out over the ocean.

"It's been a long time, hasn't it Dab?" Rigel patted Dabria's hand as the two watched a flock of gulls fight over the remains of a discarded lunch.

"Far too long." Dabria sighed and closed her eyes. "I've never gotten used to this. Two thousand years and I still can't get over it. I had a little girl, Rig, my baby, my little angel."

"She was God's, just as you are God's. We don't belong to anyone in particular, you know that. We belong to the One—the

endless depth of Universal Love. We belong to God, the Creator."
Rigel turned Dabria towards him. "You gave your life so she could
live and for that you were rewarded with this immeasurable gift of
being a guide for someone's life. You have the ability to transcend
time and space, to stand before your Creator one moment, and
guide a lost soul the next. You have been given one of the greatest
gifts of all yet your soul longs for what was instead of what is.
You must let her make this choice on her own, Dabria. It's not
our place to interfere with free will. Every day with her is an
unwritten page of a book. Every assignment a new experience for
her and for us."

Dabria sighed. "I know, I just wish, I hope, that she makes
the right decision."

Rigel patted her hand again. "Remember, whatever she
chooses will be the right choice for her. Don't ever forget that."
Rigel stood. "All that being as it may, we must teach her to see
beyond the veil. If she keeps the baby, the baby will learn while
it's inside her. If she chooses to not have the baby, she still needs
to learn. We won't be here for her forever."

Dabria stood and took Rigel's hand. "Yes, I guess it's time."
The pair shimmered, vanished, then reappeared in Ana's living
room.

Ana was eating a bowl of ice cream. "Where'd you two go?
Find another puppet so you could pull their strings? Are there
any more reluctant angels out there like me?" Ana plopped down
on the couch and sighed.

"Ana, that's enough. We've been patient with you and now
it's time for you to just accept the fact that you are who you are.

Your life is what it is and it's time to get on with it." Rigel sat down beside her. "Finish your ice cream. It's time to start your training. Today you will learn how to connect to the other side. Not just seeing us but seeing others who need to connect to you."

"You want me to be able to see even more things, see more guides like you?" Ana shovelled a large spoonful of cold comfort into her mouth.

"Not just guides." Dabria sat on her other side. "All souls, from all levels. Angels and friends and family and teachers and all those who have passed from their bodies into another plane. There are so many there to help you, answer your questions, give you suggestions, show you options—all sorts of great things so that no matter where you are, no matter where you go, you can just ask and there's the answer."

Ana looked from Rigel to Dabria. "You're joking right? You want me to talk to dead people? Like a psychic? Hold séances and shit?" Ana scraped the last of her ice cream out of the bowl and licked the spoon clean. She got up from the couch and placed her bowl and spoon into the kitchen sink. Mudo meowed as she walked back to the living room and stood before the pair. "Dead people. You want me to talk to dead people." Ana shook her head from side to side. "Unbelievable."

"Not only that," Rigel continued. "You also have to begin your rescue work. Had you passed over, you would have developed into a fine rescue worker, but you're here now and others have been taking up the slack. It's time for you to do your work."

"And just when am I supposed to do that?" She paced the

room. "While I'm sleeping?"

"Actually, that's exactly when you do it," Dabria chimed in. "That's when most of the bodied ones do it, and it's oh so much easier than doing it while you're awake because your ego can't get in the way and try to help according to how you think you should help. You help how you are supposed to help, which in the end is a better help than if you knew you were helping."

Ana gave a sideways glance to Dabria. "Does she have any idea what she sounds like?"

Rigel took Ana firmly by the shoulders. "I said that's enough. The pity party is over. You're pregnant. That's what happens when you have sex. Deal with it. You almost killed yourself ten years ago. It didn't happen. You got us instead and one heck of an offer from the head angel himself. Deal with that as you wish. For now, your insolence and impudence must stop. Try a little gratitude. We have work to do."

Rigel released her shoulders and took a step back. "I'm sorry, Ana, that was uncalled for. There are much gentler ways to deal with these things, however, it appears you don't respond well to gentle. I apologize. I should have found another way. I understand how disconcerting this must be, but you must have faith and trust us, or this is going to be a very long fifteen years."

Ana sat down again as her bottom lip started to quiver. She examined the back of her hands, then her nails, and finally the palms. She looked up at the unusual pair as a tear slipped from her eye. "A few months ago I should have died—instead I'm pregnant. A few months ago I was changing the image of a TV celebrity—now I talk to angels. A few months ago I got a promotion and a raise—now you want me to talk to dead people."

Rigel and Dabria just sat there and nodded.

Chapter 31: Reconnecting

The days turned into weeks and before she knew it Ana had become very adept at hiding her missions from her boss. She also became quite good at connecting to the other side. She hadn't told anyone of her recent situation and was aching to say something to someone. Her belly was rounding out and Brad had finally stopped calling. She knew she would have to tell him eventually, but now was not the time.

She stared out of her sliding glass doors at the ocean. She yawned, stretched, and arched her back. A Saturday at the beach was a great idea, too bad she didn't have anyone to share it with, anyone with a body that is.

"Dabria … Rigel … are you here?" Ana looked around the small apartment. "I really need to get out for a walk or something. Are we done for the day?" Ana grabbed her purse and headed for the door. "Well, it's not like you need a note or anything." She gave one final look into her vacant apartment and headed out the door.

She strode along the seawall, and before she knew it she had walked back to the studio where she had once spent so much time learning to meditate and get in touch with the universe. She had got her wish and then some. She tried the door and found it was open.

Ana stepped inside and was shocked to find how much

had changed in the short time she had been away. She suddenly felt guilty for not coming back. The last time she had spoken to Carol was the day of her birthday—the day she almost died. She hadn't told anyone from the centre where she was or what happened. She'd ignored all calls.

Ana walked farther into the waiting area. New comfy chairs lined the walls inter-dispersed with small bookshelves filled with crystals, books, bells, and baubles. The doodle she had done of Rigel was framed and on the wall facing the doorway. Ana walked over and examined it. Had it only been a few months ago since she was last here? She recalled the last words spoken in this space. "See you next Saturday." Well, she was here, and it was a Saturday, just a faraway next Saturday.

Carol startled her by hugging her from behind. "Hey, stranger! How have you been? I was wondering when you'd find your way back here."

Ana turned and hugged her friend tightly. "Oh Carol, you don't know how good it is to see you, to speak to you."

"Well, I've always been here," she said as she pried Ana's arms from around her neck and led her into the office.

"This place has really changed. What'd you do? Win the lottery?" Ana plunked down in a chair and dropped her purse on the floor.

"As a matter of fact ..." Carol's voice trailed off and she waited for Ana's reaction.

"No! No shit? You wouldn't lie to me, would you? Oh gawd, Carol, tell me the truth, what happened?" Ana waited as patiently as possible.

"Well, shortly after I called you on your birthday, I stopped off at the corner store, you know the one, next to that little vegetarian restaurant I like so much. I never gamble, but I heard a wee voice speak oh so softly and it said, 'just buy one, Carol,' so I did. I didn't check it for a few weeks, and when I did, I found out I'd won $185,000!"

Ana squealed with joy. "Oh Carol that's amazing! Did you go anywhere, do anything else, I mean I know it's not a million, but geeze, that's a good chunk of change."

"No, I stayed right here, spruced the place up a bit, did some advertising and hired an assistant. He's inside now teaching the beginners meditation class. Coffee?"

Ana instinctively touched her belly. "Best not, but I'll have some chamomile tea if you have it."

Carol grabbed the kettle and left the room. A few minutes later she returned and plugged it in. She got down two clean mugs, put a tea bag in one and added cream and sugar to the other. Then she poured herself a coffee and stirred it while she watched Ana.

"You look different. Tired, but good." Carol held up her hand as Ana started to speak. "I know about you saving that little girl in the creek. That was some pretty amazing stuff you know." The kettle whistled and Carol got up and poured the steaming water into Ana's cup. "So, aside from almost dying and then saving someone and getting banged up, what's new in your world?"

Ana took the proffered cup and placed it on the desk. "Do you want the long-drawn-out version or the Reader's Digest condensed version?" She paused and waited for Carol to decide.

Carol looked at her watch. "Reader's Digest version please."

Ana took a deep breath and slowly began. "Well, the thing is, it appears I signed a contract with the head guardian angel several years ago, someone called Rafael, and when I didn't die it was because of him, and now I have to be a sort of an angel myself but only here, with a body and no wings. Oh, and I'm pregnant and all those meditation techniques you taught me paid off. I now talk to dead people and other assorted bodiless entities."

Ana reached for her cup and waited. She knew spurting it all out like that was cruel, but it had been a terribly lonely few months and what she wanted right now was 100% acceptance of whatever she said.

Carol put down her mug and cocked her head. "You don't say." She picked up her mug again and took a big drink. "Communing with spirits and angels now are you? Oh, and a baby, too. Well, it all fits." She smiled at Ana and came around the desk. "Give me a hug mom-to-be. This is all wonderful news!"

Ana rose and melted into Carol's waiting embrace. The tension, frustration, and anger she'd felt over the past few months slowly melted away. She let herself relax into the embrace as she quietly sobbed into Carol's neck. They stood there for a moment and then slowly came apart. Carol tucked a stray hair behind Ana's ear and led her back to her chair.

"Feel better now?" Carol sat back down in her chair and finished off her coffee. Ana nodded but didn't raise her head. "Good. Well first things first. I need to meet the guides of yours, these angels. How about we ask them to come in now."

Ana looked up, her eyes wide. "What? You want me to ask them to come here? Now? You mean you might be able to see them? Oh Carol, that would prove I wasn't crazy. Can you do it?"

Carol shrugged. "I've talked to many an entity before. I don't see why these two would be any different. As long as you give me permission and they are willing to let me see them, I don't see a problem with it."

Ana looked around the room. "They aren't here, I mean I left home and didn't leave a note or anything, but I didn't think they'd need a note and I've never really had to call them before, because they were always there, well not always, but lately always, so I'm not sure how I go about getting them here, or if they are already here and I just can't see them." Ana groaned. "Oh lord, help me, I'm beginning to talk like her."

"Talk like who dear?" Dabria popped her head into the room from the outside wall. She then squeezed into the room and stood beside Carol. Rigel chose a more civilized approach and walked through the door.

"Talk like you, Dabria. How did you guys know I needed you?" She looked from one to the other, then at Carol and mouthed, "They're here."

Carol closed her eyes and began to breathe deeply and slowly. Dabria glanced over at her and made the "okay" sign with her index finger and thumb, then took her place beside Rigel. She smoothed her hair, then pretended to lick her fingers and pat down some of Rigel's stray hairs, giggled and then folded her hands in front of her.

"Ready," Dabria said.

Carol opened her eyes and smiled. "Well, I'll be damned," she muttered as she looked from the angelic pair to Ana and back again. "Not literally damned of course, but never mind."

Carol stood and walked towards them. She held an arm out in front of her, palm down, and sliced back and forth through the pair. Her hand easily moved through them and yet they appeared to be almost as solid as the rest of the room.

Carol turned to Ana. "That was rude of me. Ana, could you introduce us."

Ana complied. "Certainly. Carol this is Rigel and Dabria. Rig, Dab, this is my friend Carol."

The pair spoke in unison. "Pleased to meet you, Carol."

Dabria could no longer contain herself. "We've been wondering when she'd get tired of us and head on down here. I am so happy to meet you, that you can meet us, by which I mean see us, because it takes a lot of faith and belief to see us, not that we're invisible or anything because we aren't. Nothing is really invisible. We just vibrate at such a high frequency that most people can't see us because they don't want to see the higher parts of their lives. They get stuck in the low and then, well you know what happens then, mercy it can get so complicated. But I'm sure you know what I mean, of course you know what I mean because, well, you can see us, well not see, but sense because it's not really your eyes, but I know you aren't one of those who chooses to ignore what's right in front of them." Dabria gave Ana a small smile. "Not that our Ana is one of those either, because she isn't, never has been and you were right before about her being destined for something great, not that everyone doesn't have something great to do because they do, they just chose to not pay attention to it, or they believe their bit of greatness is less that someone else's bit of greatness, but it's really not true because what is small to some can be the world to others. Right Rig?"

Rigel stepped forward and gave a small bow in Carol's direction. "What my dear companion means is, we are very pleased that you have chosen to connect with us, and we hope you continue to do so."

Rigel winked at Ana and then smiled at Carol.

"So, Carol." Ana looked at the trio. "These are my guardian angels, my captors and my teachers. I guess you could say they're also my friends. Tell me I'm not insane."

Carol smiled at Ana. "You aren't insane. However, you are very, very blessed."

Chapter 32: Brad Returns

An afternoon with Carol had done wonders to lift Ana's spirits. She no longer had any doubts about her sanity. Connecting with entities unseen by most had become a part of her everyday life. The city filled up with tourists as Expo 86 kicked off in style with the Prince and Princess of Wales at the opening ceremonies. Tourists flew in from all over the world, bringing their families and their money with them. It would either propel Vancouver directly into the world's spotlight or bankrupt the city within the year. Only time would tell.

She took in some of the exhibits with Carol but found herself less interested with what was going on outside and was more intrigued with what was going on inside her body. She was about four months pregnant and was told she would soon experience what the doctor's called quickening. That hadn't happened yet, but she did notice that none of her pants fit her anymore.

"Look at me," she said to no one in particular as she tossed her fat jeans onto the floor. "I'm huge!"

Then she sat down on the couch and blinked twice. "Oh my gawd!" She stood up again and felt her belly. This was it. It felt like a dozen little butterflies deep inside her. The baby, her baby, was moving!

Ana looked around for someone, anyone, to talk to. "Oh my gawd! Oh my gawd! Is anyone there? Hello, can anyone hear me? I'm pregnant! I'm really and truly pregnant. I can't get rid of this baby. It's mine and besides it's too late and you know what—I don't care. I want this baby."

Ana laughed at her sudden realization and began to dance around the room. Just then her door buzzer rang. Ana pressed the intercom button. "Hello?"

A familiar voice called up to her. "Hello, Ana. It's me. Can I please come up and talk to you? It's important."

Ana hesitated for a moment and then pushed the button to open the front door of the apartment building. "Yes, of course, come right up."

She searched the rooms frantically for Rigel and Dabria, but they were nowhere to be found. The other disembodied folks she'd come to know fluttered into her peripheral vision. One of the older women just smiled at her. When Ana blinked everyone was gone.

"This is not good. Not good at all. I have an entire realm of beings that I can talk to and not one is available for guidance. What's the use of having this gift if no one will help me when I need it?"

She ran her fingers through her hair, rushed into her bedroom and searched frantically in her closet for a loose dress or baggy top. She found an old skirt with an elasticized waist band and pulled it out of the closet. Before she could look for anything else there was a light tapping at the door. She quickly pulled on the skirt, checked herself in the bedroom mirror, wiped her hair away from her face, and strode with purpose to the door.

"Be right there," she called as she passed the kitchen. She

hesitated, grabbed a dishtowel, held it in front of her, and went to the door.

"Hello Brad, it's good to see you. Please come in."

Brad smiled and made his way to the living room. He sat on the sofa, leaving the opposite chair or the spot beside him available. Ana chose the chair and carefully draped the towel over her lap before sitting down.

They both began to speak at once. "You first," Ana graciously offered. She really didn't know what to say anyway. The man sitting before her was as foreign to her as a stranger. His once handsome features were gaunt and tired looking. His hair was thinning, and he had hollow circles under his eyes. How long had it been? Four, five months since she thought she was falling for him, and now, she couldn't imagine why.

"I know, I look terrible." He managed a grin. "You don't have to ask why. That's why I'm here, to tell you." He cleared his throat and looked around. "Can I get a drink of water please?"

Ana jumped up, the towel dropped, and she scooped it back up and held it in front of her again.

"I'll be right back." She hurried into the kitchen, her mind whirling, yet her emotions were completely flat. She opened the cupboard and grabbed two glasses. Mudo jumped up on the counter. She scratched his head and whispered to her cat. "I must have lost part of my brain in one of my hospital stays," she said. "This man means nothing to me, and he should, really, truly, he should, shouldn't he?" She stopped petting the cat, patted her swelling baby bump, and filled the glasses with water. She plastered a smile on her face and headed back to the living room.

"Here you go. Now tell me, what's been happening to you? You're right, you don't look at all like yourself. What happened?"

Brad took a long drink of the offered water. "Well, I wasn't sure if I should tell you or not, being as how you wouldn't return my calls and all. I was pretty upset about the whole thing and thought I'd be damned if I'd tell you anything now." He paused and took another drink. "I'm not angry with you, Ana, just at life. The short explanation is I have cancer. I have brain cancer. The doctor said it's called a Glioblastoma multiforme or GBM, which sounds very technical. Basically, what it means is, I'm not going to be around much longer, so I've come to say goodbye." Brad didn't look at her. He simply finished his water and put his glass down on the coffee table.

Ana was stunned into silence. She stood slowly, forgetting the dishtowel, letting it fall to the ground. She sat beside Brad and took his hand in hers. "I am so sorry, Brad, truly I am. I should have returned your calls, but I thought you were just trying to, well, I, I am so sorry."

Brad just nodded and looked down at her hands and then at her bump. "It's okay, I'm here now, and you let me in so let's not talk about it." He turned and looked her in the eyes. "It's not so bad really, just that I'm not going to be much of me anymore. Not that I really was much of me before this." He gave a small smile.

"What are you talking about, Brad. You were always you, weren't you?"

Brad took a deep breath. "Yes and no. You see, I've probably had this tumour for quite some time. It grows from deep inside and it's usually always too late to do anything about once it gets to the stage I'm at. Ironically one of my main symptoms was my personality, which wasn't very nice. That, plus some memory loss here and there. I thought it was, well you know, the other." He took another deep breath. "It turns out that maybe the other wasn't there at all, it was just a brain tumour. Funny thing is, those parts of my symptoms should be getting worse, but ever since ..." He paused. "Well, ever since that last night with you a few months ago, I haven't had memory losses or heard voices or thought there was someone else inside of me."

Ana felt the tears well up in her eyes. The feelings were slowly returning. "But what about radiation and treatment, can't they take it out, can't they just go in and cut it out and zap it or something?" She searched Brad's eyes, knowing in the core of her being that he really had come to say goodbye.

"There's not much they can do. I started getting pretty bad headaches about three months ago, then the doctors took some X-rays of my head and finally they took a biopsy of my brain. It's malignant and very advanced. I tried radiation but it made me so sick. My hair started to fall out. They took another X-ray, and the tumour didn't shrink, in fact it got bigger. It's here right now." He tapped his forehead in the centre just above his eyes. "It goes all the way back to here, about the size of a squished small grapefruit." He traced an imaginary line down the centre of his skull to the top of his head near the crown. "Bitch of it is, they can't say for sure how long I've had it, or how I got it. All they can tell me is that I've got a few more weeks to say goodbye and that's it."

Ana hugged Brad and kissed him on his forehead. "I don't know what to say, Brad. I truly am sorry I didn't return your calls. I had so much going on and I ... well there are no good excuses, are there?"

"I read about you in the paper. You're quite the hero."

"Yes," she smiled. "You and I seem to have been in hospitals quite a bit lately."

They lapsed into a semi-comfortable silence, each caught up in their rememberings of the past few months.

Brad broke the silence first. "I don't mean to be rude, but you certainly have put on some weight since I last saw you. Is everything okay?"

Ana instinctively put her hands to her belly. "Yes, well, I was going to call you about this." She took a deep breath, started to speak, and took another deep breath. "I'm pregnant Brad, and I have every reason to believe it's yours."

"Mine?" he asked incredulously. "You're pregnant with my child?"

Ana didn't speak. She simply nodded and searched his face, desperately trying to read him. All she saw was a tired, beaten man.

"A baby," he whispered. "My baby." He reached over and touched her belly. "I'm not going to die after all," he murmured. "There's a baby, a part of me left."

Ana put her arm around him, and Brad slouched against her, his body weight pulling him downward until his head was on her lap, his face towards her belly. "A baby," he whispered again, then closed his eyes and began to softly weep.

Ana stroked his hair as Rigel and Dabria materialized in front of them.

"Let him sleep, Ana. He is so very, very tired." Dabria sat down beside Ana and stroked Brad's head. "He'll be coming with us soon enough, but for now, let him sleep."

Ana realized Brad had fallen into a deep slumber and looked at the pair.

"I feel like such an idiot. He had such little time, and I could have told him, made him feel better, given him some hope, but I was too damn selfish, only thinking of me. How could I be so self-centred?"

"Hush now, it's nothing to fret about." Rigel bent over and stroked the man's forehead. "You gave him the hope he needed when all hope was lost. If you'd have told him before this, he wouldn't have appreciated it, wouldn't have grasped the immensity of it all or understood a type of physical immortality that all humans share." Rigel smiled as he watched the man sleeping next to his unborn child.

"Give him a few more moments, and then wake him up. You two need to go out and celebrate tonight. It will be his last. He's only here a few more days. He'll have the strength and the clarity to make it through the night, but after this, I'm afraid he won't recognize you, or anyone for that matter."

"Can't you do anything? Can't you give him a little longer. Can you get rid of the tumour or something? There's got to be—" Ana stopped short as she watched Rigel shake his head. She knew the answers. She'd been living them since the day she was supposed to die—the day she removed the other from Brad and sealed his fate, and hers, forever. Ana nodded in resignation. "But dinner? I haven't got anything to wear and Brad, he looks like he could sleep for days."

Dabria rushed into the hallway. "Well, dear, you see, that's where we've been. I do love shopping. It's not something I was able to do when I was here, because, well quite frankly, things were a lot different then, what with making your own clothes and all. I mean we shopped for foods and sometimes for jugs and bowls at the market and now and then a sturdy pot, but never, and I do mean never, did we ever get to do anything as extravagant as buy an entire outfit, ready-made and as colourful as all of this. Well, maybe the ones that lived above the city in the hills in their fine palaces but even then they didn't really shop, but I can't say for sure as I never got to meet any of them."

Dabria pulled a lovely floral print dress out of the bag. "Just your size dear, it's maternity. I was going to get a size twelve, but I got a ten instead." At those words Ana's eyes popped open.

"A ten! You've got to be joking. I'm a size six, no more, no less." Brad moved on her lap. She whispered, "A size ten, no way."

"Oh hush, you'll look great in this." Dabria laid the dress out on the chair and pulled a pair of flat shoes out of the bag as well. Then she pulled out a new pair of Khaki pants and a new shirt. "These will fit Brad."

"How? I mean, you can barely materialize. How did you go shopping? Did you spend my money again?"

Dabria smiled and tilted her head to the side. "You aren't the only one growing and learning, dear. I'm getting the hang of this."

Rigel dropped a business card on top of the clothes. "Almost forgot, here's the name and address of the restaurant. Reservations are for 6:30 p.m., so you'd better both get cleaned up and on your way. Oh, and Ana, tonight is on us." With that the pair disappeared.

Brad opened his eyes and slowly sat up. "I'm so sorry, Ana, I just don't seem to have much strength lately. It's hard to stay awake. Coming here took a lot out of me. I feel a bit better now." He looked around and noticed the clothing.

"What's this?"

"Go shower, Brad. We're going out for dinner. A celebration of sorts if you feel up to it." Ana smiled at him. She picked up the dress. Unfortunately, it looked like it would fit.

"Actually, I feel a bit better since the nap. I would very much enjoy an evening out with the mother of my child." He paused. "Ana, you don't know what this has done for me, and I want to say it now, in case I forget. If I would have … if I could be … let's just say, you're going to make a great mother."

With that, he grabbed the pants and shirt and headed off towards the bathroom.

Chapter 33: Working it Out

Ana walked down the hallway towards Mr. Parker's office. It was time to let the boss know about the pregnancy. She was starting to show, and it wouldn't be long before she wouldn't be able to hide it anymore. She tapped on his door.

"Come in, it's open," Mr. Parker called from his desk.

Ana still hadn't gotten used to calling him Gregory or Greg. She walked into the office and took a seat in front of his desk.

"What can I do for my star junior partner today," he asked.

"Well that depends on how much you dislike disruption in the workplace," Ana managed a smile. She had no idea why she'd put it that way, it sounded far worse than what she wanted to say.

"Say what now?" Parker asked.

"I'm just going to come right out and say it. I'm pregnant. About four months along now, almost five and I need to talk to you about cutting back some of my hours, and eventually going on maternity leave. Yes, I know who the father is, but unfortunately he's very sick. It's Brad. Brad Thorn."

Ana waited as she watched the news slowly register on Parker's face.

"Well, that's a lot of news to take in," he said. "I'd heard Brad was sick, and I thought your two were an item, I just didn't realize how much of an item." He pushed his chair away from his desk and leaned back.

"I don't want to leave you without a full staff, but things are rather complicated right now." Ana waited for him to tell her she was fired. Instead Parker burst out laughing.

"A little complicated you say." His smile let her know he wasn't angry, but she wasn't quite sure what was coming next.

"Yes sir, a little complicated."

"Young lady, since I gave you that promotion you've spent almost as much time in the hospital as you have at work, yet you manage to keep our clients happy. Plus that little rescue stunt you did, it may have cost us a few weeks of sick leave, but the fact they mentioned where you worked, well that got us a dozen new clients."

He paused and thought for a moment. "I'll tell you what, being as how you're pregnant and all, how about you cut back to three or four clients for now. I'll keep you on medical benefits, don't worry about that. Then when the time comes, just let me know and your maternity leave will kick in. The government says I have to give you eighteen weeks, but that hardly seems long enough. I've got an idea though." Parker pushed the intercom button. "Send Harry in would you."

"Wow, Mr. Parker, that would be so great. I've got a little money saved up so cutting back to part time won't be too hard, especially with the nice raise you gave me."

Harry, Brad's old assistant, entered the office.

"You remember Harry, don't you Ana? He came to work for us a week ago. I gave him a couple of your old dog food accounts. Have a seat Harry."

Harry did as he was told and nodded to Ana.

"Here's what I think," Parker put the fingers of both hands together into a steeple and pushed them against each other. "I think you should spend the next few months imparting your knowledge of all your old accounts to Harry. He'll deal with them face to face and you can stay in the background and give him information. If a client wants to speak to you, we'll arrange meetings for when we know you're in the office, or you can meet on the phone."

Ana blinked rapidly a couple of times. Was he giving away all her accounts? She'd have nothing to come back to after the baby was born. Then how would she survive?

"But Mr. Parker, Greg, then what will I be coming back to?" Ana held her breath.

She glanced over at Harry. He looked excited and frightened all at the same time. This was a lot to dump on a new employee, but he held his tongue and waited for the conversation to play out.

"Oh don't you worry about that. We've been meaning to do some restructuring here. Might as well do it now. There are two other people I've been thinking of promoting to junior partner as well. With you going on maternity leave soon, that will give them the opportunity to get up to speed on your newer clients. By the time you're ready to pop, all our clients will be looked after."

He paused and before Ana could speak he held up his hand. "And no, you won't have to start from scratch when you get back. I've also been thinking of having two contact people for the larger clients. It makes it easier when things like holidays, and pregnancies, come up. And if you decide you only want to come back part time, we can work that out too."

Mr. Parker let his hands drop back down on his desk as he smiled at Ana and Harry.

"I don't know what to say," Ana paused and found the only words that fit. "Thank you, sir."

Harry finally found his voice. "Yes, thank you sir. This is an amazing opportunity."

"Okay then," Parker stood up from his desk and came around to face his employees. Ana and Harry stood up. He shook both their hands.

"Now leave me alone, I've got a lot of paperwork to do in order to get this done. Should have done it months ago. Thanks for the push Ana."

Ana and Harry exited the office with grins on their faces.

Chapter 34: Saying Goodbye

Ana pushed herself out of the chair and went to stand beside Brad's hospital bed. He was unconscious, his body willing itself to stay alive, if only for a few more moments. She thought back to what felt like just a few weeks ago when she and Brad had gone out for dinner to celebrate the coming of their child. Since then, Ana's baby bump had swollen to the size of a basketball that showed no signs of deflating any time soon. In her seventh month, the weather hot and humid, the last thing she wanted to be doing was to sit in a hospital room and say goodbye to the father of her child.

Brad's parents had flown in four weeks prior and spent the time tending to him at home. Ana had met them briefly and chosen not to get in their way. It was of no comfort to them that their grandchild was strong and healthy in Ana's womb. All they saw was their son dying at a pace that was at once too fast and too slow to bear. They had left the hospital to get some food, and Ana was alone in the room with a man who nine short months ago was alive, vibrant, and all too cocky for his own good. The shell that lay before her hardly resembled the handsome TV reporter.

Brad moaned slightly, opened his eyes and motioned for Ana to press the button on the morphine drip. She did and Brad slipped back to sleep. She felt a hand touch her shoulder and turned to see Rigel standing there.

"It won't be long now. His contract time is almost up. We are so very proud of you for being here with him. You don't have to be, you know."

Ana sighed. "I didn't have to be a lot of things, but here I am, doing what I'm doing and there isn't one damn thing I can do to change it now." She turned back to Brad and stroked his forehead. "It's not fair, you know. With that thing gone out of him, he really is a nice guy. Not at all like the creep he once was. Is this how it was supposed to be?" She turned back to Rigel who stood in the shadows of the closed hospital curtains.

"Well, not exactly like this dear, but it's very close to the original plan, and we take what we can get when the plan changes slightly." He came forward and held Brad's hand. "Not much longer now. When his parents return, he'll be ready to leave us. Don't be fooled by his lucid state when it happens. The Creator gives most of you a special gift of knowing, to those who ask, just before you shuffle off this mortal coil and ascend into your next level of being."

Ana nodded and sighed again. She was about to ask Rigel something when she heard noises in the hallway. Rigel stepped back as Dabria appeared behind him and Brad's parents came into the room. No one said a word, not even chatty Dabria.

Brad's parents stood on the opposite side of the bed from Ana. Rigel and Dabria moved to the foot of the bed. "Any change?" his mother asked.

"No, none," Ana replied. "He woke for a brief moment and motioned for more morphine." His mother looked at the contraption hung beside her beloved son's bed and nodded.

"He always looked for attention as a child, always wanted to be adored. If he only knew how much we did love him, and adored him, but he was too busy finding fault with what we did." His mother took a tissue from the box and dabbed at her eyes.

Just then Brad opened his eyes and looked around the room. "Ana," he whispered in a hoarse voice. He turned his head. "Mom, Dad. You're here, too." He smiled a sleepy smile and stared at the foot of the bed. "Who are they?" he asked and then turned back to his parents. "Mom, I want to let you know that I love you, that you did a good job, considering what you had to work with." His mother burst into tears, sank into a chair and grasped her son's hand.

"And Dad, what can I say. My only regret is not being able to show you how good a father I could be, just like you." His father took a quick intake of breath and then grasped his son by the shoulder.

"Thank you, son, and I think you would have made a fine father." The two stared into each other's eyes until Brad broke the moment by turning to Ana.

"And you, I was an idiot to treat you the way I did, but I think you know now why that was. Be good to yourself, Ana. I couldn't have asked for a better woman to carry my child and bring it into this world." Ana took Brad's other hand and kissed the palm.

"Shush now," she admonished. "Save your strength."

Brad turned away and looked at the foot of the bed. "You two look familiar, but who is that?"

His mother sobbed and his father sighed. Ana simply

watched as Azrael entered the room.

Brad's eyes lit up. "Can you see them? Can you see him? He's so big, so bright! Mom? Dad? Is this it? Am I dying?"

There was only silence as the room filled with a beautiful iridescent light. Ana suspected the only two who couldn't see it were the ones who would benefit the most from it. Brad's parents continued to stare at their son, not at the foot of the bed.

Ana broke the silence. It was her job to speak now, and she did not hesitate. "Yes Brad, your body is dying now." Brad's mother gasped.

"How dare you say that?" she said through her sobs.

A tear ran down Brad's father's cheek. "Hush now," he said. "Let Ana talk."

Ana smiled gratefully at him and then turned back to Brad. "You, however, are not dying. You are going on to the next phase of your journey. This is Azrael, he's known by a few other names, but Azrael will do for now. Go with him. Follow him into the light and be free from your pain, Brad. We love you." She kissed him on the cheek, then whispered, so only he could hear. "I'll try to find you, Brad, God willing."

Brad smiled up at her. "I'd like that, Ana, I'd like that very much." His eyes flickered and his head lolled towards his parent's grief-stained faces. "I love you," he whispered and then closed his eyes.

His parents both stared at Brad, then at Ana. Ana wasn't watching them, though. She was watching the most amazing transformation she had ever seen. In spite of all the training and crossing over she had done herself, never before had she witnessed such a sacred moment.

Brad's body shuddered as a glowing outline of his body lifted up and away from the restrictive needles and machines. She could barely make out his facial features through the brightness of his soul. He was smiling, happy, incredulous. Azrael stepped forward and touched Brad on one shimmering shoulder. "Find the light that is brighter than yours and go to it. It's time to go home."

Brad nodded and floated up and away from his body. He turned slightly to gaze down upon the body which once housed his soul. He smiled at Ana, gave a curious glance towards Dabria and Rigel, and then lightly brushed his hand over his parents' heads. The machine connected to his heart monitor began to squeal. A steady, permanent sound that announced the man once known as Brad Thorn, was no more.

Chapter 35: Another Assignment

The day after Brad's death, Ana informed Mr. Parker she'd be starting her maternity leave early. Her head wasn't where it needed to be in order to give their clients the attention they needed. He agreed, reluctantly, as long as Harry could call her if he needed help.

Two days later she attended Brad's funeral with Carol. It was a fairly garish affair with TV crews and minor celebrities in attendance. Brad's parents thanked everyone for coming and his father slipped Ana a hundred-dollar bill on the way out of the cemetery. "For the baby," he murmured.

She and Carol drove home in silence, broken only by the odd gasp as Ana tried to breathe through the kicks and punches being pummelled upon her on the inside.

"It feels like he wants to come out now."

"Is it a boy?" Carol asked.

"I don't know, it just seems easier to call it, he, instead of an it." Ana leaned back on the headrest and closed her eyes. "Just eight more weeks now." She sighed. "And I get to meet this ballet dancer or place kicker, whoever it is." The two women spent the rest of the journey lost in their own thoughts.

Carol pulled up in front of Ana's apartment building and turned off the car. "Want to come up for a cup of tea?" Ana asked.

Carol was about to say yes when Ana's door was flung open.

There stood Dabria, dressed like some 1930's chauffeur, grinning from ear to ear. "Welcome home Miss Ana. I've packed your bags, yes I did, all by myself, found your knapsack in the back of the closet. I believe I finally got the hang of this materialize in the material world thing without messing it up too badly. The bags are packed, and the plane tickets are bought, and we'll be on our way then. Oh, and don't worry, we gave you a shot of something when you were sleeping a few weeks ago. Not to worry it didn't hurt the baby, but malaria might so we can't take any chances now, can we? Not that anything is going to happen now, heavens no, not after all the plans that were changed and new ones made and oh, this is just so exciting. Hi Carol." Dabria helped a baffled Ana from the car and tried to lead her towards a waiting taxicab.

"What are you talking about, Dabria? I feel like I swallowed a small wading pool. My feet are swollen, I'm tired, I just buried the father of my baby, and I'm going to have a cup of tea with Carol, then I'm going to bed."

"No. No, I can't say as you are doing that dear, now step lively, I'm in a tremendously good mood today. Oh right, Brad sends his love, might be back in a month or two to say hello, busy relaxing and rethinking what the next journey shall be, but until that time, pregnant or not, we've got a job to do!"

Carol emerged from the driver's side and squinted in Ana's general direction. "Ana, why is there a knapsack on the sidewalk and who are you talking to? Is someone there? I can't see them." Carol squinted again and took a deep breath.

Dabria closed her eyes, concentrated with all her might, and briefly appeared before Carol. "Hello dear, nice to see you again, sorry can't chat, must run. The plane leaves in eighty-six minutes. We should be there right now but we aren't so you can see that we are in a predicament."

"I'll take her," Carol said matter-of-factly.

"You'll do no such thing!" Ana retorted. "I am not going anywhere."

Rigel appeared beside Ana just as Dabria blinked out of Carol's sight. "That's a marvellous idea Carol, thank you. We'll take you up on that offer." He waved his hand over the trunk which popped open, awaiting its cargo. He deftly hoisted the knapsack inside and shut it. "Well then, shall we?" He manoeuvred Ana back into the car, hopped into the back seat and grinned. "It's been a while since we've travelled, hasn't it, Ana." He laid his head back on the seat and closed his eyes. Dabria appeared beside him, grinning from ear to ear. "Oh this is just so exciting. I love airplane travel, it's so not like what I am used to, and being able to sit atop and whisk through the atmosphere like that is such a joy, not that just popping in and out of places isn't a joy because it is, really, but taking it slowly somehow feels so human, almost like I'm alive again. I just love it!" Dabria clapped her hands together in glee.

Carol got back into the car, started it and pulled away from the curb.

"I don't even have my passport," Ana shouted. "I can't go to a foreign country, and they won't let me fly when I'm pregnant." She turned and scowled at the pair and then at Carol. "And you're no help, no help whatsoever. I'm having a baby for crying out loud, I can't go off to some tropical country I barely know anything about. Think about it Carol, don't do this to me."

"Oh Ana, lighten up a bit," Carol responded. "You've been given the opportunity of a lifetime. You get to be a real live angel, right here, right now. Who knows what great things you are going to do over there?"

Ana harrumphed. "Yeah, maybe I'll give someone some change for a pay phone, that's pretty exciting. Oh, or maybe I'll let someone in front of me in the grocery store line, ooh, or better yet, maybe I'm spending the money that was supposed to be for the baby and flying halfway across the world to say three sentences to a total stranger that will change their life forever!"

She was furious now. Pregnancy did not improve her temperament, much as she had hoped it would. She felt on edge and was at that moment craving mango flavoured ice cream.

"Ana, I'm so proud of you," Dabria cooed. "Oh Rigel, she knows what she is going to do before she gets there, she's beginning to know! Not like the know, know that she usually knows but the other know where not many know it, though they could know if they believed they could know."

Ana groaned as the car raced along the street to the airport and then turned onto the highway. "Do you have to talk like that? I have no idea what you are talking about or where we are going or why!" Ana's patience was almost gone.

Rigel decided it was time to fill Ana in on her assignment. "Ana, this is an exciting time. You are going to a beautiful place called Sop Ruak. It's in the golden triangle, an amazing place where Laos, Burma and Thailand join. It's a little bit of a journey from the airport to the area, but I'm sure you'll love it and it's the rainy season, so you won't be too hot. You'll be meeting a young lady there. Right about now she has just discovered she's pregnant after having a brief fling with a lively British fellow she met in Chang Mai. She's thinking of ending the pregnancy and it's your job to show her that a young woman without a partner can do just fine as a pregnant woman and a mom. After all, you are going to be alone in a strange country and as big as you are, that will hopefully bring her to the realization that she is strong enough to do this alone. Besides, she won't be alone for long."

Ana sat with her mouth open. "You mean to tell me I'm flying to some God forsaken place to show some barely pregnant women my belly so she'll have her kid?"

"Oh dear, it's not just some kid." Dabria could barely control herself. "Oh no, and it's definitely not forsaken by God or anyone. It's quite beautiful there, that much I do know. And this baby, well if she has it, will be a very close friend to someone of a similar age who eventually stars in a movie and can see dead people, very much like the way you see them, except yours are usually happy, but the ones he sees are not that happy. Oh, the movie business certainly does get some things wrong, but for the most part at least it gets people talking, if you think talking is a good thing, which I think it's because it gets people thinking and thinking leads to understanding and when you mix some emotion and beliefs in there it makes the world a very wonderful place indeed." Dabria sat back, then shot forward again. "We're here! Quick we don't have a moment to spare."

Carol pulled into the drop-off zone and before the car was stopped, Dabria and Rigel were outside, knapsack in hand, anxiously motioning for Ana to come along.

"Go with them, Ana. It will be an adventure, one you can tell your child when he or she gets here. You'll be safe, you have those two to protect you."

"God help me." Ana sighed.

"Yeah, that too." Carol laughed. "Now go, or you'll miss your flight. She waved as Ana stepped through the doorway, off on yet another assignment.

Chapter 36: Welcome to Thailand

The plane ride was uneventful, despite Ana praying they wouldn't allow her to fly at her stage of pregnancy. She slept fitfully, complaining to her seat companions that her feet were swelling, and her fingers were little sausages. Her aisle mates, an elderly Asian couple, simply smiled and nodded and they returned to their own private conversations. There was a brief stopover in Hong Kong, where Ana contemplated jumping ship, but continued on despite her misgivings. The baby continued to kick and punch and gave Ana's inside's a blistering workout before the plane touched down in Bangkok.

The airport was clean and cool, and Ana was grateful for that. She adjusted her knapsack and headed towards the main door.

"Now what?" she whispered into the air around her. "Where is this Golden Triangle anyway?" No sooner had the words been spoken than a short, thin young man approached her and tugged on her elbow.

"You want Golden Triangle? I take you there. No worry." He led her through the front doors and to a waiting taxi. The hot humid air hit Ana like a wet wool blanket, and she stopped dead in her tracks.

The man tugged gently at her elbow. "No worry, you get used to it." He opened the door to the cab. He spoke rapidly in

Thai, the only words Ana could make out were Golden Triangle, or so she thought.

Dabria and Rigel were nowhere to be found, not like on her other adventures. This time she appeared to be completely alone. The cab ride was not unlike her adventure in Paris except this time she was all alone, and she was more concerned with her baby than where she was going. Her driver smiled at her in the rear-view mirror, tried to speak to her in broken English and then eventually gave up. Some streets began to look familiar, as if she'd just been on them, but she put that off to jet lag. Finally, after passing the same hotel three times, she tapped the driver on the shoulder and glared at him. He laughed, took a sharp right and pulled in front of what looked to be a bus terminal. He pointed to the amount on his meter and held out his hand. Ana reached into her purse, took out the exact amount, and paid the man.

Her knapsack actually felt comfortable on her back as it helped balance out the weight in her front. She was able to breathe a bit better now and made her way through yet another set of sliding glass doors. The station was bustling with people milling about everywhere. There were obvious tourists, native travellers, and the odd families clustered together, waiting for arrivals and departures. She made her way to what appeared to be a ticket line up and waited her turn.

"Golden Triangle please," she said as she opened her purse. The woman behind the counter barely looked up.

"One way or return?"

"Oh, return please." Ana was glad the woman spoke English. They exchanged money for tickets and the woman pointed to a door at the far end of the building. "Number nine, go down there, wait."

Ana gathered up her things and did just that. Outside the building was another small line of people. Some of the travellers had Canadian flags sewn on their backpacks and spoke with Southern US accents. It made Ana smile. She had heard of that happening in Europe but never here. Then again she knew very little about Thailand. A few cats scampered around the garbage cans. She noticed immediately that they were not your average alley cats. They appeared to be purebred Siamese. She stared at them until a young woman with sad eyes came up to her.

"Amazing isn't it?" She pointed towards the cats. "My name is Amy. Is this your first time in Thailand?" She glanced at Ana's belly and then up into her eyes.

"Um, yes," Ana began, "very first." She held out her hand. "My name is Ana, pleased to meet you. Are those really Siamese cats?"

Amy's eyes lit up as she smiled. "Yes, of course. It surprises most people until they realize where they are."

Ana looked at her, puzzled. "What do you mean, where we are?"

Amy let out a small laugh. "Don't worry, my first time here I did the same thing. The locals must think we are so ignorant, going gaga over a bunch of stray cats. We're in Thailand, formerly known as Siam, thus the Siamese cats." Amy grinned at Ana. "Cool huh?"

Ana smiled back. "Yes, very cool. Are you going to the Golden Triangle?"

Amy sighed. "Yep, I have ten days left on my visa and then I have to go home. Just in time, too."

"In time for what?" Ana asked. "A special occasion?"

"I wish," Amy muttered. "It's no big deal. So where abouts in the Golden Triangle are you going? Chang Rai, Chang Mai?"

"Not sure actually." Ana pulled out her ticket and read it. "Looks like I'm going to Sop Ruak. You know where that is?"

Amy grinned again. "No way! That's where I'm going. I want to walk into Burma if I can. That is, if I can still buy a day visa. Want to come with me?"

"Um, sure," Ana replied. "Any place good to stay up there?"

Amy laughed. "It's pretty rough. There's a few small motel type structures but it's mostly tin huts and roof showers, or at least that's all there was that I could afford last time I was here in 1985."

"You've been here before?" Ana looked at her incredulously.

"Yep, a few times actually. I moved to London right from high school, and with airfare so cheap I've been working off and on for the past five years and travelling for the rest of the time. But this is my last trip, it's time to go home after this. My parents will be happy, they haven't seen me in three years, or is it four?" Amy scratched her head. "No matter, hey you want to ride up together and maybe share a room. We can afford something a little nicer if we split the cost."

Just then a bus pulled in, came to a noisy, smelly halt, and opened its doors. The driver stepped out, scratched his leg, and announced the bus would be leaving shortly.

"How long is the trip," Ana asked her new companion.

"It should take about five hours by what the map reads, but with all the stops and stuff, we'll be there first thing in the morning."

"In the morning." Ana looked up. "What time is it now?"

"It's almost 10 p.m. by my watch. We should get settled in and on our way just in time for snoozing. Make sure you get a seat near the back and don't let anyone push you around either." She pointed to Ana's obvious pregnancy. "Use that to your advantage, you'll need it."

Ana nodded and stepped aboard the bus. It was going to be a very, very long night.

Chapter 37: Peeing and Pregnancy

Ana slept rather well despite the frequent stops, the new country, the high humidity and the fact she was sleeping in a sitting position. Her new friend Amy kept the various farm animals and small children that boarded the bus away from her and although Amy slept some, she spent the rest of her time watching Ana's belly move in ways that normal bellies don't.

Ana awoke near Chang Rai and was startled to find the wide assortment of people and animals crammed onto the bus. Amy smiled at her. "It's the quickest way for the locals to get to market sometimes when they don't have their own vehicle. They sell fresh eggs and chickens and fabrics and such."

"Are we almost there?" Ana's bladder was filled to bursting and she didn't see any place on the bus to relieve herself.

"Almost, one more stop after this. Won't be long now. You gotta pee?" Amy was feeling the urge herself.

"Yeah, you could say that."

The last leg of the journey was spent watching the people on the bus, the people outside the bus, and the amazing scenery. The city noises faded and once again the bus headed north. Soon the bus pulled into a small parking area and stopped.

"This is it," Amy chirped. "I'll grab your pack, let's get outta here before he starts heading back."

Ana pushed herself out of her seat, winced at her stiffness

and followed Amy down the aisle and out of the bus. The heat was more bearable now, but then again it was about seven in the morning. "It's not much of a town yet, which is why I like to come here. It's more of a location, or a point of geographical interest than anything else." Ana waddled behind, her right hand pushed into the small of her back.

"Umm Amy, I really need a bathroom." Ana stopped for a moment and looked around. There were a few souvenir shops open, but nothing that resembled a gas station or a restaurant.

Amy led her over to one of the vendor's stalls and spoke what sounded like Thai to a short, frail looking woman. The woman nodded and motioned for Ana to follow her. Behind the souvenir shack was an alley type road and behind that a small lean-to, or so Ana thought. The woman pushed open the door, walked into a shack-like area and turned right into the gloom. Ana followed and found herself walking through a kitchen with a shower curtain at the end of the room. Behind the shower curtain was another room, barely. It had a small window with a broken screen and a hole in the concrete floor. The woman motioned for her to go in and left. Ana stared for a moment and then realized she was expected to squat and somehow pee into this little hole—without falling down, without missing, and most importantly, without complaint. This was definitely not the corner gas station.

She pulled down her maternity pants and panties and slowly tried to lower herself while her right hand steadied herself on the wall. Once she got into a semi squat position she realized her clothing was in a direct line between her and the pee hole.

She put her left hand down to move the fabric and wobbled precariously.

So far so good. Now to pee. Ana willed herself to relax and began to empty her overfull bladder. She relaxed a little too much and felt her bottom drifting dangerously close to the pee spattered opening. She took her right hand off the wall and braced it behind her to stop the fall. She felt as if she were playing some demented game of twister and the baby inside her was about to push her off her spot. Ana's balancing act was getting harder to maintain and the pee stream didn't look or feel like it would be letting up any time soon. She also realized that she was now aimed slightly forward and was splashing the edge of the hole, with some splatters escaping over the ridge and onto the concrete platform. "Oh God," she groaned as her stream finally slowed to a trickle. By the time it stopped her right wrist and arm were trembling from the weight. She released her pants and panties and tried to use her left hand to push herself up from the squat position. If she put her hand behind her, she would end up falling on her behind. She tried moving it in front and was faced with the choice of placing her hand in her own pee splatter or making a valiant lean towards the wall. She chose the wall. It was not a good choice.

Her left hand reached out, only to find she was much closer to the right wall than the left and she immediately tilted farther back and over to the left. Her left hand instinctively went down to stop her from falling backwards. Her right calf began to spasm, and she felt the baby do a tap dance on her bladder. The result was instant; more pee.

She cried out, "Shit! No!" as the small yellow stream hit her panties dead centre. "Oh Jesus, now what." It was too late to try and save them, the little bit of piddle was all that was left. Now what was she going to do?

"Dabria … Rigel … where are you?" she whispered. "I could use a little help here!" She was now completely and totally embarrassed, stuck in a crouched crab position with soggy panties and no visible way of getting herself up and out of this strange room. She heard a sound behind the shower curtain and called out. "Amy is that you?"

A small head peeked through the curtain and grinned at her. The girl was about eight years old, thin and pretty.

"Ah, hello," Ana said, wondering how in the hell to ask this strange child to help her. The girl seemed to understand her predicament and came slowly into the room, bowing her head up and down, not looking into Ana's eyes. She stood directly in front of Ana and then turned around, back straight. Ana had no idea what to do next. Was this some sort of odd Thai tradition where the children of the household kept visitors company in the bathroom but were polite enough to not look? After a few tense moments the girl turned her head slightly, patted herself on her shoulder and said, "You take, help you."

She finally understood what the girl wanted. Ana took what she thought was her cleanest hand and pushed off from the floor, the weight of her belly carrying her forward. She connected with the girl's shoulder and held on for dear life. The girl swayed slightly but did not move. Ana then pushed off with her left and let her weight rest on her right hand and the girl's shoulder while she frantically tried to pull up her pants. She succeeded in getting them up to her knees, only to realize the squat position was not conducive to pulling up soggy underwear. She sighed, reluctantly put her left hand on the girl's shoulder, and slowly pulled herself out of the squat position. Once standing she quickly pulled up her garments and stepped away from the hole.

Without saying a word, the girl left the room. Ana followed, completely mortified by the experience. When she stepped outside into the light she was greeted by the smiling face of a very pregnant woman. There was no doubt she was the girl's mother, so strong was the resemblance. No wonder the little girl had known what to do. It was what she did for her mother, who was obviously due any day.

She thanked the girl and was surprised when the woman handed her a moist cloth. Ana gratefully took it and wiped her hands clean. The two women nodded to one another, and Ana headed back over to where Amy was standing.

"I thought you had to go, too." Ana said.

"I did," Amy replied. "In the bushes, right over there."

Ana shook her head. "I need a shower, a sink, and a soft bed. Where can we find one of those?"

Amy tilted her head across the street and up a bit. Ana followed her gaze and saw row upon row of tin shacks in a rectangle around a common area.

"Oh no, not there, please, there must be a motel or something around here."

"That's all I can afford right now. There's a guesthouse up the road, has some indoor rooms, sheets are clean and there's only eight guests allowed so the bathroom is fairly accessible. We could try there, but it's about one-hundred baht a night."

"One-hundred baht? What's that in dollars?" Amy asked, it seemed like an awful lot of money for a clean bed and a shared bath.

"About $2.50 I think, give or take a few pennies. I've got one hundred left before I head home, and I want to make the most of it."

Ana laughed. "Two dollars and fifty cents, give or take a few pennies. Oh, it sounds like heaven. Much cheaper than Paris. Let's go!"

Ana waddled off down the street with Amy beside her.

Chapter 38: Secrets Shared

The guesthouse was indeed clean, if not a little less modern than Ana had expected. Mama, as her guests called her, was a short, squat, balloon of a woman with a huge grin and hugs for everyone. Once the girls were settled into their double room she came around with fruit shakes for both of them.

"Eat, eat," she said, as she handed them each a tall cool glass of pureed fruit and ice.

Ana took a sip and closed her eyes as the cool concoction trickled down her throat.

"Mmmnnn Mama, this is delicious," she said.

"You like," Mama said. "Good, thirty baht. Will put on bill." And with that she left the room. Ana and Amy laughed and sat on their beds to finish their drinks.

"So," Amy began. "Why are you here? It's not often you see pregnant women wandering around Thailand, especially at your stage, unless they live here, or they were born here."

Ana hesitated. "I'm on an assignment actually. Research of sorts, for a special project. What about you? What are you doing wandering around Thailand? Aren't you with friends?"

Amy sighed, her eyes blinking as she looked to the left. "I was with my boyfriend, but we had a fight, and we went our separate ways. We were down in Koh Samet. It's an island off the coast, very rustic and quaint, and something happened. We fought and I took the first boat back to the mainland and then up to Bangkok where we met."

"May I ask what the fight was about?" Ana watched Amy's face and saw her eyes were welling up with tears.

"It was stupid, really," Amy sniffled a bit, swiped at her eyes and sat up taller. "We were staying in one of the huts on the beach. It was only like a dollar a night. You got electricity for ten hours a day and the food was fresh picked or caught that day. It was great. Rick got upset with me because I got a tattoo. He said it was stupid." Amy pulled the V-neck in her T-shirt over to reveal a small heart and a quarter note side by side above her heart. "I love music, it's what I do, it's what I study, it's who I am. I thought it was no big deal, but he was all upset because of …" Amy's voice trailed off.

"Anyway, it doesn't matter anymore because I'm going to take care of things, go back to the States and work on my music career. This is my last holiday, only four days before my visa runs out, then it's back to London to pack up my things and then home to California."

The baby kicked. Ana put down her glass and leaned back on her elbows. "Damn this kid is active." They both watched as Ana's belly wriggled. "It's like something out of the alien movie." They both laughed. "You can touch it if you want. It actually feels kind of cool."

Amy hesitated. "No, I'd better not. It's personal, something for the father and the rest of your family to share. Where is the dad?"

Ana sighed and sat up as straight as possible while junior

continued to kickbox her bladder. "We buried him yesterday, at least I think it was yesterday, could have been the day before." She was so tired. "We weren't really together anyway, just one of those things that happens I guess."

"Yeah, things happen," Amy replied. "Sorry about your loss."

The baby kicked, noticeably moving the fabric of Ana's shirt. Then it kicked again. Amy moved forward and watched in amazement. "Well, maybe just a quick feel." She put her hand flat on Ana's belly and waited. Nothing happened.

"It figures." Amy chuckled. "I should keep you around so I can get some sleep at night." Just then the baby gave a two-footed push against the walls of Ana's abdomen. Amy laughed and pulled her hand back.

"Woah, that was amazing." Ana just nodded, then lay back on the bed.

"So, what are you going to do then?" Amy asked. "About the baby I mean. Are you keeping and raising it on your own?"

"Yep, it appears I am," Ana replied, though not quite sure how she was going to accomplish that while she was being escorted around the planet by a couple of invisible wing jobs.

"Are you scared?" Amy asked, lying back on her bed and staring up at the ceiling.

Ana thought for a moment. Scared wasn't the right word. "No, not scared. I think the word is trepidatious."

"Trepidatious? Is that even a word?" Amy laughed.

"It is now." Ana laughed. "I mean, I am tense about it, anxious, but not necessarily scared. It's like this was somehow, in some weird way, was supposed to happen and no matter what I do, it will happen, and I've decided to go along for the ride."

"Oh." Amy closed her eyes and took a deep breath. "I'm pregnant, too. That's kind of why I took a liking to you. I wanted to know how you could traipse around a foreign country alone and pregnant. I can't even face the pregnancy, let alone what you are doing."

Ana perked up. So this was her assignment, number forty-nine according to her calculations.

"Well, you just listen to your instincts and do it." Ana paused and sat up. "Look Amy, I'll tell you the truth, because quite frankly I'm tired of making up lies or hiding behind what I do. I'm not doing any research. I am on assignment, though. My assignment is you. You see, your baby, the one you are carrying right now, chose you to be its mom, and he's going to grow up to be a good man, and that's mostly because of you. I also know that he will play a big part in some other kids' lives and he'll bring them some sort of stability because it's what he is. A good, stable kid with his head on straight. All I know is he's going to help some people out, who would stray into a life that is pretty messed up. Sometimes you get to be the student and sometimes the teacher. From what I've been shown, your kid is ninety percent teacher, and that goes for what he is going to teach you, too."

Ana stopped talking. How the hell had she known all that stuff? Dab and Rig had given her some insight, but not all that. It was like she knew what was going to happen but didn't know until the moment she opened her mouth. The baby kicked and brought her back to the situation at hand.

"Amy, are you okay?" Ana leaned forward so she could see her new friend's face. Tears were sliding down Amy's face and into her ears, but she didn't make a sound.

Ana stood up and went to sit beside Amy when Dabria and Rigel appeared and motioned for her to step outside the room. She followed them outside.

"So now you show up!" Ana said in a loud whisper. "I had no idea what to do in there and now she's crying, and I don't know what to say now and this damn kid won't stop kicking me!" Ana gently tapped her belly where the feet were digging in the hardest. "Stop that!"

Dabria giggled and hugged Ana. "We are so proud of you, dear. You were perfect. Absolutely perfect."

Rigel took her hand in both of his and shook it. "Bravo Ana, we couldn't have coached you any better. It was brilliant the way you opened up and just spoke truth. It's a gift we had hoped you had, and you do. Our work will be so much easier from now on."

Ana stared at the pair. "Can we go home now?" She was bone weary, hungry, and her feet were quite swollen.

"Not yet dear, you deserve a little vacation." Dabria straightened Ana's hair and fussed with it until it hung neat and tidy. "Why don't you stay for a day, visit some of the site. You know there is this amazing pyramid not far from here, well it's not really a pyramid but it's amazing and almost every layer was built by a different country because the borders change more often than some people change their minds, and you can see the different types of cultures that built upon it so as each one built something it got smaller and smaller as it got near the top so it looks like a pyramid but it isn't really or maybe it is, I'm not so sure what it is now, but I know it's pretty." Dabria grinned and then disappeared. "Must run now, have fun!"

"Why does she always fuss over me like that. It's very annoying." Ana took a deep breath.

Rigel stood there, his usual stoic self. "Let's go for a walk, then you can rest." Ana followed him out of the enclosed yard and into the street. "I talk, you listen ... deal?"

Ana nodded.

It was almost noon now and the market stalls were filled with clothing, vegetables, meats, and cooked foods. Locals and a few tourists were purchasing snacks and dry goods.

"It's going to rain soon so I'll make this quick."

Ana looked up at the blue sky and shrugged. "I want to go home, Rigel."

He acknowledged her words with a raised hand and spoke. "I have to tell you something about Dabria. It's confidential and I don't want you letting on that you know. Deal?" Ana nodded as they walked through the market.

"Many, many lifetimes ago, you were born into a small village near Galilee. You were born at the same time as one of the world's greatest prophets and healers. You were even a playmate for a time, but your father took you away. Your mother died giving you life. A choice made by her before she came into body. You see she had lived many lifetimes and had learned much and accomplished many of her soul's goals. She was to become a guide, an angel as you call them. A spirit free of chemical and physical bondage we experience as humans."

Rigel paused as a young woman showed Ana a pair of cotton pants with a huge waistline and draw string. Ana paused for a moment and then shook her head no. The pair continued to walk.

"Something wasn't quite right, though. The soul of your mother was not content, even though this was the journey she had chosen. She often fretted about you and wondered where you were, how you were doing, to the point that she was assigned to you to watch over you. That was over two-thousand years ago. Since then she has guided and mentored over five-hundred-fifty souls, helped over nine thousand cross over, and been a mother figure to newly appointed guides. She works hard and rarely complains, except for one thing."

Ana started to speak, but Rigel held up his hand to stop her.

"Dabria wants to be human again. She wants to live a life in body and give up two-thousand years of rescue and guide work. She missed something and desperately needs to fill that void. Ana, Dabria was the woman who gave her life to give you life all those centuries ago."

Ana stopped and stared at Rigel. This time he did not stop her when she spoke.

"And that's why she mothers me, because she was once a mother that I never knew?" The baby gave a solid kick to Ana's bladder and then did a little flutter kick before settling down. "Rigel, this kid is always kicking me. When it comes out I can't wait for the doctor to spank its bare bottom!"

She smiled and rubbed her belly gently. "So, she was my mom." She let the words sink in and absorbed their full meaning. "I guess I could be a little more understanding and let her fuss and ramble on. I really don't mean to hurt her feelings. It's just that she can be so damn annoying."

Rigel chuckled. "Think of it as entertaining and it makes it much easier." He took Ana by the elbow and led her back towards the guesthouse. "Get some rest, eat and spend some time with Amy. She needs you, and believe it or not, you need her, too. Your plane leaves Bangkok in two days. We'll make sure Mudo is fed and cared for, and we'll see you at home soon." Rigel opened the door to the guesthouse, kissed her cheek and disappeared.

Chapter 39: Mudo Troubles

The remainder of the trip went well. Ana and Amy exchanged addresses and phone numbers and the two became fast friends. Amy had, as Ana hoped and as was her assignment, decided to return home and keep the baby. Ana's explanation of why she was in Thailand and what Amy's child was to become, was accepted without question. The two had decided to leave Thailand together and hugged at the departure terminal. Ana slept off and on the entire plane ride, except for the odd bathroom break brought about by her rambunctious offspring doing a jig on her organs.

When she arrived, Carol was waiting for her at the arrivals pick-up zone. Ana didn't even bother to ask how she had known to be there. She simply accepted the offer of the ride and filled Carol in on her trip and how things had gone. All in all she was feeling less concerned about people knowing she could talk to dead people, know things as she spoke them, and that she chatted with guides and angels. Now she was more concerned about her child. The baby had stopped kicking her somewhere above the Vancouver airport and hadn't moved since. She decided to take it as a good sign; baby was content, and they were almost home.

Mudo greeted her at the doorway with howls and meows and excessive cheek rubbing and tail flicking. He was not pleased that she had been gone so long and had shown his displeasure by digging up one of her plants, tossing it unceremoniously onto the floor and pooping in the pot. Ana ignored it, tossed her backpack on her bed and headed for her bathroom. All she wanted was a hot shower.

The scent of her own shampoo pleased her, reminding her there were some things in her life that didn't change. She rinsed her hair, applied conditioner and lathered up her belly with soap. As she was rinsing she noticed the water was pink and gasped. She quickly rinsed herself off, towel dried and called her doctor. He wasn't available, but the nurse was comforting.

"Just relax honey and go lie down. Sometimes the stress of travel can bring on spotting. Put on a fresh pad and monitor it. If it stops, you're fine. If it actually starts bleeding, call us back."

Ana thanked her and hung up. She had never used maxipads and had no idea how to get some without leaving the apartment. She made her way to the kitchen, past the dead Dieffenbachia, and made a phone call.

"Hey Carol, it's Ana. Can you do me a favour and bring me over a maxi-pad or two?" She then explained that she had to go lie down. Carol promised to be there shortly, and Ana went to survey the damage to her plant. Mudo was lying on the floor, pawing at his mouth. Ana bent over, picked up the shredded plant and tossed it into the garbage. She'd deal with the poop later.

In the bathroom, she folded toilet paper and stuck it into her panties. It would do for now. She lay down on her bed, rubbed her belly and began to sing the mockingbird song. She felt a slight movement and continued to sing. The baby moved an arm, jabbing her in the ribs with its little fist. She closed her eyes and drifted into a semi-sleep state.

She was awakened by two things at once, the sound of raspy breathing and her door buzzer. She got out of bed as quickly as she could, let Carol in the building and unlocked the door. She went to investigate the other noise. She found Mudo lying on the floor of the kitchen, his eyes slightly bulged, gasping for air.

"Oh God," she cried as she picked him up, pulled herself to a standing position and headed for the door.

Carol met her in the hallway. "Hey, I have those maxi-pads, why aren't you in bed?" She took one look at Ana's face, then at the cat. "Oh no, what happened? Did he eat something he shouldn't have?"

Ana shrugged through her tears. "I don't know, I wasn't here and now he's sick. Damn cat, one moment I want to kill him for ripping out my plant and the next I'm worried he's going to die. Can you take us to the vet?"

Carol turned around and headed towards the door. "Sure I can but aren't you on bed rest?" Ana mumbled something about things happening for a reason, grabbed her purse and headed out the door with her ailing cat.

"I can't do this," Ana said to herself more than anyone else. "I can't have any more death or tragedy or uncertainty in my life. I'm going to be a mother for heaven's sake."

Carol turned to her. "Ana honey, once that baby is born you are going to have a lifetime of uncertainty. Best you get used to it now."

She pulled into the emergency vet clinic and Ana was out of the car and in the clinic before Carol was even out of the car.

She thought Ana moved pretty fast for a pregnant woman.

The receptionist noticed the extreme distress of the cat, put her caller on hold and took the cat from Ana. She hit a buzzer on the desk beside her and paged one of the vets to come to the examining room stat. She told Ana to have a seat and carried the gasping Mudo through a set of swinging doors. A few minutes later she returned and sat beside Ana.

"Has he eaten anything he shouldn't have? Gotten into any medications?"

Ana shook her head no. "I've been away for a few days, so I really don't know. He dug up a plant of mine, it was shredded but it didn't look eaten."

The nurse nodded. "What type of plant was it?"

Ana thought for a moment. "I think it was a Dieffenbachia. I got it a few months ago, a get-well gift when I was in the hospital." The nurse nodded and headed to the back room.

"Oh gawd Carol, what have I done?" Ana sobbed as the baby inside her began its familiar dance. "At least the baby is okay." She placed a hand on her belly and waited.

Fifteen minutes passed before the vet appeared. He did not look happy.

"Do you know this is the fifth cat I've treated this week for plant poisoning? What is it with you people, you think that everything on the planet reacts to things the way you do? Well, it's not so. That cat of yours almost died. We've rinsed out his mouth and throat and he appears to be stabilized, but his breathing is still laboured. I want to keep him overnight to make sure he'll be all right. I trust you've destroyed that plant." The vet turned on his heels and returned through the swinging doors.

"Wow," Carol said as he walked away.

"Yeah, wow," said, still staring at the doors he'd gone through. "He was totally cute!"

The two burst into laughter as the receptionist returned to the front counter. "Dr. Riley wants to keep your cat overnight if that's okay with you."

The pair walked up to the counter, still grinning. The stress of the past few days had an odd effect on Ana, and she was feeling rather giddy. "Yes, yes that would be fine." Ana reached for a pen and wrote on the back of one of the clinic's business cards. "Here is my home number and the name of Mudo's regular vet if you need his records. I'll come by in the morning and pick him up. Won't I?" she glanced over at Carol who nodded.

"Yes, we'll pick him up tomorrow morning, thank you." She steered Ana towards the door by her elbow and added, "Now let's get you home and into bed. Doctor's orders."

"Yes ma'am," Ana replied and gratefully let her friend lead her to the car, to her home, and to the relative calm and safety of her bed.

Chapter 40: The Feline Physician

Ana slept for over ten hours and awoke feeling groggy and disoriented. She padded to the bathroom, peed, and tried to put the last few days into some semblance of understanding. Doing what she did, connecting with people and contributing something positive to their lives was a definite plus. Even being able to communicate with angels and guides and those who had passed on, wasn't such a bad thing. In fact she felt rather calm and grounded after each session. It wasn't even the tiredness she felt some mornings when she knew she'd been doing her rescue work. It was the not knowing. Now that she knew so much, she found that she recognized she knew less than she could ever imagine. Ignorance was truly bliss.

She made her way into the kitchen, poured a glass of juice and leaned against the wall. She saw the plant-less pot and remembered Mudo. The emergency clinic was only ten blocks away and she knew she could walk it, but she didn't want to carry Mudo all the way home. She dialled Carol's number and got her answering machine.

"Hi Carol, it's Ana. I'm just going to hop in the shower and then walk down to the clinic to get Mudo. Can you come and pick us up there, say around eleven?" She hung up, showered and was ready to go in twenty minutes. She grabbed her purse and headed for the elevator. As the elevator doors closed, Ana's answering machine picked up a call.

"Ana, it's Carol. I can't make it by eleven. I hope you are still in the shower. One of my students had an emergency and I'm just sitting with her now. I'll call the clinic around eleven if I'm through." The answering machine clicked off just as Ana stepped out into the late morning sunshine.

The walk took more out of her that she thought it would. She stopped to rest every three blocks, stretching her back and patting her belly. Junior was wriggling up a storm. By the time she reached the clinic she had a fine film of perspiration coating her body and she was slightly out of breath. The receptionist took one look at her and rushed around the counter.

"Are you okay?" she gasped as she led Ana to a chair in the waiting room. "Sit here, I'll get you a glass of water."

Ana didn't think her conditioned warranted such attention, but she sat, nonetheless.

The receptionist returned with a glass of water and Dr. Riley.

"Are you okay, Mrs. ..." He left the rest for her to complete.

"It's Miss and call me Ana, and yes I'm fine." She took the water and sipped slowly. "I'm not sure what the fuss is all about. I'm just a little winded from the walk."

The vet took her wrist and checked her pulse. Once done, he laid her hand gently on her lap. "It's a little fast, but normal." He gave her the once over and turned to leave.

"Ummm, thank you," Ana called after him. He waved her comment away with his hand and returned to the back room.

"Is he always so friendly?" Ana asked sarcastically.

The receptionist blushed and replied. "I shouldn't be telling you this but ever since his wife left him a year ago, he's been a real bear. Personally, I think he needs someone new in his life to shake things up a bit." She returned to her place behind the counter. "You're here to pick up a pet?"

"Yes." Ana stood and walked towards the counter. "Mudo, my cat, ate something he shouldn't have."

"Oh yes, right, he's doing better. His mouth and throat are still swollen but he should be fine in a few days. You really have to be careful with those types of plants. They have little crystal-like shards in them and are very dangerous for cats; little people, too." She motioned her head towards Ana's belly.

"Oh my, really? I didn't know that. I'll make sure all my plants are safe for everyone from now on."

The woman handed Ana a bill and told her she'd be right back with her cat. Mudo was brought to her wrapped in an old towel—groggy, but otherwise looking healthy and far from death's door.

Ana placed him on the counter and paid the bill. "Can I borrow your phone to call a friend to pick me up?" The receptionist handed her the phone and watched as Ana dialled. No answer, but she left a message.

"I'll just wait here if that's okay?"

"Sure, make yourself comfortable."

Ana went back to her chair and put Mudo on her lap. He curled up on what was left of her lap and placed his head on her belly. As soon as he got comfortable the baby kicked him. Mudo repositioned himself and drifted back off to sleep. No sooner had his eyes closed when the baby booted him again. Ana chuckled and scolded her unborn child. She picked up a magazine and flipped through it, wondering where Carol was.

No sooner had she thought that when the receptionist came over to her. "Your friend Carol just called, she's very sorry but she can't pick you up. Told you to take a cab and she'll buy you lunch tomorrow."

Ana sighed. It was close to lunch now. She might as well take Mudo home and have a bite to eat as she hadn't had breakfast either. Just then Dr. Riley came through the swinging doors dressed in street clothes. He looked puzzled at Ana still sitting there.

"Did you need to see me for anything?" he asked.

"No, not at all," Ana replied. "I was waiting for a friend but she can't make it so I was just going to see if I could call a cab." She smiled up at the vet.

"Hmmm," he said, checking his watch. "Look, I've been on call here since six and I'm ready to leave now. I could drive you and Mudo home if that's all right with you."

Ana tried to stand with Mudo in her lap and failed. "It's really not necessary," she said as she fell backwards into her chair. "We'll be fine."

Mudo yowled as Ana made a grab for him with one hand while she tried to push herself up with the other. Dr. Riley caught the cat with one hand and Ana's wrist with the other and helped her to her feet.

"Actually, I insist I drive you home. I want to make sure this cat actually survives the trip."

He managed a smile to show he was joking.

"Well, you are the doctor, Doctor." Ana followed him to the door.

"Call me Richard," he said as he flipped the In/Out sign beside his name to Out.

"Richard it is then."

Mudo fell asleep as soon as they got to the car, the raggedly towel still wrapped around him. Richard and Ana made small talk as they drove. They talked about how long they had each lived in Vancouver, how they liked the city and where their favourite restaurants were. When they arrived at the apartment building he insisted on helping her get Mudo into the apartment. "I want to see what other deadly plants you have up there," he commented with another smile. Ana decided she liked that smile.

Once inside the apartment Mudo wriggled out of the towel and headed for his food dish. There was still some kitty kibble left and he ate slowly.

"So, where did you put the plant?" Richard asked as he walked into the living room.

"In the garbage. Want to see it?" Ana asked.

"No, that's quite all right. I see Mudo has left a present for you as well." He pointed to the dirt and the poop in the pot. "You really need to dispose of all the dirt, or he'll keep going there." He lifted the pot and brought it into the kitchen. "Do you have a garbage bag to put this in?"

Ana opened the lid to her kitchen garbage. All that was in it was the plant. "There should be enough room in here," she said and stepped aside as he shook the dirt and Mudo's contribution into the bin. When he was done, he placed the pot in the sink, tied up the bag and started towards the door.

"You have a garbage chute?"

"Down the hall and to the right."

As soon as he was out of earshot she called for her teachers. "Rigel, Dabria, are you here? What's going on? Is he an assignment? Is this #50 or what? Rig. Dab. Where the heck are you?"

She looked around the apartment squinting to see if she could sense them. Nothing.

Richard walked back into the kitchen. "Who are you talking to?"

"Oh, just the cat." She bent over sideways and stroked Mudo's head. "Thank you so much for saving him. I really didn't know it was harmful. I got it as a present when I was in the hospital."

He motioned towards her belly. "Problems with the pregnancy?"

"No, nothing like that, I was ummmm, well I had a brain aneurysm and got better and here I am."

"Wow, how long ago was that?"

Ana glanced at her belly. "Oh about thirty-two weeks ago, give or take a few days."

"You mean you were pregnant and had the aneurysm and have recovered to this state already. Amazing." He shook his head.

"Yeah, that it was." The two stood facing each other in awkward silence.

"So," he leaned against the wall then stood back up again.

"Are you doing this solo or is there another man in your life besides Mudo."

Ana laughed. She had never thought of Mudo as the man in her life. "Yes and no, is the easy answer." She couldn't miss the look in his eyes. Her stomach grumbled loudly. "Oh, right. I really need to get something to eat." The baby gave a noticeable kick.

"Are you sure you're only thirty-two weeks? You sure look bigger and that baby sure can kick. I think it's hungry, too."

"Yes, according to the doctors it's thirty-one or thirty-two weeks, give or take and yes, he's quite the little soccer player."

"Why don't I take you for lunch then." Richard managed a full-blown smile.

Ana decided it was time to be forward. "Are you asking me on a date, or do you feel sorry for the poor single pregnant girl?"

He stopped smiling and spoke slowly. "The only one I've felt sorry for lately is me, and you have something about you that I'd like know more of. I'm not one for picking up pregnant women either. I just, well I was rude to you the other day and you took it so well. Then I saw you sitting there with that cat on your lap, and you looked so approachable, I just thought, why not. So yes, I'm asking you out on a date, that is, if you want to eat with a grumpy dog doctor."

Ana smiled at him. "I think I would enjoy lunch with a fabulous feline physician, and I know the perfect place just around the corner."

Richard stepped back to let her pass, and with a slight bow and wave of his arms said, "Lead on fair lady, lead on."

Chapter 41: Dating the Doggy Doctor

Lunch turned into another lunch which turned into dinner and within two weeks Ana was seeing Richard on a daily basis. They had many things in common and enjoyed each other's company. He laughed heartily when she told him she'd only graduated last year from promoting dog food to promoting people and she found the dog food easier.

She told him about Brad, the aneurism, the accident at the river and how she discovered she was pregnant. She glossed over the parts she thought he might find a little weird. He was thirty-four, had been married for ten years and his wife had left him because of differing opinions on when, where and why to have babies. She wanted to move to the country as soon as possible and start having babies before it was too late. He, on the other hand, wanted to stay in the city, try and patch up their rocky relationship and have children out of love, not because of a ticking biological clock.

She left him the previous year and was currently three months pregnant. Their divorce would be final in one month's time, and his ex would be married the following week.

Mudo regained his health, still searched for the missing dirt pot, and mostly slept and ate his way through the days. By Ana's eighth month of pregnancy she looked like she was about to burst with twins. The doctor said it was normal, she was carrying up front and it just looked bigger than she really was. In truth, it was hard to tell she was pregnant if you walked up behind her. She let Richard feel the baby kick, and the baby responded by kicking even more enthusiastically.

One day, after a slow walk along the beach enjoying the crisp fall air, they returned to Ana's apartment for a hot drink. Ana looked at him and blurted. "It's been almost a month. Are you ever going to try and kiss me or is this strictly friendship?"

Richard laughed at first, taken aback by her question. Once he stopped laughing he cupped her face in his hand and kissed her gently on the lips. Ana responded in kind.

"Like that?" Richard asked.

"Yes," Ana whispered. "Like that."

She moulded her body into his as best she could considering her circumstances. They kissed a moment more and then Richard broke the moment by pulling away.

"Ana," he whispered. "We can't do this."

"Why?" Ana leaned in for another kiss.

"No." He held her shoulders. "It's just that it's been such a long time for me and just being here with you, like this, now, well it's arousing all sorts of things in me. I have never met a woman like you before. You are so alive and so strong and so confident. I want to scoop you into my arms and keep you safe always, but I know you don't need me to keep you safe."

Ana looked at him and spoke in a husky voice. "Is that all I'm arousing in you or is this belly of mine a bit too much of a distraction."

To answer her he took her hand and placed it on his crotch.

Ana's eyes opened wider as she took in a quick breath of air.

"Oh my!" She leaned in and kissed him passionately. This time it was she who broke the kiss.

"Richard, maybe you're right." She searched his eyes for some sort of clue, a sign to say this was all going to be right. "I mean we hardly know each other. I'm carrying another man's child and I look like a beached whale. I mean, I don't even know if we are right for one another. You are such a good man, but a month is such a short time, maybe we'd better stop now. Just leave well enough alone."

He looked at her and surprised himself by the words that fell from his lips. "I don't need any more time. I know how I feel about you. I've known since the day you brought your cat into the clinic."

They kissed again, this time more slowly, with less urgency, but just as much passion. Ana took Richard by the hand and led him into the bedroom. She'd never felt as brazen as she did now, but nothing was going to stop her. Richard followed and then hesitated at the doorway.

"Ana, I …" his voice trailed off.

"Shhhh." She pressed her finger to his lips. "No words, please, this is awkward enough for me."

He followed her quietly into the room and lay beside her as she indicated. They closed their eyes and let their tongues, hands and bodies explore each other. Ana flashed back to the last time she remembered making love, the incompleteness of it, the frustration. She would not experience that today, not with this man. She rolled onto her side, and he snuggled into her in the spoon position. Within moments they were naked and moaning softly as they experienced each other for the first time. Bodies moved in unison, and for once, the baby stopped kicking.

Dabria and Rigel turned away from the door and made their way into the kitchen.

"Well, that certainly didn't take long." Dabria tsked. "Is Nizroth around here somewhere?"

"No." Rigel shook his head. "That was just pure human nature. Two people who are lonely and in need of physical comfort. There just might be a little love there, too."

"Do you think it will last?" Dabria sighed. "Let's go to the roof, it feels wrong being in here right now."

The pair effortlessly appeared on the roof as Rigel answered her question.

"It's free will. They may be together for the rest of the week or the rest of their lives. Remember, this part of her life is unwritten, unscripted, unplanned. No contracts, no expectations, no anything; a blank slate. The child is another story, there needs to be a decision soon."

They sat in silence for a time and then Dabria spoke. "You know the one once known as Brad wants to come back. It is his child, and he does deserve a second chance, after all he had one short life with two of him in one body and you think it would only be fair to let him have a life in the body he helped create. His request was to experience life in body before birth, so we have time, don't we?"

Rigel shrugged. "It's not up to us Dab, you know who makes the final decision. I've seen the list. There are over two dozen who qualify to be the child of the woman with an unwritten script for the rest of her life. It's not a common occurrence Dab, as you well know."

Dabria sighed. "I wish I was on that list."

Rigel patted her hand gently. "I know Dab, I know."

Chapter 42: One Final Assignment

Ana awoke the next morning feeling refreshed and happy. Richard was gone, but there was a note on her pillow. *You sleep like an angel. I didn't want to disturb you. Call me at the office when you get up.*

Ana read the note, sighed and rolled up on her side. Today was a good day to be alive. She made her way out of the bed and padded into the bathroom. She rubbed her belly and sang to it as she showered, telling it how happy she was and what a great life they were going to have. Richard was everything she'd ever wanted in a man and last night had helped ease her fears of being alone. Richard was there for her. Sure, he hadn't said I love you yet, but he had told her he knew how he felt. That must mean love, right?

She towelled off and put on a loose dress. She brushed her hair, put on some makeup and went into the kitchen to make some breakfast. She fed Mudo, got the paper from in front of her door, and proceeded to make herself some fresh-squeezed juice.

There was nothing interesting in the paper, just more of the same. The business section didn't normally catch her eye, but today it did. The headline said that a developer was coming into the area and putting offers in on an entire city block. *Bigger and better, onwards and upwards and all that marketing crap,"* thought.

She looked at the article again and realized the block in

question was the exact same street where Richard had his vet clinic. She picked up the phone and dialled his office. The receptionist informed her that he was in surgery and would be out by eleven, would she like to leave a message. Ana left her information and dialled Carol's number.

"Hi, this is Carol." Ana waited, thinking it might be the answering machine. She had a hard time telling some days.

"Hello? Anybody there?"

"Oh Carol, it's you, sorry, it's hard to tell sometimes."

"Hey Ana, sorry, I thought I was at work, forgot where I was for a bit. How are things, hun? Everything okay with you, the baby, Richard?"

"Yeah, everything is good, actually Carol it's great!" Ana tried hard to contain herself. "Carol, we did it, it was wonderful. Best I've ever had, and I think he loves me!"

There was a slight pause before Carol spoke. "You did it? And you think he loves you?"

"Yes, yes, I'm almost sure of it. He said he already knew how he felt about me and then he kissed me so passionately and with so much feeling, it just has to be love. It has to be. You know how some men are, they just can't say it, but I feel it, I really, really feel it."

"Well, if you feel it, it must be real, right?" Carol tried to hide the scepticism in her voice.

"Yeah, I do Carol, I really do. I'm not sure if I love him but I really love being with him and he's such a good man." Ana paused and then remembered the article. "Oh, and some big developer is coming into the area and trying to buy out all the small businesses on the same street where his clinic is. Can you believe it? I can't wait to hear what Richard says about it. I'm sure he'll sell, but where would he move to?"

Carol absorbed all the information and then spoke. "First off, don't rush into this love thing just yet, you've only known the man for a month, and you are highly emotional right now, what with the baby due soon. As for the developer, you can't stop progress, or so they say. Has Richard ever mentioned where he'd like to have a practice?"

Ana thought for a moment. On one of their first dates he had mentioned that one of his dreams had been to move to somewhere exotic, somewhere in Africa or South America so he could help out the locals with their pets through vaccination, neutering and spaying. He just didn't have the money to do it.

"Well, come to think of it, he did mention something about going overseas, but now that we're together, I'm sure that option is far in the future."

"What do you mean by together?" Carol asked. She knew Ana was prone to jumping ahead to the future and wanted to make sure she didn't get hurt because of her own expectations. "You've been together for a little over a month. Sex doesn't make a commitment. It may to you, but it doesn't mean that to everyone, especially men."

"But Carol," Ana began. "He made love to a really pregnant woman. That's got to count for something. Nice guys don't just bed a woman this pregnant and then take off. Do they?"

"Nice guys don't usually do that, you're right." Carol took a deep breath. "Honey, why don't you talk to your angel friends and see what they have to say. I'm not a good authority on men as you well know. If you don't see one around me, there's a reason for it."

Ana and Carol both laughed. Carol was picky when it came to men. If they didn't meet her criteria she wouldn't even go out with them. If they made it to a first date, there had better be some connection or the man was quickly sent packing. Ana on the other hand fell in love with the potential of every man she dated. Carol only looked at the present package.

Ana's stomach rumbled. "Well, baby and I are hungry, so I'd better go make something to eat. I'll talk to you later and let you know how things work out."

"I'm happy for you, Ana, really I am," Carol said. "Just be careful. Men do not think like women. Don't set yourself up for a fall, okay?"

"I won't. I'll talk to you later." Ana hung up thinking happy thoughts while Carol stared at the receiver on her end and wondered what her friend had gotten herself into this time.

* * *

Dabria and Rigel popped into the room as Ana sat down to a meal of toast and eggs. She was staring at a calendar. "Morning all," Ana mumbled between mouthfuls. "I think I'm overdue. My last doctor's appointment said I was now due around October 25th. Today is the 25th, therefore, I am overdue. Come on out little one!" Ana patted her belly.

"Morning Ana," Dabria said.

"Good morning dear," Rigel said as he took the chair opposite her. "Big day today."

Ana chewed her toast. "Oh really, why? Am I giving birth today? Do tell!"

Dabria spoke up. "No, not today dear. Today is one of your last assignments for a while. We're going on a little trip."

Ana finished off her breakfast and downed the rest of her juice. She wiped her mouth with her sleeve and stood awkwardly, taking her plate and glass to the kitchen sink. "Really? When and where to? I hope it's not too far. I want to be back by tonight and make a nice dinner for Richard."

"Actually Ana, it might take longer than that." Rigel moved in beside her. "We're going to a Red Sox game."

"Red Sox, as in Boston?" Ana rolled her eyes. "I don't even like baseball!"

Dabria stepped in and Ana knew she was in for a long explanation. "Wait!" Ana said. "At least let me sit first." Ana waddled into the living room and sat on the couch. "Okay, go."

Dabria smiled and began. "Ana this is going to be such an exciting game. It's the 1986 world series and it's the first time in, oh gosh about sixty-eight years, since they've done this well, and you know right now everything is tied up at two and two and that's the most exciting time to go see a game, and the Boston fans are the most loyal and deserving in the whole world, except for maybe a few A level league teams up north, but that doesn't count in the big leagues for when you are going after the big win, and mostly the ones who will be there are the ones that can afford to fly up there because it's in New York and not in Boston, but

Boston fans don't mind all that much. It's going to be quite the event Ana with popcorn and hotdogs and lots of shouting and cheering and everyone sending out all these great wishes for their team to win and well, you really need to be there. Even though it's been sixty-eight years, which isn't long if you're dead, but when you're alive it's a pretty long time, and they really deserve it, there are some other things going on so I don't want you to get too excited during the game because it's going to get very tense and so many things are going to add up to go wrong and in the end there is going to be one very disappointed little boy and you have to cheer him up or he won't go on to invent some pretty amazing things and the world will have to wait at least a decade more, so just pack up your overnight bag and a few other things and we'll get going." Dabria patted Ana's tummy and headed out of the room.

"Say what?" Ana said. "You want me to go to a Red Sox baseball game in New York and the Red Sox don't get to win? What kind of inventions?"

Dabria came back with a small bag and Ana's purse. "Not to worry dear, I packed it all for you. Let's get going then. There's a charter flight leaving in an hour, and you have to be on it. Regular airlines probably won't let you fly what with being as big as a small country and all, but we found this nice small airline that really needs passengers, we should be there by nightfall. Come on then, let's go."

"Wait. I can't go yet. I'm waiting for a call from Richard." Ana let Rigel help her up from the couch.

"You can call him from the airport, dear." Dabria filled up

Mudo's food dish. "This really is one of your last assignments until the baby is born. There may be a few minor ones here and there, but Rigel and I can watch out for those if you get too tired, so you really must hurry because this is the big one. Come one then, don't dally." Dabria opened the door and waited for Ana to walk out.

"But Rigel, Dabria, I don't want to go. I have some things I need to talk to Richard about and I can't do it from New York. Why New York?" Ana asked as the elevator opened and she stepped in.

"That's halfway across the world almost, or at least on the other side of the country. I mean, it's afternoon there and it's only morning here, what time are we going to get there?" Ana waited for an answer as Rigel guided her out of the elevator, into the street and into a waiting taxi.

"And who is going to feed Mudo?" Ana asked, not really expecting an answer as so far no one had said anything to her since they left the apartment.

"Dab just gave him something and Carol will come over later," Rigel answered. "I'll just pop into her place now and let her know you're gone."

With that, Rigel disappeared, and Ana was left with Dabria. She knew she'd get no answers from her, not any that made sense anyway.

The rest of the trip was made in relative silence, with Dabria commenting on the odd person, building, car, or flower that caught her attention on the way. The taxi pulled up to the far end of the terminal and Ana had to hurry to get to the check-in gate. Dabria waved her off as Ana walked down the aisle to board the plane. Pregnant or not, she was not looking forward to an all-day trip to watch a baseball game that was destined to disappoint so many.

Reluctant Angel

Chapter 43: World Series Wisdom

The flight to New York was uneventful. The baby kicked half-heartedly during take-off and arrival and slept for the rest of the trip. The taxi ride to the stadium was mildly annoying, but only because at her stage of pregnancy, sitting for a long period of time was more uncomfortable than not.

She found a ticket in her purse and headed into the stadium. The Red Sox were winning three to two and there was some commotion going on as Roger Clemens had just been pulled as pitcher for the Sox. Ana found the whole situation to be a little beyond her understanding of the game, let alone her appreciation of the fact it was a world series game.

She made her way to her seat and sat beside a young boy and his father. The boy was decked out in Red Sox gear, including the jersey and hat. Ana could tell that they boy didn't have any hair, despite his head being covered. She also noticed the dark circles under his eyes, but the eyes themselves twinkled with excitement. His team was winning, and he was having the best time ever.

"Hi there," Ana said as she sat down. "Got here late. What did I miss?" She directed her question to the boy, though the father nodded in acknowledgement and smiled as he looked at his son.

"We're winning!" the boy responded excitedly. "You aren't a Mets fan are you?" He eyed her as if she were an enemy spy.

"Nah, I flew out here for the Red Sox, never was much of a New York fan." The boy's grin widened even farther. Ana held out her hand. "My name's Ana."

His father turned and held out his hand. "The name's Austin, and this here is my son, Cory." Ana shook the man's hand. "Pleased to meet you both."

"My doctor said my chances of getting better were about as good as the Red Sox winning this World Series. I wasn't supposed to hear it, but I did and now we're winning so that means I am going to get better!" Cory bit into a hot dog, coughed a little, then continued to chew and watch the game. Ana looked over at his father. She could see the pain in the man's face, but his lips turned up into a smile as he patted his son on the head. "Hey, no matter what, you are going to get better little man."

Just then a roar went up in the crowd. It was the eighth inning and the Mets had just tied the score, three to three.

Cory looked up at his Dad and then at Ana. "Don't worry, they'll win, I know they will. I talked to God today and asked him to make it so. Mommy says God listens to little kids."

Ana smiled. "I have it on good authority that your mom is right. Sometimes we don't get exactly what we want, but we do get exactly what we need."

Ana and Cory chatted in between batters as the eighth inning passed and managed to give a few exciting moments to the crowd. The ninth managed to slip by without a run being scored. Ana found out that Cory had been a die-hard Red Sox fan, like his father and his grandfather before him, since he learned to walk. As it was a tie game, the players headed back to the field for an extra inning, and even though Cory looked tired, his eyes still held that sparkle that said he was going to stick it out to the end of the game.

By the end of the top of the tenth inning, the Red Sox had taken a five to three lead over the Mets.

Cory was ecstatic. He pulled out his baseball card collection and showed them to Ana. "This is Dave Henderson, he's the one that had the home run. And this is Wade Boggs, he had the double and this one here," Cory looked exhausted. He had to stop and catch his breath. "This one is Marty Barrett."

By the bottom of the tenth Cory was curled up on his dad's lap, eyes keenly watching the action on the field. It did indeed look like the Red Sox would win. There were two out, it was the bottom of the tenth and the Rex Sox were winning. They were one strike away from breaking their championship drought.

Then everything changed. Calvin Schiraldi gave up three straight singles. Then a wild pitch by Bob Stanley gave the Mets two more runs and the game was tied at five all. Cory curled face first into his father's chest, not wanting to look.

Cory finally turned to watch. "He'll get this one out, I know he will." The little boy looked up to the sky then out at the field. It looked as if the tenth inning would end in a tie. Then it happened. Ana held her breath as she watched some player named Mookie Wilson hit a slow ground ball to first. Cory lay with the back of his head against his father's chest, his eyes became moist as he watched his hopes for a win disappear. As the ball rolled between Bill Buckner's legs, the tears began to fall. He was barely able to see Ray Knight score the winning run from second.

Ana watched Cory as his father held him tight and rocked him in the stands. She didn't know what to say but she knew she was here to say something. She closed her eyes and said a silent prayer, "Please God, tell me, show me what to do for this little boy."

She heard a small voice inside her head. "Tell him what you know is truth."

Ana sat for a moment and watched as Cory gathered himself together and swiped at his eyes and wiped his nose. Ana waited until he looked her way. "You okay?" she asked, knowing he wasn't. Cory nodded.

"Can I tell you something?" she asked more to his father than to the boy. Austin nodded and helped Cory sit up straight on his father's lap.

"I want to share something with you about me. You see I almost died once. Only I didn't know I was dying. But I lived even though the doctor's said I shouldn't be alive." Ana paused to make sure the boy understood what she as saying. "The point is, that no one, not my doctors or my family, thought I was going to make it. I was going to die, and they were just waiting for it to happen. But I didn't die, Cory. I didn't die because I didn't know I was supposed to die. You need to remember that. You need to live like you don't know you are sick. I don't believe you are supposed to die. I don't believe some silly baseball game can decide your fate. You need to believe, no matter what, that you are going to get better, and even when you think you are getting worse, don't give up, okay honey. Please, don't give up."

Cory's tears stopped and he looked at Ana with clear eyes.

"Were you really supposed to die? And now you're going to have a baby?"

"Yes, and now I get to have a baby." At that exact moment the baby kicked Ana hard enough to move her belly. Cory saw it and laughed.

"Wow, your baby sure is strong." He reached out his hand and then pulled it back.

Ana smiled. "Go ahead, it's okay. You can touch my tummy. The baby doesn't mind." Ana guided his hand to where she knew the baby's feet were. The baby obliged by kicking hard against Cory's hand, hard enough to bounce it off Ana's belly. Cory giggled and looked up at his dad.

"Did you see that, Dad?" Cory's grin was almost as big as when the Red Sox were winning.

Austin nodded. "Ana, thank you for sharing that with Cory. Sometimes we get a little distracted and we focus on how sick Cory is, instead of how well he could be. Thank you for the reminder. Now I have to get this little fellow back to the hotel and to bed." With that, the pair stood and left the stands.

Rigel and Dabria appeared on either side of Ana. "Good work, Ana." Rigel patted her on her knee.

"We're proud of you." Dabria gave Ana a hug and then released her.

The three of them sat there quietly as they watched the crowds leave the stands.

"Do they get to finally win?" Ana asked, not really wanting to hear the answer.

"No," Rigel said. "Not this year."

"Does Cory get to grow up and be a man?" Ana took a deep breath and held it.

Rigel stood and helped her up. "Let's just say that it will take about another eighteen years for that to happen, the World Series win. But, young Cory will be there with his son to see it happen."

Ana smiled and with the guidance of Rigel and Dabria, made her way out of the stadium, back to the airport and eventually back into the comfort of her own bed.

Chapter 44: Goodbye Dreams

Ana fell straight into bed when she got home and did not wake up until the next morning when the phone rang. She struggled out of bed, but the answering machine got it before she did. The man on the other end was not happy.

"Ana, where the hell have you been? I've left five messages yesterday and nothing. You'd better be deathly ill, giving birth, or unconscious somewhere, because I do not appreciate your lack of communication. I'm worried and upset. Call me." Ana picked up the receiver just as the answering machine beeped to inform her the message had been recorded. She looked at the flashing light to see seven messages. Six must be from Richard. Who could the seventh be? She pressed play and listened. The first one arrived shortly after she'd left. It was Richard saying he had some news. The next three were also Richard, each one getting less patient, more irritated, more frustrated. It was the next message that caught her attention because it was Richard's ex-wife.

"Ana, you don't know me, but I wanted to talk to you. Richard told me about you the other day, and I'm happy for you, but darling you must realize that all that he has is because of what we built together. I'm just calling to let you know that I expect you to convince him to sell out and take the offer from the clinic in Chile. As much as we weren't speaking during the last part of our marriage, I do want what is best for him. Besides, I get half the sale of the business. He did tell you we were partners, didn't he? Must run now, do think about what I just said." Then the line when dead, followed by a beep.

Ana stood there, stunned, trying to figure out what this woman had been talking about. Then the next message started.

"Ana, damn it where are you! I'm worried sick, and I don't know if I should be worried at all, damn I just realized I barely know you at all. I wanted to talk to you about something. Call me when you get this message."

Ana listened again to his recent message, then sat in a chair and called his home number.

"Hello?" The phone was picked up before it completed its first ring.

"Hey Richard, it's Ana." She wasn't given a chance to say anything more.

"Good God Ana, where the hell have you been? You called my office yesterday morning and then disappeared. I've been going back and forth between fear and anger, worry and frustration. Thank goodness you're okay, you are okay aren't you?"

Ana couldn't help but laugh. "Yes Richard, I'm just fine, so is the baby." Before she could explain any further he jumped in.

"Well where the hell were you then? I've been worried sick, and I have some very important news for you and some things to discuss and after our last night together I wanted you to know, well I didn't know what I wanted you to know, but damn it, Ana, why couldn't you have called?"

"I was in New York Richard and—" he interrupted again.

"New York! Who the hell let you fly to New York? I can't

believe you would do something so stupid."

Ana was furious. "How dare you call me stupid! I wouldn't do anything to harm myself or my child. I had an assignment, and I went and now I'm back and I'm fine so just stop it!" Ana took a deep breath. This was not something she was any good at.

"What do you mean an assignment? What is going on Ana? I thought you weren't working." Richard waited for her answer.

Ana took another deep breath. "Well it's not really work, it's just something I do. Can we talk about this in person? I'd really feel better if you were here. Then we can discuss your news."

Richard thought for a moment. "No, I think your lack of communication and your hiding things from me has given me all that I need to know. As for my news, I'm selling the building. There's been a lot of interest in downtown properties since Expo started and they offered me a deal I just can't refuse. I'm handing my practice over to a friend of mine, and I'm going to Chile."

Ana was stunned. "You're what? When? I thought that ..." Her words trailed off.

"You thought what? That you could lie to me about what you do? That you could just seduce me and then take off? Men have feelings, too, Ana and we don't like to be forgotten, ignored or lied to." Ana felt the baby kick as a tear came to her eye.

"Richard please, let's talk about this, please. Come over, or I can come there, just let's not fight." She waited for his response.

A full minute passed. No one said a word. Ana held back her tears as the baby tap danced on her bladder. Finally she broke the silence.

"Richard?"

There was the sound of a deep intake of breath and then he spoke. "Ana, you know, meeting you has been one of the best things that has happened to me since my wife left. It's not great that this sale has to go through before our divorce is final, but even with the money she gets, I'll have enough money to pursue my dream. I care about you, more than you probably realize. As much as I want to be able to step up and be with you and be a dad to your kid, I don't think I can do that. The other night was magical. Truly it was, however, yesterday and today made me realize two very important things. One is that I do care about you and two is that I am not ready to care that much for anyone just yet. I'm sorry, Ana."

Ana felt a sob escape her. It had all felt so good, so promising. Her life was getting better. Richard was her savior, the man who would help her get herself back on track. The man who would be dad to her baby. The man who would be her lover and her friend, and now none of it was true. She closed her eyes and felt Mudo winding around her ankles. He gave her a questioning meow and looked up at her tear-stained face.

She remembered the message from his ex-wife and spoke softly into the phone. "If that's the way you need it to be, then go. You have a chance to fulfill your dream, you should go do it."

The baby did a happy dance on her bladder and Ana realized if she didn't pee now, it would be too late.

"Ana, I can come by later if you like, or maybe we could—"

"No, you're right," Ana cut him off. "It's best this way." She stood up and leaned against the wall. "I have to go now, Richard. Take care of yourself."

272   Reluctant Angel

She hung up the phone and made her way to the bathroom as fast as her body would take her.

* * *

Carol sat on the edge of the couch and handed Ana a tissue. "Honey, I told you to be careful. You can't fall in love with every man you have sex with. It's just not, well it's not normal. You're supposed to fall in love first, or just have fun and let it go."

Ana sniffled and blew her nose. "But he was so right for me!" she wailed.

"You've known the man for a little over a month for goodness' sakes. You know your cat better than you did him!" Carol got up and went into the kitchen to make another pot of tea. "All you knew about him were the basics: he was recently divorced, never a good thing for starters, he was a vet, and he had a dream to someday go somewhere warm and spay and neuter Fluffy and Fido. That and the fact that he was handsome, and didn't mind keeping a pregnant woman company, in more ways than one." She rinsed out the pot, tossed a new tea bag in and waited for the kettle to boil.

"Carol …" Ana stopped.

"Oh, don't try and defend him or yourself," Carol began. "I've seen you like this before, well maybe not exactly like this, not pregnant and all. Remember that loser boyfriend you had. What was his name? Chris wasn't it? Doped up all the time, always looking for a way to drag you into it. Poor soul that he was, never had a chance."

The kettle boiled and Ana's voice could barely be heard over the noise. "Carol …"

"And just in case you were thinking of getting back with him, there's something I was going to tell you last week, but you were so busy with Doctor Doolittle that I didn't have the heart." Carol unplugged the kettle and poured the boiling water over the tea bag. "It's about Chris, Ana, he died of an overdose last week. I really am sorry to break it to you this way."

Carol emerged into the living room and sat the tea pot on the table in front of them. "It was heroin I think. Someone who knew you had dated him came into the centre the other day and told me. I'm sorry honey, but I might as well tell you now and get all the bad news out of the way at once."

"Carol …" Ana's eyes were wide. "Carol, I …" She looked down at the stain on the crotch of her dress.

Carol's eyes followed hers and then looked up at Ana. "Does it hurt?" she asked.

Ana shook her head no, slowly dabbed at the moist spot, and held it up to her face to get a better look. Then she gave it a sniff. "It's not blood," she said with an air of authority. "No, not blood or even pee."

Then she looked up at Carol. "Chris is dead? My Chris?"

Carol nodded. "Honey, I think your water just broke. We should get you into some dry clothes and call your doctor." Carol helped Ana to her feet. A dark stain crept across the couch. "Yeah, definitely call the doctor. Are you having contractions?"

Ana let herself be led into the bedroom. Carol grabbed a towel off the rack on the way past the bathroom and rushed ahead to set it down on the bed. "Sit here honey, I'll help you change." She lifted the dress over Ana's head being careful not to let the wet spot rub up against her. "What do you want to put on?" she opened the closet door then rushed out of the room. "Where did you put the maxi-pads I bought you? We'll need a couple to keep you dry." Carol rummaged under the sink and found them. "Got it!"

She returned to the room and saw Ana staring straight ahead.

"Ana honey, are you okay? This is exciting, the baby is coming!" Carol went into the dresser and pulled out a clean pair of jumbo panties. "One good thing, you won't have to wear these much longer." She tossed the panties at Ana and started to laugh. She stopped when she saw fresh blood on Ana's hand.

"When did that start?" Carol sat beside her friend and turned her head so she could see her eyes. "Ana, it's going to be all right. I'm going to call an ambulance, okay?"

Ana nodded. "Thanks for the towel. I would have ruined my bedspread. Will you look after Mudo?"

"You bet kiddo. I'll look after Mudo, and I'll call everyone who needs to be called. Where is your address book?" Carol looked around the room, and then stopped. "But first, I need to call the ambulance."

Carol rushed out of the room and into the kitchen. She dialed 911, gave them all the information and went back to help Ana. When she returned Ana was lying on her side, the towel and parts of the bedspread were soaked in blood. "Oh God," she muttered as she went to her friend. "Hang in there, honey, help is coming. Don't you worry about a thing." Ana's eyes were far away and unfocused. "Stay with me kiddo, the hospital is only five minutes away they'll be here any minute."

Dabria and Rigel appeared at Ana's side. Carol caught a shimmer out of the corner of her eye and sensed she wasn't alone.

"Okay you two, I have no idea what is going on here, but this is not good. Can you do something? Anything?" Carol watched as the air around Ana appeared to shimmer, but she couldn't see the pair as she had the other day. She did, however, hear a soft voice in her head.

"Go gather what she'll need for the hospital. The overnight bag is on the floor in the closet, the address book is inside. She'll need toiletries, too. Please get them from the bathroom."

Carol rushed to the closet, grabbed the bag, and headed into the bathroom to pack what she thought Ana would need, not knowing how long she would be.

"Ana. We're here dear, don't be afraid." Rigel lay a hand on Ana's forehead and her eyes focused on him.

"What's happening, Rigel? Am I going to die? I don't want to die. I'm so cold." She closed her eyes and then opened them again.

"You aren't going to die dear, you are having a baby. There's just a small complication, both here and out there." Rigel continued to stroke her head as Dabria paced the room.

"Complication?" Ana asked.

Dabria came over and knelt down beside her. "Ana dear, it's not really a complication, just a bit of a well, yes it's a bit complicated but we have been told that you shouldn't worry because it's not really that much blood and before you know it we'll have some new blood for you, and you'll feel just fine again. I know all this almost dying is probably getting to be a little hard on your body, I mean goodness it would be hard on any body, especially a pregnant woman's body and you are definitely pregnant but not for long now dear and soon you'll have your baby, and it will be all wonderful again. As for the other part, well we've decided to let Raphael decide who your baby will be as there are quite a few who would want it and only one that can be it, as we don't want to create another mess like what happened with Brad because that was just too messy for any contracts to be sorted out and then, well you know what happened in the end. It just wasn't right, so yes, only one will be chosen."

Ana's eyes fluttered. "Oh God, I am dying. Everything you said just made sense."

Carol came back into the room. "You aren't dying honey. The ambulance—" Carol was cut off by the sound of the door buzzer, "is here right now. Hang in there."

Carol rushed to the hallway and hit the button to let them in. She flung open the door and ran back to the room to be with Ana.

Mudo ran out the door and into the elevator as the paramedics stepped off and made their way into the apartment. A tenant was waiting for the elevator on the main floor. When the door opened, Mudo dashed through the closing front doors and out into the street.

Upstairs the paramedics loaded Ana onto a gurney and advised Carol to come with them, just in case.

Chapter 45: It's a Girl!

Ana regained consciousness just as they were rolling her into the operating room. "Where am I?" She was frightened by all the masked faces and wasn't sure why she was there.

"Everything's going to be okay. We have to go in and get the baby out, but she's strong and a fighter. We're going to put a mask on your face now and we want you to relax. It's going to be all right Ana, just breathe and relax."

Ana felt something on her face and struggled slightly, then as the gasses overtook her she drifted off. Her body at least, was in good hands.

Rigel and Dabria stood at Ana's head and waited patiently. Within a few moments Ana's spirit left her body and stood with them. She stared at her hands and then at her body on the table.

"Aw geeze, am I dead? Oh, this just isn't right." Ana looked around, everything looked gauzy, out of focus.

Rigel laughed. "No dear, you aren't dead. You are quite alive and about to become a mother. We need to talk to you, keep your mind off things, let the doctors do their work."

"This is so exciting," Dabria blurted. "I've never been present at one of these before. "I'm so excited, I don't know what to say!"

And then she stopped talking. Both Ana and Rigel stared at her waiting for words to come flowing out. Nothing came.

Dabria just stood there, transfixed, staring at Ana's belly as they cut her open and began the process of removing the baby.

Ana turned to Rigel. "Never been present at what, a birth?"

Rigel took Ana by the shoulder and turned her away from the open abdomen on the table before them.

"This is a very extraordinary event Ana, and you the focus of it. You see, you aren't supposed to be alive. You changed all that when you were eighteen. Now you've had almost eleven more years of life. Everyone who comes in contact with you, everyone you interact with is fresh and new. There are no contracts left for you, except the one to serve as an angel here on earth."

Rigel paused to let his words sink in. The doctors were almost done cutting. He continued. "To be born to a mother who has no karma, so to speak, is something so fresh, so clean, so unimaginable to most, that many would give up numerous lifetimes to be that baby, your baby."

Ana thought about that for a moment. "But I thought the soul entered into the baby at conception, at least that is the way I was brought up." She tried to see what was happening on the table, but Rigel kept her out of the line of sight.

"Sometimes it does happen that way. Sometimes a soul will only need the experience of growth in human form from egg and sperm to embryo. Others only want to stay until the moment of birth in order to form a bond with the mother. When these souls leave the baby, then the one who is to live that lifetime steps in, sometimes at the precise moment of birth. There are so many needs and so few humans to experience them in, that we do take turns. Now this birth—this is very special. Your child has no contracts other than the few it agreed to before coming into human form. No contracts binding it to you because you have no contracts left. Whatever you do, will not affect this child or it's life path. Yes, you must be a good mother and teach and explore together and grow together, but no matter what you do, this child will remain on its chosen path and will not stray off. You two are only bound together out of love, not out of commitment, and that is a truly beautiful gift."

Ana thought for a moment and felt a need to go back into her body. "Who is it going to be? Do we know, has it been chosen?"

Rigel shrugged. "It could be one of many. The options are carefully weighed, the applicants screened and just today we had another want to be chosen."

"Who are they?" Ana felt her hold weaken and saw a baby from the corner of her eye. The doctors were stuffing her with what looked like paper towels and pulling them back out soaked in blood.

"Well, I really shouldn't say, but you won't remember this anyway." Rigel put his arm around her, turning her away from the sight on the table. "One of them is Brad, he really does want another chance."

Ana thought for a moment. "That would be a little odd, giving birth to a son who was my baby's father?"

Rigel chuckled. "Ana honey, you're having a girl, in fact you've already had her." Ana felt a little spark of excitement and then went back to her questioning.

"How can that be? Brad was a boy, a man."

"Souls don't have a sex Ana, we just are. Dabria and I look this way because this is what we were in our last incarnation. We can also change our look if we like, it's not a set thing."

Ana nodded. "Who else then?"

"Well, there's Chris. He wanted another chance with you, a chance to make things right. There's also a couple of people that recently died in disasters, like the one in Chernobyl. Oh and Mark Twain."

"The writer, Mark Twain?" Ana was curious but wanted to see what was happening to her body. The baby was wrapped in a blanket and placed in a bassinet. The doctors had almost finished sewing Ana back together.

"Oh yes, I forgot to tell you that earlier. Mark Twain was born when Hailey's comet passed in 1835. He died the next time in came around in 1910. Just this past April that comet went whizzing past Earth again. They think it might be poetic if Mr. Twain's soul could come back 76 years after it left his body, you know, like the comet coming around Earth every 76 years."

Ana just stared at Rigel. Just when she thought life couldn't get any weirder, it did.

"Almost time for you to get back there," Rigel said. "Oh, then of course there may be Mudo. He has yet to make a choice between life and death. Silly cat ran out into the street when the ambulance came. It's unusual to graduate a cat soul into a human body, but this is an unusual case as he was actually a soul fragment from a Venetian monk. They are deciding now if he is eligible or if they should just pop him back into your apartment, very much alive. His guardian angels are torn."

"Wait," Ana said. "My cat has guardian angels, too. Are they cats?"

Rigel laughed. "That's a lesson for another time. Right now you also need to know your great, great aunt wants to come back and reconnect with family. Then there's Martin." Rigel paused.

"Martin? My old boyfriend from high school, Martin?" Ana looked puzzled.

"Yes, well you didn't keep in touch. He was hit by a train a few years ago. He thought he could beat it." Rigel put his finger to his temple as if trying to remember something.

"Oh yes, and there is also an ascended being who wanted to become human for a time, but I think that was rejected because it's been out here for over two-thousand years. Oh, I almost forgot, there's also—"

Ana didn't hear the rest. She was violently dumped back into her body and sat upright gasping for air.

"Hello Ana, how are you feeling?" A kindly nurse put a cup of ice chips to Ana's lips. "Take some of this, you'll feel better."

Ana lowered herself back down on the bed. "I had the strangest dream." She tried to focus her eyes. Her limbs felt heavy.

"That was no dream. You have a beautiful baby girl. She's in the nursery right now with your friend, Carol." The nurse took Ana's pulse. "You sleep a little more and we'll take you up to your room to meet your baby."

"Okay," Ana said, just before she slipped back into unconsciousness.

* * *

Reluctant Angel

Ana awoke an hour later in her private room. Rigel was there.

"Rigel, my baby, is she …" Ana couldn't say it.

"Yes dear, you have a beautiful baby girl, quite the little angel." Rigel's smile went from ear to ear.

"Can I see her? Where is she?" Ana sat up and looked around the room. An IV drip was in her arm and her catheter was still in place. "Oh gawd," she groaned.

A nurse came in and helped her to a sitting position. "Best to get you up as soon as possible, then we'll bring you your baby. Hang on and we'll get you unplugged." The nurse removed all the various tubes running into Ana's body and then helped her stand. "How's that? You'll feel a little woozy at first. Just ring that bell there when you need help to go to the bathroom. My name is Julie and I'll be here in a jiff. Now let's get you back into bed and bring you your baby."

The nurse bustled out of the room humming.

"Lie down Ana, they'll bring your baby to you soon," Rigel said as he fussed over her.

Ana lay back on her pillow as a nurse wheeled the baby into the room. Carol was right behind her. She rushed in and gave Ana a big hug.

The nurse lifted the baby from the bassinet and handed her to Ana. "We were told you want to breastfeed, so let's see how the little one does and then you both need some sleep."

Carol stepped aside to let Ana hold her baby. "She's so beautiful." Ana looked at the nurse. "Is she okay, I mean with being born late and all the blood and all?"

"She's just fine hon, just fine. Now let's see if she's hungry."

Ana opened her gown and held the baby's head near her nipple. The little lips immediately found purchase and began to suck as if its life depended on it. After four or five mouthfuls, the baby slowed down and snuggled down for a good feed.

"She is gorgeous, Ana." Carol watched her friend nurse her baby from the side of the bed. "Just gorgeous. What are you going to call her?"

Ana smiled. "She looks like a little angel, doesn't she." Ana smiled and inhaled the sweet smell of her newborn's head. "Yes, I think that's it. I'll call her Angelique, Angie for short."

Carol smiled. "How very appropriate."

Ana smiled at her friend and then at Rigel. She looked around the room. "Where is—"

"I've already called your folks," Carol interrupted. "They'll be here any moment now.

"I was going to say, where is Dabria?" Ana looked around the room and then to Rigel. He simply shrugged. Dabria was known to disappear from time to time.

Ana looked down at her now sleeping baby. There would be plenty of time for questions later. Now, she was a mother, and that was all that mattered.

Afterword

Back in 2004 I had some dental surgery and the dentist sent me home with Darvon (propoxyphene) for pain. I remember being alone, getting up off the couch and heading into the kitchen to get another pain pill. Then I realized, I didn't remember if I'd already had one, and my mouth still hurt.

In my drugged state I was wise enough to simply grab a Tylenol and go back to the couch. Once I settled, I wondered what would happen if I took too many pain pills. I closed my eyes and the first chapter of *Reluctant Angel* unfolded before me.

Darvon was banned in 2010. In larger doses it can cause respiratory depression, hallucinations, a major drop in blood pressure, and when used with alcohol, lead to death. Needless to say, I never took another Darvon again. However, it did plant the seed for this book.

Toni Morrison, the 1993 recipient of the Nobel prize for Literature, once said, "If there's a book that you want to read, but it hasn't been written yet, then you must write it."

So I did. I remembered the first chapter in its entirety and started to write *Reluctant Angel*. I completed it in 2006 and I put it aside until later. I was a single mom and life got busy. I honestly forgot about it.

Fast forward fourteen years and I, like everyone else on the planet, found myself in the midst of a pandemic. We were told to stay home, and only see people within our bubble. With little to do and lots of time to do it in, I went through all my short stories and put them into a collection called, *Read My Shorts*.

But the pandemic wasn't through with us yet, so I dug out *Reluctant Angel*. While it needed a lot of editing, the plot and storyline were still strong enough for me to believe in it. Several revisions and edits later, here it is.

I hope you enjoyed the read. I have a soft spot in my heart for Ana and her daughter. So much so, that my next step will be to write a novel about Ana and Angie. I can't wait to see what adventures they have!

Acknowledgements

The world would be a strange place if we didn't have kindred spirits to connect with. I am so grateful for mine. You know who you are, and I am forever grateful you are in my life.

When I completed what I thought was my final revision, I sent it off to be edited and then to beta readers. My deepest thanks go out to Jonas, Elaine and Audrey for all their assistance in pointing out what needed to be fixed in my novel. You are more than an editor and beta readers; you are my friends, and I am thankful you are on my side.

I want to thank my daughter, Nicole and my friend, Teri, too. Back in 2006 my daughter and I visited Teri for our summer holiday. They were gracious enough to leave me alone and entertain themselves for the entire time, while I sat in a hot room and typed. You two are the best. Thank you for respecting my needs.

I also want to thank my mom. She was a teacher and read to me whenever possible. She instilled a love of books and words and ideas into me at such a young age, I had no choice but to follow my passion and become a writer.

Finally I want to thank you, the readers. The entire time I was writing and revising this novel I thought about what you would want to read. I hope I've lived up to your expectations with this novel.

As you travel down the road of life, may angels light your way and help to lessen your load.

About the Author

Darcy Nybo developed a love for writing in Grade 2. She still has the first story she ever wrote. She also believes her writing skills have improved somewhat since then.

Darcy has several awards for her short stories and for many years made her living as a well-known freelance journalist. She was voted one of the best writers in the Okanagan three times.

Today she is a sought-after editor, writing coach and writing instructor. Darcy teaches creative writing and all its aspects at colleges and universities in British Columbia, Canada. She loves helping writers find their voice and navigate the world of writing. She runs two word-related companies: alwayswrite.ca and artisticwarrior.com.

In her spare time, Darcy loves to spend time with her family, including her daughter and granddaughter. When she's not doing that, you'll find her near the water, puttering in her garden, painting, and of course, reading and writing.

Other books by Darcy Nybo

Short Story Collections
Okanagan Tall Tales
Read My Shorts

Children's Books
The Great Grape Adventure (activity)
Emma Jean Finds a Friend
Bark, Swat, Crunch!

All books are available on Amazon.

Wholesale orders are also available.
Please email publisher@artisticwarrior.com for more information.

Made in the USA
Las Vegas, NV
20 November 2021